Christie Barlow is  author of twenty-
iconic Love Heart
Home at Honeysuckle Farm and *Kitty's Countryside Dream*. She lives in a ramshackle cottage in a quaint village in the heart of Staffordshire with her four children and two dogs.

Her writing career came as a lovely surprise when Christie decided to write a book to teach her children a valuable life lesson and show them that they are capable of achieving their dreams.

Christie writes about love, life, friendships and the importance of community spirit. She loves to hear from her readers and you can get in touch via X, Facebook and Instagram.

facebook.com/ChristieJBarlow

x.com/ChristieJBarlow

bookbub.com/authors/christie-barlow

instagram.com/christie_barlow

Also by Christie Barlow

The Love Heart Lane Series

Love Heart Lane

Foxglove Farm

Clover Cottage

Starcross Manor

The Lake House

Primrose Park

Heartcross Castle

The New Doctor at Peony Practice

New Beginnings at the Old Bakehouse

The Hidden Secrets of Bumblebee Cottage

A Summer Surprise at the Little Blue Boathouse

A Winter Wedding at Starcross Manor

The Library on Love Heart Lane

The Vintage Flower Van on Love Heart Lane

Puffin Island Series

A Postcard from Puffin Island

Standalones

Kitty's Countryside Dream

The Cosy Canal Boat Dream

A Home at Honeysuckle Farm

THE LIGHTHOUSE DAUGHTERS
OF PUFFIN ISLAND

CHRISTIE BARLOW

One More Chapter
a division of HarperCollins*Publishers* Ltd
1 London Bridge Street
London SE1 9GF
www.harpercollins.co.uk
HarperCollins*Publishers*
Macken House, 39/40 Mayor Street Upper,
Dublin 1, D01 C9W8, Ireland

This paperback edition 2025
1
First published in Great Britain in ebook format
by HarperCollins*Publishers* 2025
Copyright © Christie Barlow 2025
Christie Barlow asserts the moral right to
be identified as the author of this work
A catalogue record of this book is available from the British Library

ISBN: 978-0-00-870803-0

Printed and bound in the UK using 100% Renewable Electricity
by CPI Group (UK) Ltd

For Andrew Snook.

Our paths have crossed for over twenty-five years, and as you hit the big 6-0, I was left pondering... What do you get the man who has everything? Apparently, all I could come up with was this lousy dedication!

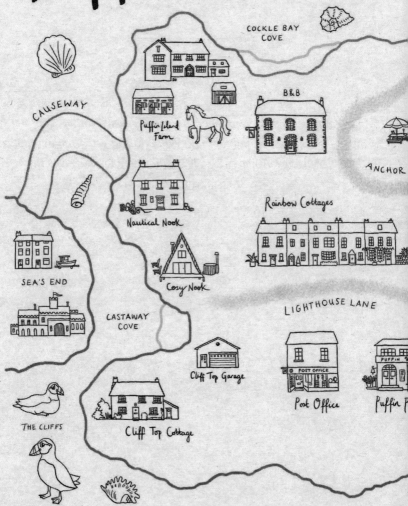

Prologue

Puffin Island
October 1950

'The fog is coming in thick and fast,' Betty Rose said from where she was standing in the window of Lightkeeper's Cottage, which overlooked Blue Water Bay. A raging storm was something the residents of Puffin Island knew only too well, and the red and white lighthouse that stood six hundred feet from the harbour was a steadfast sentinel in the gale, its towering frame silhouetted against the turbulent sky. The lighthouse's beacon flickered intermittently, struggling to pierce the dense fog, each rotation casting eerie shadows through the swirling mist.

'Mack is going to be busy tonight and with any luck Eric will be back soon. I don't like the thought of him out at sea in these weather conditions.' She hugged her mug of tea, hoping she'd spot her husband Eric, a fisherman, walking across the harbour soon.

'Never mind the fog, the baby is coming!'

Betty swung round to see Selby standing in the doorway, looking pained, clutching her stomach.

POP!

Selby's waters broke with the urgency of a dam giving way. One minute ago, the two women were savouring the perfect mix of tea and cake, and now they were staring at a puddle on the living-room floor.

'I just knew when I woke up this morning that I felt a little strange.'

'Are you in pain?'

'Am I in pain? YES!' Selby winced as the tightening across her stomach took her breath away.

'How fast are the contractions coming?'

'Fast enough.'

Betty looked again towards the window before hurrying over to the chart on the wall. She quickly traced her finger down the dates on the left-hand column. As soon as she reached today's date, she followed the tide times across the chart. 'Selby, the midwife is never going to be able to cross the causeway. The tide is in and the fog is only going to get worse.'

Selby's hands were cupped around her stomach as she gave out another groan. 'We need to get a message to Mack.'

Mack Sinton was the principal keeper at Puffin Island Lighthouse. It was in the blood; his father, grandfather and great-grandfather were all keepers before him. There were three other assistant keepers he worked alongside and they had shifts of six weeks on, two weeks home. This was Selby and Mack's first child and Mack's home leave had coincided with the baby's due date. They hadn't planned for the baby coming early.

With the weather conditions worsening by the second, Betty knew that Mack was going to have his work cut out for him and that the keepers certainly wouldn't be wasting time looking in towards the bay. Even if they did, it was unlikely they would be able to see the semaphore flags being waved from the harbour. One keeper would be operating the fog signal whilst the other tended to the light. And besides, there would be no way he could leave the lighthouse. The safety of the sea had to be his first priority on a night like this.

Betty was already listening out for the fog signal – an explosive charge at set intervals to alert the ships and guide them safely on their way.

'I'm not sure we can get a message to Mack,' she said gently.

'Betty, we have to try. I want him to know,' Selby pleaded.

Betty paused for a second, thinking quickly. 'Okay, I'll try.'

Rushing into the hallway and grabbing her coat from the wooden stand, Betty thrust her feet into her boots and clutched her gloves. 'Where're the flags?'

Selby pointed to the bag of semaphore flags next to the dresser.

'I will be ten minutes maximum. While I'm gone, I want you to make yourself comfy on the bed. Try and stay calm.'

Selby nodded. 'Can you remember how to use them?'

'Of course. I stood by your side at the end of the pier

watching you communicate with Mack in the first few months he was posted.'

It was part of the weekly routine to keep the men stationed in the lighthouse connected to their loved ones. Every Sunday at ten a.m., the friends and family of the lighthouse keepers stood on the end of the jetty at the harbour and communicated by the alphabetic flag signalling system, watched through a telescope by the keepers. The signalling system involved those in the harbour holding the yellow and red flags in certain positions to communicate messages.

Slinging the bag of flags over her shoulder, Betty opened the front door and hurried towards the bay. As the storm worsened all she could hear was the wind swirling around the cliff tops and the waves crashing against the rocks. Finding exactly the same spot as they had used every Sunday, she started signalling, desperately waving the semaphore flags in a frantic attempt to get anyone's attention in the lighthouse. As Betty's arms flailed in a wild dance, she spelled out the urgent message letter by letter.

S-E-L-B-Y I-S I-N L-A-B-O-U-R

But there was nothing, not even the hint of a sign from any of the keepers, which wasn't altogether surprising as the weather conditions were worsening and their attention was undoubtedly occupied.

'What are you doing out here? It's freezing.' She turned to see her husband Eric in his usual oversized black duffel coat, walking across the sand towards her. 'We were lucky to get the fishing boat back in these conditions. It's brutal out there. I can't wait to get home and throw some logs on the fire.'

4

'It's Selby. She's in labour. I'm trying to alert Mack but having no luck.'

'I'm not surprised. He'll have his work cut out for him tonight.'

Just at that second, the first explosive sounded from the lighthouse, causing Betty to jump.

'You aren't going to get Mack's attention now.'

Betty leaned in and gave her husband a kiss. 'The midwife can't cross the causeway, so I'm going to have to deliver this baby.'

'What can I do to help?'

'You can row me over to the lighthouse.'

Betty and Eric spun around to see Selby standing there, huddled inside her coat. 'I need Mack.'

Betty took her hand. 'Selby Sinton, you are mad. It's too dangerous! The explosives are being fired and the fog is becoming denser. Not to mention that the sea is choppy.'

'Please, it's only a short distance.'

Eric looked towards Betty then back at Selby. 'I honestly don't think…'

'Please,' she begged. 'I need to be with my husband, I don't want to do this by myself.'

Betty couldn't even begin to imagine how terrified Selby must feel. The baby was three weeks early.

'If you won't row me, I'll row myself.' Selby was strong-willed but as another contraction hit her and she let out a cry, her wail could be mistaken for a seagull's caw echoing all around them.

Betty took control. 'Eric, get the boat. I'm coming with you,' she added, turning to Selby. 'You can't give birth by yourself.'

Dubiously, Eric looked out at sea. It was only a short distance to the lighthouse but Betty knew that if anything happened to Selby on his watch, he would never forgive himself … and neither would Mack. The cannon was fired again.

'Hurry, Eric, get the boat before we can't see anything,' ordered Betty.

Putting on a spurt, Eric hurried to the boat house. He untied one of the rowing boats and grabbed two oars before pulling it onto the sand and down to the water. After he helped Selby into the boat, she bent her head and hugged her knees.

'I'm not sure this is a good idea at all,' he whispered to Betty.

'I'm not one hundred per cent either, but what can we do except hurry?' They held each other's eye before Betty climbed into the boat and squeezed Selby's hand. The water was choppy, the air was cold and the temperature had dropped considerably in the last hour.

Eric began to push the boat into the water then waded through the shallows before he climbed in and began to steadily row.

He rowed in silence, except for the tiny whimpers that escaped from Selby, and it wasn't long before they reached the lighthouse and Eric grabbed the rope at the side of the jetty.

'Betty, can you climb out first? Try and keep yourself steady so the boat doesn't rock.'

Once Betty was safely out of the boat she turned and extended her hand towards Selby. Slowly Selby climbed the ladder with Eric bringing up the rear after he'd secured the boat with the rope.

'Thank you for getting us here safe.' Betty touched Eric's arm before looking up at the tower.

'When shall I come back for you?'

Betty looked towards Selby. 'Maybe forty-eight hours. I've left the flags on the harbour. Can you grab them and signal tomorrow around ten a.m.? I can give you an update.'

He nodded and kissed his wife. They all jumped as another cannon went off, followed by a siren.

'Why the siren?' asked Betty, looking concerned.

'There must be a boat that's lost its way and is too near the rocks. You need to get inside and get Selby settled,' replied Eric.

Just at that moment, they heard shouting, and they all recognised Mack's voice.

'Mack,' shouted Eric, his voice echoing all around. 'Mack,' he shouted again.

A panic-stricken Mack appeared, looking between all three of them as if he wasn't quite sure they were real. 'What are you all doing here?' His eyes locked on Selby. 'Tell me everything's okay?'

'I'm in labour. I didn't want to have the baby on my own.'

Mack exhaled, bringing his wife in for a hug. 'Get yourself into my living quarters. There're fresh towels in the cupboard. I'll be with you as soon as I can, but we are in the middle of a crisis.'

The explosion went off again. Stricken, Mack looked behind him. 'There's a boat that's hit the rocks, and it's possible there are women and children on board.' Mack was obviously torn. 'I'm so sorry, but I have to go. I have to help them.' Mack hugged Selby again. 'I love you.' He walked backwards before turning and disappearing in the fog.

'Mack, wait, I'll come with you.' Eric hurried after him, leaving Betty shouting, 'Be careful.'

As Betty led Selby through the door to the inner chamber of the lighthouse and towards the spiral staircase, she realised that getting up the stairs was possibly going to be as much of a challenge as the birth itself.

'Are you able to make it?'

Selby glanced upwards. 'I'm going to have to.'

Slowly she ascended, clutching the hand rail and taking a short rest every few steps.

'We're nearly there,' Betty encouraged.

As they reached the top of the staircase, Selby pointed. 'That's Mack's room.'

Betty opened the door. The minimalist room – the walls grey, just like the fog that swirled outside the window – held only a single bed, a wardrobe and a bedside cabinet with a framed photo of Selby. Thankfully the space was heated.

Betty helped Selby to the bed and she sat down. She took off her scarf and wriggled out of her coat, which Betty promptly hung on the back of the door.

'I can't bend in the middle,' Selby said, sounding helpless as she sat on the edge of the bed looking at her boots.

Betty smiled as she pulled them off then plumped up the pillow. 'Do you want to lie flat or sit up a little? What's most comfortable for you?'

Selby pushed herself backwards and lay down. 'This feels as comfortable as I'm going to get.'

'This is going to be a first for both of us. I've never delivered a baby and you've never given birth.'

'Are we able to swap roles?' asked Selby, managing a smile.

'I think it's a little late for that. I'm going to find some clean towels and get some water. I'll be right back.'

The next contraction took hold and Selby grasped the bed linen. The time between the contractions now suggested that the baby was well and truly on its way.

'I want Mack,' she hollered.

Betty bustled her way back through the doorway and placed a bowl of water next to the bed along with a pile of towels. She wetted the flannel and dampened Selby's forehead.

'He'll be here as soon as he's able,' reassured Betty, 'but in the meantime...'

As Selby clutched her bump again in agony, it was clear she wasn't going to hold on to this baby for much longer. She raised her knees and hitched up her skirt, and Betty helped to take off her tights and underwear.

'I'm going to have to take a look at what's going on down there. Is that okay with you?'

Selby nodded then reached for Betty's hand and squeezed it so tight that Betty started to lose feeling in it.

Selby cried out in pain. 'It's coming!'

'Try and keep calm and breathe through the contractions. You are doing really, really well.'

'I want to push.'

'Push on the next contraction.'

9

The next contraction was soon here. Selby moaned through it and Betty wiped her brow whilst holding her hand, then took another look.

'The head is crowning. I can see the head!'

'I need to push again.'

This baby wasn't hanging around. Betty knew the next contraction was already on the way judging by the pain on Selby's face. On the next push Selby gave it everything she'd got. Gaining leverage by pushing one leg against Betty's hand, Selby gave a guttural scream and with one last push, a slithering bundle of life slid into Betty's hands. She quickly wiped the mucus from the baby's mouth and nose, and the baby let out a cry. Betty's relief was instant.

Selby was worn out, tears of relief streaming down her face.

'You have a baby girl and she's beautiful.' Wrapping her up in a towel, Betty gave the newborn baby to Selby.

Hearing footsteps hurrying up the stairs, Selby shouted, 'We have a baby girl!'

Both were expecting to see Mack standing in the doorway. Instead, a grief-stricken Eric appeared.

'Betty, I need a word.'

Betty knew that the look on his face heralded terrible news, and with a slumping feeling she stepped outside the room and pulled the door closed. 'What is it? Has something happened?'

In a whisper, Eric said, 'There's no other way to say this.' He briefly closed his eyes and took a breath. 'Mack has been swept out to sea trying to help the boat that crashed against the rocks.'

Betty closed her eyes and hugged her husband, clinging on to him for dear life before pulling away slowly.

'Are you telling me Mack is dead?'

Eric nodded. 'Yes. There's no way he could have made it to safety. The waves took him and we lost sight of him. No one could save him.'

Betty looked towards the door then back at Eric. She swallowed and blinked away the tears. Taking a deep breath, she slowly walked back into the room and closed the door behind her. There were a couple of seconds of silence before Eric heard Selby wail, her grief cutting through everyone's core.

Chapter One

Puffin Island
Present Day

With just thirty minutes until the gallery opened, Dilly Waters decided to kill two birds with one stone and head to the tearoom at the bottom of Lighthouse Lane. The scent of freshly baked scones greeted her as she pushed open the door, the small brass bell above her head jingling softly.

'Clemmie!' Dilly called out, spotting her best friend behind the counter, busy arranging pastries with her usual flair. 'I don't suppose you have a vintage decorative bowl I could borrow? And I would love a cinnamon roll.' Dilly walked up to the counter looking hopefully at her friend.

'You've come to the right place. One freshly baked cinnamon roll...' Clemmie popped it into a bag. 'And what size bowl would you like?'

'That is the question. I'm not quite sure. I may need small, medium or large, depending.'

'Depending on what?' Clemmie noticed the mischievous smirk on Dilly's face. 'Delilah Waters, you are up to something. I know that look.' She narrowed her eyes. 'In fact you look … how would I describe it … quite cocky.'

Dilly looked over her shoulder to make sure there was no one else in earshot before leaning in towards Clemmie. 'Cocky indeed,' she chuckled. 'It's to cover up a penis.'

'Woah! For a second there I thought you said penis.'

'That's exactly what I said but I'm not sure how big it's going to be.'

'Whose penis?' Clemmie shook her head in wonderment. 'I think you better explain.'

Grinning, Dilly whispered, 'I'm organising a new art class. I thought I'd spice up our artistic endeavours a bit. It's been something I've been thinking about for a while.'

'And you thought instead of painting a simple bowl of fruit you'd have a naked man lying behind it?'

'Exactly that.'

'That's nuts! I wasn't expecting you to say that at this time in the morning.'

Laughter escaped from Dilly's mouth. 'I see what you did there! I think it'll be great fun. Friends, a few glasses of prosecco and a healthy dose of artistic inspiration mixed with awkwardness.'

'Should be a masterpiece in the making, both on canvas and in our memories!'

'It's all legit and tasteful. I'm just waiting for the agency to confirm which model will be available. Then all I will need is the students. But I'm thinking of it as more of a social occasion, a girly get-together.'

'I'm in!' replied Clemmie without hesitation. 'And I don't think we'll have any trouble persuading the gang. Amelia and Robin will sign up and I'm sure we can coax Verity along too.' Amelia, Clemmie and Dilly had been best friends for as long as Dilly could remember. They'd grown up together on the island and even went to college together. Amelia was a wannabe writer who owned The Story Shop, the bookshop on Lighthouse Lane. And Robin was the chief baker at Beachcomber Bakery. She had moved to the island ten years ago and immediately became part of the Puffin Island family. Verity was the newest addition to the island and had instantly slotted into their group. She worked as an assistant at the Cliff Top Veterinary Surgery.

'Fabulous!'

'And how is business doing?'

'Really good. The art is flying from the gallery. There aren't enough hours in the day to paint but I feel like I still need something more in my life to keep me occupied in the evenings since...' She trailed off as a wave of sadness overcame her.

'I know, and you are doing brilliantly,' said Clemmie supportively.

'I couldn't have got through it all without my friends. It's still a little tough some days but I just remind myself how brilliant I am and how far I've come.'

'Exactly! You're brilliant and you can't blame yourself for what happened. These scammers come in all shapes and sizes and yours was particularly handsome. He knew exactly what he was doing.'

Nearly two years ago, Dilly Waters' life took an unexpected turn when a famous musician staying on Puffin Island had purchased several pieces of her whimsical puffin- and lighthouse-themed paintings. His stay was documented by Netflix and when it aired, Dilly was catapulted into overnight fame, appearing on radio shows and TV programmes and even being recognised by strangers wherever she went. Her social media had also exploded and her once quiet gallery on Puffin Island suddenly became a bustling success with her paintings flying off the wall faster than she could create them.

A strikingly handsome man strode into her gallery a few months later, his confident presence catching Dilly's attention straightaway. His tailored suit clung perfectly to his athletic frame and a playful smile danced on his lips as he met Dilly's gaze. Captivated by his effortless allure and the intoxicating mix of genuine interest and flirtation in his words, Dilly was hooked immediately. They fell madly in love very quickly and he soon moved in with her.

But like all good things, it soon proved too good to be true, and it all came crashing down in spectacular fashion.

'I was *this close* to handing over my inheritance to that monster,' she said, holding her thumb and index finger just millimetres apart. 'I still can't quite believe I fell for him the way I did, hook, line and sinker.'

'I never liked him,' admitted Clemmie.

'Neither did most of the island. Nobody warmed to him, not even my dad.'

'Still, you weren't to know that Giles Fox was a romance scammer. He was very good at what he did and he was in it for the long game.'

'He broke my heart and I don't think I'll ever trust another man again.'

'You will, but maybe not just yet. It's understandable. What he did takes a lot of time to get over.'

'But in the meantime, the fun of the art classes will keep me occupied. Would you put up a poster for me on your information board?'

'Absolutely I will. I bet your classes will become very popular.'

'Let's hope so and thank you.'

'Classes? What sort of classes?' Betty, Clemmie's grandmother and owner of the tearoom, breezed into the shop with a wide smile on her face.

'Dilly's new art classes will be right up your street,' teased Clemmie.

'I'm so bad at art that I can't even draw a stick man.'

'Life drawing classes,' added Dilly, waiting to see Betty's reaction.

'What I don't know about life at my age isn't worth…' She stopped in her tracks. 'Ohhh, you mean…' Betty looked around before mouthing the words, 'Naked men.'

'Exactly that,' confirmed Dilly.

'Yes, we are going to be drawing a naked man, with a bowl of fruit strategically placed for modesty,' added Clemmie.

'I've asked Clemmie to round up the troops. Shall I keep a space for you, Betty?'

Betty blushed, causing Clemmie and Dilly to burst into laughter.

'Of course. I think I might just give this art malarkey

another go!' She gave them a wink. 'I'm not missing out on any fun.'

'That's my granny!'

Betty swiped her grand-daughter playfully before turning back to Dilly. 'You'll be the talk of the island with your new art classes along with this. Have either of you seen the newspaper? This might be something you're interested in.' Betty looked at Dilly then opened the paper and tapped the article. 'There's a lot of history in that place for you.'

Dilly stared at the article.

Historic lighthouse up for sale with the best views over Puffin Island

An incredibly rare opportunity has come up to buy Puffin Island Lighthouse, overlooking Blue Water Bay and the harbour.

The spectacular 110ft lighthouse, eight storeys high, was originally built in the 1830s and was in operation until 1993. One of the first lighthouses to be automated back in the 1920s, it has been a listed building since 1985 and has recently been converted into a residential dwelling with the opportunity for a commercial venture.

The ground floor has a living room, while the first, second and fourth floors house bedrooms, with a family bathroom on the third, boasting a Victorian tub and spectacular views. The fifth and sixth floors house a dining room and kitchen while the top floor – the lantern room itself – has a balcony offering magnificent views across the water.

'"The property will be sold by auction in a few weeks'

time,"' Dilly read out loud, her voice tinged with surprise. 'Can you believe this? That's so soon.'

'Are you tempted?' asked Betty. 'Especially given your connection with the lighthouse? Your grandfather was chief lighthouse keeper there for many years and your mum was born there.'

'I've always wondered whether it would ever come up for sale. I'd spoken about it to Mum before she passed away. We always pondered what it would be like inside.'

'What about your dad? He's the owner of the boat house, do you think he would be interested in it?' asked Clemmie.

'I wouldn't think so, but I'd sure like to look around.'

'Now's your chance.' Clemmie pointed to the bottom of the article. 'There's an open day on Monday for potential buyers.'

This was an interesting bit of news. 'Potential buyers,' repeated Dilly, walking over to the window and staring out towards the lighthouse. Clemmie and Betty joined her.

'Your grandfather's death was tragic,' murmured Betty. 'I can still remember that heart-breaking night like it was yesterday.' Her voice cracked. 'Selby had just given birth when she learned that Mack had lost his life trying to save the passengers from the boat that had smashed against the rocks. It was the worst storm we've ever encountered on Puffin Island.'

'I can't even begin to imagine the emotions of that night. Welcoming a new baby into the world and losing your husband at almost exactly the same time,' added Clemmie.

Betty wiped a tear with a napkin. 'Selby was a strong,

remarkable woman. One of a kind. I don't know how she got through it all, but she did.'

'Probably with the help of good friends like you,' said Dilly. 'She was the best grandmother anyone could have ever wished for. Didn't she move in here soon after Mum was born?'

'Yes, Selby and Eva moved in straightaway. Unfortunately, due to Mack's death they were given notice on the cottage. It's one of the downsides of being a keeper's wife – the cottage stays with the job. It was difficult for her to give up the place they'd called home, especially as it was full of memories of Mack. It broke her heart a second time. But we all rallied around and helped as much as we could. Selby took several jobs to get back on her feet; she worked shifts at the pub, cleaned the hotel, worked here at the tearoom. We all took it in turns to look after the baby. Twelve months they stayed with us. Then she rented Seaside Cottage and as you know, lived her days out there.'

'It must have been hard to wake up to a view of the lighthouse each morning,' said Dilly.

'Selby took comfort in it. She believed Mack was always looking down on them.'

'And do we know if there are any contenders who are going to bid for the lighthouse?' asked Clemmie.

Betty shrugged. 'I've not heard about anyone specifically being interested, but I think that any potential buyers will be keeping their cards close to their chest. It'll be interesting to see. You're not toying with the idea, are you? Are you thinking of bidding?' she asked Dilly.

Dilly couldn't deny that thoughts had been turning over in her mind since Betty pointed out the article, and she was already envisioning the possibilities. Even though her dream had always been to open a chain of galleries across the country, what mattered to her even more was supporting young, emerging artists in her local community. She had an inheritance sitting and waiting, and if she used it to buy the lighthouse she could convert the ground floor into a gallery. Her current gallery could be transformed into a community space where up-and-coming artists could showcase their work, and she could host workshops to nurture their talent.

'I'm thinking this is possibly fate.' Dilly looked towards Clemmie. 'As I said to you only last week, I'm looking for other premises so I can support the community and display local artists' art. The current gallery is limited in space so this would be a perfect solution.'

'But if you live in the lighthouse, you'll be isolated. How would you feel about that?'

'It's not quite the same as it was in the 1950s. At least I wouldn't have to row across every day. It's easily accessible and only a five-minute walk, if that. Now there's a short road to the lighthouse, and the jetty that people can walk along. It even has a parking space and a small walled garden. Of course, I would need to look around it first though. I know my grandparents didn't own the lighthouse but it has special meaning to me and it's been a huge part of our family history. It's also the reason I paint quirky lighthouses and puffins.'

'You'll be flying high above the gulls with eight storeys to roam about in,' added Clemmie.

'What about the upkeep though? That's not going to be

cheap, and it's listed, which means there will be a whole list of rules and regulations,' chipped in Betty.

'People live in listed cottages all the time. The island is full of them, including your own.'

'That's very true.'

'Besides, we all know that work has been done to the outside of the lighthouse in recent years, so it's really only the inside I need to worry about.'

'There's only one thing for it – you need to take a look round on open day and see what you think after that,' said Betty. 'I bet most of the islanders will have a nosey around anyway, including myself.' Suddenly Betty looked saddened and Dilly suspected she knew why.

'Was the last time you were in the lighthouse the night my grandfather passed away?'

Betty nodded. 'Selby and I left the morning after the storm, just after your mum was born. Returning will bring back a lot of memories.'

'It will, and hopefully, if I like what I see, new memories can be made.' Dilly looked over the article again. 'But can I ask you both to keep my interest to yourselves for now? I'm going to talk it over with Dad and have a sit down and look at my funds. I might just be dreaming but how cool would it be to own the lighthouse?'

'Very cool. I'll be very jealous,' admitted Clemmie. 'Hopefully one day my own inheritance will come in.' She gave her grandmother a wry smile.

Betty interpreted her smile correctly, giving her grand-daughter another playful swipe. 'It'll be no time soon,' she said. 'And of course we will keep this to ourselves.'

'Thank you. Now if I can borrow that bowl I came in for? Then I need to go and open up the gallery.'

Five minutes later Dilly was walking up Anchor Way heading towards Quaint Quarters. She opened the door to her gallery and stuck one of her posters in the window, advertising her brand-new art course. As soon as she flipped the sign to open, she grabbed her painting smock from the peg behind her desk at the back of the gallery, then added fresh paper to her easel before switching on the radio. Every day she sat at the back of the gallery, painting, while potential customers wandered in and out. But as she sat down on her stool and looked towards the blank canvas today, there was only one thing on her mind – the lighthouse. Was this potential purchase too extravagant? She'd always been sensible with money, but she questioned whether she would really be in a position to bid for it. But the more she thought about it, the more she wanted that lighthouse. She glanced towards the framed photograph of her mum and grandmother that was sitting on the shelf behind her desk. The idea of someone else owning that beacon, a cornerstone of her family history, didn't sit right with her. Would they even appreciate the lighthouse's legacy as much as she did? Would they know about the countless nights her grandfather dedicated to keeping the light burning bright?

Still looking at the photograph, Dilly made a decision, there and then. Opportunities like this didn't come around often, so no matter what it took, she was going to make sure she won the lighthouse.

Chapter Two

As Dilly sat back she started to feel emotional, staring at the painting she had just finished. Already, she knew this one held a special place in her heart and she couldn't wait to showcase it in the gallery. She'd decided to title it 'Sail Away with Me', and it was her new favourite. The deep blue sea stretched from the bay to the lighthouse and in the distance, puffins hovered on the cliffs. The different highlights, shading and vibrant colours brought the sentimental image to life.

The couple that stood in the tower at the top of the lighthouse represented her grandparents, and on the path at the top of the cliff she'd painted a couple walking hand in hand, which paid tribute to Dilly's mum and her mum's partner, Anton, who had both been killed in a car accident. It had taken her five days to create this latest piece of art, having started it the very morning she'd learned the lighthouse was up for auction, and the thought of winning that auction hadn't left her mind since. Taking her usual pen she signed the bottom of the painting before fetching the small ladder from the studio at the back of the gallery along with the picture hook, hammer and tape measure. She'd decided that the painting was going to hang on the new signature wall of brand-new releases, knowing it would catch the eye of potential buyers as they walked past the gallery.

Climbing to the top of the ladder, hammer and hook in hand, Dilly balanced the canvas at the top of the ladder against the wall just as a sudden wave of dizziness washed over her. The room began to spin, her vision blurred, and Dilly tried to steady herself, gripping the ladder tightly … but it was too late. Her head felt light and her knees buckled, and the last thing she remembered was the picture falling to the floor before everything went black.

'Hey, Dil, are you okay?'

As Dilly slowly regained consciousness, the room around her swirled like a Jackson Pollock painting. Through the haze she glimpsed a familiar figure leaning over her.

'Am I dead? Did I just score a one-way ticket to the afterlife?' she murmured, her gaze taking in the figure before her, who slowly sharpened into the guy whom she'd secretly desired in her early twenties. 'It can't be you. I must be dead. Are you dead too? At least heaven has excellent taste in company.'

'You are not in heaven, but you have spectacularly face-planted in the middle of the gallery.'

Dilly realised with a jolt she was very much alive. She

blinked, then blinked again. As fate would have it, she'd fainted at the feet of none other than her art teacher from college. The painting had been tossed into the air, the ladder had fallen over and Dilly was frozen like a deer caught in headlights, still staring up at him with a mix of embarrassment and nostalgia. 'Mr Harrington, is that actually you?'

'It is.'

'Well, this isn't awkward at all.' Dilly tried to get up quickly but felt dizzy again.

'Don't move for a moment. Can I get you some water?'

Dilly pointed towards the door at the back of the gallery marked 'private', which led to the kitchen. She watched as Mr Harrington disappeared and soon returned with a glass of water, which he placed on the desk.

'Let's get you to the chair.' He extended his hand and helped her up before hooking his arm through hers. He walked her slowly towards the chair.

Dilly took in his aroma as she caught his eye. She recognised that smell. It was a subtle, lingering scent that released a cascade of memories from the past. He held her gaze for a brief moment before Dilly gave herself a little shake, catching another whiff of his aftershave in the air.

She swayed a little before she took a sip of water. The painting was lying face-down on the floor and Mr Harrington walked over and picked it up.

'Luckily it doesn't look damaged. What a magnificent painting it is. Is that the Puffin Island lighthouse?'

'Thank you, Mr Harrington, and yes, it is.'

'Will you stop calling me Mr Harrington? It makes me sound ancient when in fact I'm only around six years older than you. It's Max. Is this going up here?' he asked, gesturing to the spot on the wall she'd designated for the painting.

'Yes,' she replied, watching him pick up the fallen ladder.

'Are you hurt?'

She shook her head. 'Just embarrassed.'

Picking up the hammer and hook, he placed them at the top of the step ladder before grabbing the tape measure. Dilly watched as Max focused. He took hold of the tape and measured the gap between the other paintings on the wall with such precision. It had been a little over five years since she'd seen him last – it had been the 15th of July, the day she left college – and still he looked exactly the same, though maybe a little thinner in the face. He had the most gorgeous hazel eyes, with thick, long lashes any woman would die for and a head of brunette curls that was swept back in a headband like the one footballer Jack Grealish wore. Max wore navy shorts, showing off his tanned, muscular legs, and battered boat shoes. His tight-fitting T-shirt had Dilly blushing at the sight of his toned torso.

With the painting now hanging on the wall, Max stepped back and admired it. 'I love it. There's an air of romanticism with the couple walking on the cliff, the boat bobbing on the water, the swirling vivid blues conveying a beautiful sunny day. The multi-layered cliffs and those puffins are also very dream-like. It all ties in beautifully together.'

Dilly's smile grew wider. Max was talking about her painting with such passion. He genuinely loved it, she could hear it in his voice. 'I must have had a good teacher.'

'Talent like this has nothing to do with me and everything to do with you. You always stood out from the crowd. I still remember your very first painting in class.'

Dilly laughed. 'The bowl of fruit.'

'It looked so real. It was unbelievably good and so much better than mine. In fact, it put my painting to shame and that's why I didn't show mine to the class.' His eyes twinkled and Dilly felt that tiny rush in her heart that she had felt in every art class at college.

'How do you even remember what I painted all those years ago? I can't believe it stayed with you.'

'Because it was a masterpiece.'

She pointed to the wall at the back of the gallery. There it was, her very first painting, hanging in pride of place behind her desk.

'You still have it?' Max looked amazed. He walked towards the painting. 'It's exactly how I remember it. I'm surprised it's not been sold. You'd make a fortune from that with your fame.'

'It's not for sale. That's where it all started. I can still remember that day. I was worried mine would be the worst painting of the class.'

Dilly had walked into her first art class with a mix of excitement and apprehension, clutching her new set of paints, wondering whether she could actually paint. As she looked around the room, she saw her classmates confidently setting up their easels and talking about their previous creative masterpieces. A wave of doubt had washed over her as she worried that her skills wouldn't measure up to their apparent expertise.

'You had nothing to worry about,' Max said. 'And look at you now, world famous.'

'I wouldn't quite go that far.'

'I would. I saw you in that Netflix documentary and then you seemed to appear in every art magazine I picked up. I couldn't believe my eyes when I switched on the TV and there you were on breakfast telly. I'm really happy for you. You were always one of the talented ones and not many people are lucky enough to make a living doing something they love.'

'You did. You taught art and sold your art.'

'Not anymore. Things have changed for me.' Max didn't elaborate but Dilly noticed a flicker of sadness in his eyes. He swiftly changed the subject. 'And how are you feeling now?' he asked. 'Have you eaten this morning?'

Dilly shook her head. She hadn't fancied breakfast for several days. In fact, over the last couple of months, she hadn't felt like eating much at all. 'If I'm being honest, I've neglected myself a little.' Since discovering what a rat Giles was, she'd fallen into a rut, consumed by hurt and anger. There was a time she used to love cooking meals, sourcing local produce from the deli and devouring gorgeous treats from the bakery, but her appetite had dwindled of late, more than likely due to all the stress and discovering her relationship wasn't what it seemed.

'I've been skipping breakfast for a while,' she admitted.

'You need breakfast to set you up for the day and you need to look after yourself.' Max reached into the bag that was slung across his body. 'Here, I have a couple of croissants. Take them. I've just picked them up from Beachcomber Bakery.'

'I couldn't possibly. That's your breakfast.'

'You need them more than me; it's not me who's fainting.'

'One each?' she offered with a smile, suddenly feeling ravenous.

He smiled back and handed her the bag. 'If I remember correctly, you liked croissants. Every morning you queued up in the bakery opposite the college.'

'I did,' she replied, pleased that he had remembered.

'You've done amazingly and all this … it's so impressive. A gallery! Congratulations on your success.'

'You deserve some of those congratulations. After all, you did have a little something to do with my career choice. You inspired me. Made me believe I could make money from painting. You played a crucial role in my journey.'

'That's lovely of you to say, but I disagree. You were always going places. I often wondered whether you'd stuck with your painting. I'd look out for you in the Sunday supplements and then one day there you were. Your name was up in lights.'

'You did?'

'Of course I did.'

'You should get your easel out while you're here. There's so much beautiful scenery on the island and you were always such a fantastic artist.'

He smiled at her. 'Beautiful scenery indeed.'

His smile was just as radiant as she remembered and his gaze was just as intense as it had always been. There was a familiar flip in the pit of her stomach, the same flip that she had experienced all those years ago.

'I'm so glad all this has worked out for you. You deserve

it all. I wish I could stay longer and chat, but I need to get going.' He pointed towards the door. 'But are you okay? Do you need me to call anyone?'

Dilly shook her head. 'Honestly, I'm fine. I've just been working a little too hard of late. Are you sure you can't stay for a coffee?' She hoped he didn't notice the hope in her voice.

'Tempting, but I need to be somewhere and I don't want to be late.'

'It was lovely to see you again.'

'And you. It really is.'

Checking his watch, Max edged backwards towards the door but then stepped forward and pressed a soft kiss on Dilly's cheek. There was a brief moment of surprise, followed by a shared smile that captured the blend of admiration and the awkwardness of the moment. It was only after Max walked out of the gallery that Dilly realised she had never asked him how he was, or why he was here on the Island, and suddenly she wanted to know rather desperately. She really hoped she would see him again. She touched her cheek. Even after all these years, Max Harrington had her completely flustered.

Chapter Three

Two days later, Dilly woke to the calls of the seagulls and the sound of waves crashing through her open window. Already feeling the warmth of the day, she pushed back her duvet and swung her feet to the floor. All of a sudden there it was again, that light-headed feeling. She stayed sitting until finally it passed and then slowly got to her feet. She knew there had been a virus going around – was it possible it was finally catching up with her? Painting into the early hours also likely hadn't helped, but it had to be done as that was when she painted best, the one time of day with no distractions. Moving to the window, she pulled back her curtains. The view was perfect; the sun was already high in the sky, the sea was rolling into the bay and the lighthouse stood on guard. She smiled. This was exactly the reason she loved Puffin Island and, with the gallery closed today and the sun shining brightly, she planned to embrace the beautiful weather and paint near the harbour. It was the perfect spot, not just for capturing the scenery, but also for catching up with her dad throughout the day. She really wanted to run past him her thoughts on buying the lighthouse.

With a surname like his, Ralph Waters was probably destined to work on the waves. He grew up on Puffin Island, just like the four generations before him, and he'd started working at the local boat house at sixteen. He had now been the proud owner for nearly thirty years.

His youthful days had been filled with family sailings on his father's yacht, and he was given his first boat by his father for his seventh birthday. She was five feet in length and called *No Fin Better*. Ralph was hooked, and it was clear from that moment on that boats were going to be his life. Through his teens the boats he captained grew, until he proudly purchased his first yacht, aged eighteen. She was in need of repair and Ralph spent every minute and penny on that boat until she was ready for sea six months later.

Last night Dilly had gone to sleep with two things on her mind. Firstly, excitement had taken over. Even though she didn't know the state of the interior of the lighthouse, in her mind she had the auction won, the new gallery opened, and she was living happily in her new home. Secondly, Max Harrington. His visit had taken her completely by surprise. Her love of art had started at school and after her exams, she knew it was exactly what she wanted to do with her life. Studying art at college was the natural next step and even though her mother and father were separated by then, they were both very involved and very supportive of her choice of career. They had outlined the pros and cons, the main con being that it was difficult to make a living out of selling paintings, but ultimately Dilly believed in herself and her ability to make it, and so they did too.

Art college was one of the best periods of her life and a huge part of that was down to Max. On a weekly basis he'd shared art books with her. He'd encouraged her to study different artists and their style, and to experiment with colour. Just like Max, Dilly loved contemporary art and wanted to paint with warmth and humour, and that's when the idea of whimsical puffins and coastal paintings was born. Paint what you know and what you love was always Max's advice, and so that's exactly what she had done. After art college her dream of opening a gallery had become a reality, and with her recent success, Dilly felt inspired to give back and nurture young talent who felt the same passion for art. She wanted to use her experience to help others, and with a second premises she could make her own gallery even bigger and better, and use the original gallery specifically to showcase other local artists' work and offer classes to nurture emerging talent in the community.

Hearing her phone ping, Dilly looked at the screen. It was a text from Clemmie.

> I've rounded up the troops for Art Class but I had to text you, you are NEVER going to guess who has just walked into the tearoom!

Dilly suspected she knew exactly who'd just walked into the tearoom, which meant that Max was still on the island. She liked the thought.

Before she could reply, another text came through, this time from Amelia.

I'm sure I've just seen our college crush walk past the bookshop! Remember Mr Harrington?

Dilly could never forget him because it wasn't just a college crush for her, it was something much deeper. But she never shared those feelings with her best friends, feeling too embarrassed to admit she had fallen for someone so off limits, given that Max was both her teacher and married. Nobody other than her diary ever knew, but Dilly had fallen completely in love with him.

It wasn't just because he was goddamn sexy; he was also the whole package. He wasn't like boys her age, who got their kicks out of racing their cars over the causeway in the middle of the night. He was mature, dressed in style, held intelligent conversations and was passionate about art. Max was always the professional, and he never crossed any boundaries, but that never stopped Dilly wondering what it would be like to kiss him … on many occasions.

Still smiling at Clemmie's text, Dilly wondered whether to burst her bubble or play along. She went for the latter.

I've no idea, do tell!

The reply came instantly.

Sexy Mr Harrington! Still as sexy as ever too!

Dilly pinged back, smiling.

> I think I remember him!

> Who could forget him?! What are you doing with your day off today?

> The sun is shining so I'm off to paint at the harbour!

Dilly also planned to call in at the tearoom and grab her father's favourite guilty pleasure … a chocolate flapjack.

———————

A couple of hours later, with her easel under her arm along with a foldaway stool, Dilly loaded her paints and brushes into her bag and set off towards the harbour, calling in at the tearoom on her way. Leaving her stuff at the gate, she passed through the open tearoom door to find there wasn't a vacant table in sight inside.

'Business is booming!' she called to her bestie.

Clemmie swung around and greeted Dilly with a smile. 'I shouldn't complain but it's been non-stop since we opened. The good weather brings people out in their droves.'

'It's your own fault for having such a good reputation.'

'Probably!' Clemmie smiled. 'So…' She raised a brow suggestively. 'Mr Harrington is in town! You do remember him, don't you?' Clemmie was wiping her hands on her pinny as Dilly had pointed to the chocolate flapjacks she wanted from the glass dome on top of the counter.

'Mr Harrington…?' Dilly feigned a confused look.

'You are kidding me, right? Your hot art teacher. The one we stalked at lunchtime to see where he ate. We'd hang around the art block hoping for a glimpse of him and…'

'Oh, *that* Mr Harrington. I think I remember him. Still hot, you say?'

'Not aged a bit, and still has that sexy stubble going on. And those eyes! Anyone could get lost in those eyes.' Clemmie put her hands on her heart before leaning in and looking around the tearoom to make sure no one was listening.

Dilly leaned in too. 'You've gone all secretive.'

'There's something else I noticed about him, too.'

'Which was?'

'He's no longer wearing his wedding ring.' Clemmie's eyes widened.

That was an interesting piece of information, and one Dilly could kick herself for not noticing herself.

'Maybe he'd been for a swim in the sea and had taken it off,' replied Dilly, thinking out loud.

'Or maybe he no longer has a wife.' Clemmie gave Dilly a pointed look.

Back at college, they'd all Googled Mrs Lydia Harrington. She came from a family of plastic surgeons who owned an exclusive clinic for the rich and famous on the outskirts of the Cotswolds. According to Google, they were one of the richest families in the United Kingdom. Within the first couple of years of being married to Max, Lydia and her siblings had opened up a couple more clinics, one being in Northumberland on the outskirts of Sea's End, the nearest town to Puffin Island. Dilly, who had never contemplated plastic surgery in her life, had wondered how many people in and around the Sea's End area would ever consider it. But when Clemmie had pointed out that the ferries brought in clients from abroad just like the tourists to Puffin Island, they knew that Lydia was on to a winner.

'They were like chalk and cheese,' continued Clemmie.

'Who were?'

'Mr and Mrs Harrington. She was all manicured nails, Jimmy Choo shoes, Mulberry handbags and expensive cars, whereas Mr Harrington was so…'

'Normal, down to earth, rode to college on an old bicycle, had the most gorgeous floppy hair, eyes you could get lost in, a heart-melting smile and that sexy tiny scar at the top of his cheekbone.' Dilly realised she might have admitted a bit too much and coughed and looked away.

When she looked back at her friend, she found Clemmie had cocked an eyebrow and had a knowing look in her eye. 'A second ago you didn't know if you actually remembered him and now you remember his sexy tiny scar at the top of his cheekbone?'

'It's all come flooding back!' As had Dilly's hormones, which had been dancing through her body every time she thought of him … which had been a number of times since he'd walked into the gallery. In fact, he'd been the last thing she thought about before falling asleep last night and the first thing she thought about when she'd woken up.

Dilly handed over the cash for the flapjacks. 'I'll take these to Dad. I'm going to run past him my idea about bidding on the lighthouse.'

'I think it's a brilliant idea. Everyone on the island will be delighted it's gone to an islander rather than an outsider, especially with your connection to the lighthouse.'

'It just depends on the finances. I'll have to work out what my highest bid can be and pray no one can go higher, but I'm sure there will be a number of property developers who will want to snap it up.'

'What will be, will be, and anyway you don't have to make a decision until you've had a look around.'

'I've got a feeling I'm going to fall in love with the place. Thanks for these.' She held up the white paper bag. 'I'll catch up with you later.'

As Dilly walked towards the harbour in the beautiful weather, the soft breeze carried the salty scent of the sea. She stared out towards the fishing boats that bobbed lazily on the sparkling water, their reflections dancing in the sunlight. The whole place had a sense of calm. This part of Puffin Island was quieter than the main bay but just as picturesque.

'Dad!' Dilly called out, spotting him through the open doors of the boat house.

The old boat house had been a huge part of Dilly's life. As a child she would often accompany her dad to work and she was well used to the scent of aged wood filling the air, mingling with the faint, briny aroma of the sea. Outside the boat house there were oars, life jackets and fishing gear hanging on the walls, and inside an array of boats and equipment was neatly stored, ready for use. As usual, Ralph was covered in grease and paint and wearing the same old overalls that had definitely seen better days. His footsteps echoed softly on the wooden floor and a smile spread across his face as he came to greet her at the door.

'Here she is. My favourite daughter. I wondered if you'd be out painting today.'

Dilly balanced her easel against the doorframe and dropped her bag to the ground before she kissed her dad on the cheek. Holding up a white paper bag, she said, 'I've got your favourite flapjack, and I wondered if you had five minutes. I want to talk to you about something.'

'Now that sounds serious.'

'Just looking for a little bit of advice. I'm not sure if my heart is overruling the common sense in my head and whether I should let it.'

Ralph pointed to the rock just in front of the boat house down by the water. The rock had been home to so many special conversations between them, a place they'd sat together over the years, contemplating the world and making sense of life. As soon as they were perched on top of the rock, Dilly passed one of the flapjacks to her dad and took the other, catching the crumbs with her hand as she took the first bite.

'What's on your mind?'

'I've been thinking about something important...'

'I knew this day would come and I've been dreading it. Go on.'

'What are you on about? You've lost me.'

'You've achieved great things as an artist and this is only the beginning. I want you to know I am so proud of you. I knew you would outgrow Puffin Island and need to be in London, Edinburgh or even Paris to carry on growing and catapulting your art around the world.'

Immediately Dilly realised why there was anxiety etched on her dad's face. 'London, Edinburgh or Paris? You have to be joking! Who could ever give up all this just to earn a little more money and possibly be a little more famous?' She smiled. 'Dad, I'm going nowhere. This place is my life, and *you* are here. I could never leave Puffin Island. It's my home.'

Tears welled up in Ralph's eyes. 'I can't tell you how relieved I am to hear that. You do know your mum would be so proud of you, too.'

'I know. It still hurts every day that I can't just speak to her.'

Ralph nodded. Dilly admired her dad. Even though her parents had divorced when she was young, they'd still had the utmost respect for each other and had always put her first. Something she knew must have been tough for her dad, especially as her mum had moved on so quickly with someone else, soon after they'd split.

She pointed towards the lighthouse. 'I want to talk to you about that place.'

'The lighthouse?'

'You know I've been infatuated with the lighthouse since I was a child.'

'You have. Selby used to tell you exciting stories about it.' Ralph gave a little chuckle. 'I can remember the time you decided you were going to run away from home when we wouldn't let you stay up past your bedtime. You sneaked out but Betty clocked you from her cottage and followed you to Blue Water Bay. You'd decided you were going to hide out in the lighthouse, but your plan was floored as there was no road or jetty to it back in those days, and you were too small to even hold an oar to row a boat across. You sat down in one of the boats on the sand and Betty found you sulking.'

Dilly laughed. 'I can remember when Betty brought me home and the looks on both your faces, as you thought I was fast asleep in bed.'

'After that incident, your mum spent many years checking in on you nightly to make sure you didn't do it again.'

'Got to love a headstrong child.' She playfully nudged her dad's elbow. 'There's a profound sense of history and family heritage to that place.'

'Yes, there is. The lighthouse stands as a testament to your grandfather's diligent service, guiding ships safely to shore.'

'And my mother's unique beginnings.'

'When I was married to your mum, we researched the history of the lighthouse, and specifically the storm that raged the night she was born. Every source agreed it was the worst storm ever to hit Puffin Island. There were a number of lives lost that night, including your grandfather's.'

Suddenly Dilly was choked. 'I can't imagine how Granny got through it all. I was talking about it with Betty a few days ago.'

'Selby Sinton was a strong woman. She didn't suffer fools, but she was a fair, lovable woman. You already know that though.' Ralph smiled. 'When I first started dating your mum, she often put me in my place, but I have to admit she was always right.' Ralph glanced across towards the lighthouse.

'Did you know the lighthouse is up for auction?'

'Yes, I saw the article in the newspaper. That place will generate a lot of interest. I'm sure a lot of wealthy people will bid. I just hope it stays in keeping with Puffin Island's style and way of life.'

They both fixed their gaze across the water.

'Dad, that's where I come in. I'm thinking of transforming the premises on Lighthouse Lane into a community space, somewhere I can hold art classes and showcase local talent. I could do it if I moved my own work to somewhere new – the lighthouse, in fact – and established a new gallery there. It fits perfectly with the themes of my paintings of lighthouses, puffins and the sea.'

Ralph swung his gaze towards his daughter. 'Are you serious? You're thinking of bidding on the lighthouse?'

'Owning the lighthouse would mean preserving a piece of our family's legacy. I think I really need to do this.'

'It's true, if you owned the lighthouse the history it holds would be carried forward to future generations.'

Dilly smiled. 'Future generations are a long way off, but yes, if the price is right, I could make it my own and preserve it the way it deserves. I have my inheritance from Mum just sitting there, and I need proper living space because my flat above the gallery has been feeling increasingly cramped. The lighthouse has eight storeys, and I quite like the idea of living amongst the clouds.'

'You'll have the best view of Puffin Island, there's no doubt about that.'

'I can wave to you every morning from the top of the tower,' she said, smiling. 'It might be just a dream and I'm sure other investors will be in a better financial position than me, but something's telling me I have to try. It's just … I've no idea what it's going to be like on the inside and how it would actually be living in the lighthouse.'

'There will be rules and regulations to follow regarding the upkeep, but since they've built the road to the lighthouse, and the jetty, it at least makes it more accessible. I think you'd attract a lot of tourists who will be curious to see what's inside. Have you worked out your financials?'

Dilly shook her head. 'Not yet, that's this week's task, as I've no clue what anyone will be bidding or what it's even worth.'

Ralph looked thoughtful, his brow furrowed. 'It's going to be the most sought-after location on Puffin Island. You need to take a look around first, get a feel of the place. Then, if you like it, go for it. You don't know unless you try.'

'The open day is next Monday. My only worry is: what if I fall in love with the place and I don't win?'

'That's simple. It just means that it wasn't meant to be and something else will come along.'

'I know, but I already want it so badly. My latest painting features the lighthouse, and I had my grandparents in mind when I painted it. I think that was a sign. I would even go as far as saying it's my best yet.'

'All of your paintings are the best,' her dad said supportively.

'I'm about to work on something a little different,' she admitted, looking towards her easel. 'It's something for me, like nothing I've ever painted before.'

'Are you going to share?'

Dilly smiled. 'I'm attempting a portrait … of Mum. More of a serious painting.'

'I'll look forward to seeing it. And I'm looking forward to seeing how it goes with the lighthouse.'

'Fingers crossed. For now, okay to set up here for the day?' Dilly nodded to the small stretch of sand in front of her. 'I want to be close by.'

'Of course you can. You've come a long way in the last year and handled yourself so well.'

Dilly knew exactly what her father was referring to … Giles Fox. Her father had never warmed to him and had expressed his doubts on numerous occasions. He often mentioned that he just didn't have a good feeling about Giles, even though he rarely interfered in her personal life. His concern had created a small rift between them, one that lingered in the background for a while, causing Dilly to downplay the seriousness of her relationship when talking to her father, even though Giles was still a significant part of her life at the time.

'I'm never going to let myself fall for another man again.'

'You will, but next time it'll be the right one. Someone you deserve and who deserves you.'

As her dad spoke the words, Max Harrington popped into her thoughts. She wondered if her dad would remember him. She'd often spoken about him during her college days. 'You'll never guess who walked into the gallery yesterday.'

Before her dad could answer, the boat house phone rang out in the office. Ralph looked over his shoulder. 'I need to get back to work, but first let me introduce you to Luke's replacement. He's here for six months until Luke hopefully tires of travelling the world and comes back.'

'Youngsters of today,' joked Dilly, standing up and brushing herself down. She followed her dad inside to the office where a man was standing with his back to her. He hung up the phone and turned around, locking eyes with her.

'Max, let me introduce you to my daughter, Dilly.'

Dilly was stunned and Max looked just as surprised to see her as she was to see him. Why was he working in the boat house? Max was a brilliant, passionate artist who had mentored hundreds of student artists. The contrast between his past career, filled with creative brilliance, and his new job performing manual labour in the boat house was striking.

She took in his tousled hair, slight stubble and olive-green overalls, as his eyes widened and the penny dropped that she was Ralph's daughter.

'What are you doing here?' she asked, the unexpected sight of him giving her that usual flip of the stomach.

'Do you two know each other?' asked Ralph, suddenly aware something more was going on here.

'Dad, this is Mr Harrington, my old art teacher.'

'Max, it's Max,' added Max, looking as if he'd quite like to sink into the ground and disappear.

Dilly's eyes flitted towards Max's left hand. Clemmie was right, there was no longer a wedding band. That, combined with the fact that he was apparently painting boats for a living, had her completely confused.

'Max. Sorry, it's just habit. Dad, this is the best art teacher in the world. The teacher that shaped me into the artist I am today—'

'I don't think I can take the credit for that,' interrupted Max.

'I think you can. You remember, Dad, I used to talk about my fantastic teacher, the one who let me borrow his art books?'

Ralph smiled. 'You did. What a small world it is.'

'But what are you doing here?' Dilly was still clueless as to how he'd ended up here.

'Painting boats. I'm here for six months.'

Dilly glanced towards the hull of the nearby boat, which had a tin of brown paint and a large paintbrush sitting next to it. 'That must be monotonous. Sorry, Dad, didn't mean to offend.' She knew how condescending that must have sounded. 'But why?' she asked again, then realised she was putting Max on the spot and backtracked. 'I'm sorry, that was an intrusive question and none of my business, I do apologise.'

Max nodded his head. 'That's okay. Are you feeling better today?'

Ralph looked surprised. 'Feeling better? What's all this?'

'I fainted,' admitted Dilly.

'Just as I walked into her gallery yesterday.'

'You fainted? You said you'd been feeling ropey. Have you seen the doctor?' asked Ralph.

Dilly shook her head.

'Dilly! You must.'

'It just comes and goes. I probably just need to eat more. With all I have to do, I forget to eat sometimes, but when I faint it reminds me.'

Ralph looked horrified.

'Dad, I'm joking! I only fainted the once and I promise I'll take better care of myself.'

'Please do.'

The phone rang again and Max turned to answer it as Dilly and her father stepped outside.

Dilly leaned towards her father. 'Why would Max Harrington be painting boats, with his talent? It doesn't make any sense to me.'

'You don't need to make sense of it. What goes on in other people's lives is their business and not up for speculation. As long as his work is good, I'm happy. Which it is. So I have no complaints.'

'I'm not speculating, I'm just curious.'

'It's still none of our business.'

Dilly raised an eyebrow in question. 'You know more than you're letting on.'

'What I know about my employees is confidential and not open for discussion,' her dad reminded her, his voice protective.

Dilly narrowed her eyes. 'Okay, I was just curious, but you should know that you getting all defensive makes me think something bigger is going on.'

When Ralph didn't add anything else she threw up her arms in a gesture of surrender.

'Fine, I'll let you both get on with your work. But before I forget to ask, would you be free to come with me on Monday to look around the lighthouse?'

'Oh, Dilly, I'm so sorry. I'm away for the week. I'm travelling around the Scottish Highlands to look at a number of boats. Maybe we could contact the seller and arrange a separate viewing?'

'I don't think that's how it works but I can ask.' She tried to mask it but knew that the disappointment in her voice didn't go unnoticed.

'Did you just mention the lighthouse?' Max asked as he walked out of the office. 'I've booked another boat in,' he said to Ralph. 'I know we're strapped for time but I can do it over the weekend, as I've no plans.'

Ralph nodded his appreciation. 'Thank you and yes, we were just talking about the lighthouse.'

'I've seen it's up for auction.'

'I've got it into my head that I'm going to win it, live in it and open up a new gallery.'

'Wow! Wouldn't that be living the dream.' Max walked out in front of the boat house and stared out over the sea towards the lighthouse.

'I wanted my dad to come to the open day with me, but he's in Scotland.'

'I can come; when is it? I mean if that's okay with you, Ralph. I could shut the boat house for an hour or go during lunchtime.'

'I think that's a great idea.' Ralph placed a hand on his shoulder. 'With all the building maintenance work you've done in the last twelve months, you'll have just the right eye for any major costs or works that might be needed. We would appreciate that, wouldn't we, Dilly?'

Dilly again was taken back by this little piece of information. Artist to building maintenance worker was not what she had expected for Max's career trajectory. 'If it's okay with you?'

'Of course! I should be able to give you a fair idea of

how much things will cost if it's in need of repair or modernising,' continued Max.

'Thank you,' she replied, perplexed. She pointed to her easel. 'I'd best get to work as well. I'll hopefully catch up with you before Monday.'

Ralph carried Dilly's easel to the spot she indicated on the sand and she opened up her stool before setting out her paints and the water pot. But she didn't take her eyes off her dad.

'I can feel you watching me,' he said, laughter in his tone.

Dilly looked over her shoulder and saw Max moving around inside the boat house. 'What has happened in his life? Divorce, I assume?' she questioned. 'But surely that wouldn't mean such a huge career change.'

Ralph remained silent.

'Dad?'

'Sometimes people need a break, and a little breathing space. Max has proved himself already and like I said, it's his work I'm concerned with, not his private life. Now, that's all I'm prepared to say on the matter, aside from saying that no one who has ever worked here before has ever painted the hull of a boat as well as he has.' Ralph smiled, placing a hand on his daughter's shoulder before he turned and walked back toward the boat house.

Dilly's eyes followed him then moved to where Max was sitting on a stool painting the hull. The concentration on his face turned to a warm smile as he glanced over in her direction. Dilly mirrored his smile, but she was still wondering what exactly had gone on in his life since she saw him last, and why he had ended up here on Puffin Island.

Chapter Four

Dilly looked out over Blue Water Bay as the glorious afternoon came to an end. The sky was painted in shades of orange, casting a warm golden glow over the water. Paddleboarders glided gracefully over the calm, glassy surface. Children with fishing nets splashed near the shallow water of the shoreline and seagulls circulated overhead. The gentle breeze carried the scent of the saltwater and the sound of the puffins' mooing could be heard from the nearby cliffs.

Dilly tossed down her paintbrush in frustration. She'd been painting for three hours solid, but the painting just wasn't working. She'd been too distracted wondering why and how Max had ended up working at the boat house, knowing his salary would be nowhere near that of a teacher. He was intelligent, capable, and it baffled her that he would settle for such a modest job. Her curiosity was heightened by her dad's peculiar reaction when she had asked him. The fact that Ralph, usually an open book, had become uncharacteristically tight-lipped had only made it more intriguing.

Tilting her face up to the sun, she exhaled deeply and closed her eyes, savouring the gentle warmth on her skin. She ran her fingers through her hair, gathering it all together. With a practised motion, she twisted the strands into a messy bun, the loose ends framing her face. She reached for a clean paintbrush that was lying in her bag and secured the bun with the makeshift hairpin.

'Hard at it, I see.'

Dilly jumped to find Max beaming down at her.

'I wish! I've been painting for hours but my creativity just isn't flowing today.'

'Any particular reason why?'

'It's just one of those days,' she replied.

'And what's the title of this painting?'

'"One Moment in Time".'

Max studied the painting intently. It was whimsical, capturing a vivid scene with high cliffs rising majestically on both sides as the lighthouse stood proudly in the centre, guarding the rocks below. In the foreground a couple sat on the sand, sharing an ice-cream, their black Labrador paddling at the water's edge. The painting radiated a sense of carefree joy. 'And you say that's creativity not flowing? It looks amazing to me. Fairytale art at its best.'

Dilly noticed him screw up his face a little.

'I know that look! You always screwed up your face like that when you thought something could be better.'

'No, I didn't.'

'Oh yes, you did. Come on, what would you do differently?'

'This is your painting.'

Dilly held out the brush towards him. 'Do what you used to do.'

'I was your teacher then but not anymore. These days I'm sure it's you who could teach me a thing or two and I don't want to ruin the work of a world-famous artist.'

'Come on, your opinion matters to me.'

For a moment, Max hesitated, until Dilly moved off the stool and perched on the nearby rock. She gestured towards the painting. 'For me it's just missing a special something,' she said.

Dilly watched as he dipped the paintbrush in the water, his gaze shifting from the lighthouse to the sky. With a steady hand, he swept the brush over the palette, dousing it in vibrant orange. He then applied gentle strokes to the canvas, capturing the essence of a breath-taking sunset with hues of burnt orange.

'Wow! That looks stunning,' said Dilly admiringly.

Max looked up towards her. 'A sunset sky always evokes a sense of romance.' He handed her back the brush then stood up.

'It's like the old days. You'd always rescue my artwork.'

'Your artwork never needed rescuing. In fact, sometimes I thought you should be the one teaching.'

'That's very kind of you to say, but look how you've transformed this painting.' Dilly wanted to ask so many questions. She was still very curious about what had brought him to Puffin Island. 'If you're working for my dad, are you staying locally?'

'I am. I'm currently staying at Smuggler's Rest, but tomorrow I'm moving up there.' Max pointed to the top of the boat house. 'I'm renting it from your dad for the time I'm here.'

'That'll be handy for work. When I win the auction, we can wave across the harbour to each other.'

Max smiled. 'What was it they used in the past to communicate with the lighthouse keeper from the land?' He exhaled deeply as he tried to remember.

'The semaphore flags. Betty used them to try and alert my grandfather when my grandmother was in labour.'

'I suppose there were no other forms of communication back then. Could you imagine reading that message?'

'He didn't see the flags, due to the storm, so you'll never guess what my granny did. Picture the scene: a storm, a choppy sea and freezing conditions. Not ideal for what came next, which was my granny enlisting her best friend, Betty, and Betty's husband, who was a fisherman, to row them across to the lighthouse during her labour as she didn't want to give birth without my grandfather being there.'

'That's what I'd call brave.'

'Me too. Unfortunately, tragedy struck just as they arrived.'

'How?'

'The storm got worse and a boat crashed into the rocks.'

'Not their rowing boat?'

'No, they managed to arrive safety at the lighthouse and soon after my grandmother gave birth, with Betty by her side. But my grandfather missed it because he was helping to rescue the passengers whose boat had smashed against the rocks. Sadly, he didn't make it. He got swept out to sea and he never got to meet his daughter, my mum.'

'I can't even begin to...' Max stopped in his tracks. 'That's so sad.'

'It was. To make things worse, my granny was forced to move out of the cottage that came with my grandfather's lightkeeper job, and so she had to move in with Betty. Having lost her husband and her home in quick succession, it took her a while to rebuild her life, but she did it.'

'Your family is made of strong women. I have to admit, I did see the news about your mum's tragic accident. I'm really sorry for your loss.'

'Thank you.' She looked out towards the sea. 'Some days are more difficult than others, but on the bad days I tend to throw myself into painting a little bit more, so I guess there's a silver lining.'

'I'm the opposite. I've always found that on my bad days I can't paint. And recently, there's been more bad days than good.'

Dilly immediately noticed his mood slump. 'I'm sorry to hear that. Is there anything you want to talk about?'

Max shook his head. 'This place is my breather whilst I work out what to do next.' He paused. 'I'm really glad I saw the advert for the job at the boat house. Your dad is a very supportive man and I'm grateful he's given me this chance.'

There was a certain sadness about Max and Dilly found she wanted to lift his spirits back to where they had been only moments earlier when he'd had a paintbrush in his hand. Max didn't want to talk, and she didn't want to push him, but maybe in time he would confide in her.

She wondered if it had to do with his marriage breakdown. She remembered how her own life had shattered when she'd discovered that Giles was a complete fraud. At first, she couldn't talk to anyone about it, feeling she'd been fooled by his charm and good looks. Dilly had thought their chance encounter was like something out of a movie, with genuine love blossoming between them. She believed that when you knew, you knew, and there was no reason to take things slow if you were utterly in love. However, once she discovered what Giles really was, a romance scammer who nearly took her inheritance, she had to muster all her strength to keep it together.

She questioned everything he had ever said, the way he'd looked at her, and all the times he'd claimed to love her. It was devastating to realise everything had been a lie. Dilly couldn't fathom how anyone could play such a convincing game without genuine feelings, but he had. Despite a part of her wanting to believe he had some fondness for her, she knew it wasn't true – that's how scammers operated – and her heart was shattered into smithereens. She was merely collateral damage in his quest for money, and the only thing he hadn't anticipated was being found out. Feeling foolish, she was glad she had played down their romance to her friends and family in the last few months before his scam was revealed. She was just thankful her dad never said the words, 'I told you so.'

'Are you hungry?' she asked.

'I am.'

'Good, because I'm suddenly famished,' she exclaimed, her stomach rumbling loudly, prompting shared laughter. 'I'm craving a towering stack of fluffy pancakes smothered in Nutella. How does that sound to you?'

'I'm game if you are,' he replied with a twinkle in his eye. Her stomach fluttered with a sensation completely unrelated to hunger. Shaking herself slightly, she reaffirmed to herself that the next six months were solely about her. After Giles, she had no intention of entering into any relationship, her focus instead on expanding her business and, hopefully, winning the lighthouse.

'Then I know just the place.' She grabbed her bag. 'This way.'

'Dill, you can't leave all your equipment here. It'll be stolen and sold on the web before you could blink.'

Dilly felt an instant warmth spread through her chest. He was the only person who had ever shortened her nickname. She had been Delilah to her mum her entire life, and her dad and closest friends called her Dilly, a nickname she also embraced professionally. But hearing him call her Dill brought back memories of the past, of after-class chats about art, visits to the local galleries, the books he had shared with her, and the closeness they had felt sitting next to each other, painting.

She grinned. 'This is Puffin Island. The last crime committed here was when Clemmie, Amelia, and I were around ten years old, sneaking extra pick'n'mix into our paper bag without paying. I still feel a twinge of guilt about it. Trust me, this will be fine.'

They strolled across the sandy shore, their feet sinking into the soft surface as they navigated through parasols and the last of the sunbathers soaking up the sunshine. Blue Water Bay buzzed with tourists, and as they walked towards the Cosy Kettle they caught whiffs of coffee and the lively chatter of nearby children engrossed in building the grandest sandcastle on the beach.

'That coffee smells so strong.' Dilly wriggled her nose.

'Do you fancy one?' asked Max.

She shook her head. 'It's strange. Until recently, I was a huge coffee drinker, and all of a sudden, I don't want anything to do with it. In fact, right now I'm really craving a milkshake. They make the best ones here.'

'And your favourite milkshake?'

Dilly scanned the chalkboard outside the Cosy Kettle. 'I'm torn between going double chocolate with my pancakes and shake, or opting for strawberry ... but then the vanilla one is calling my name, too,' she mused aloud.

Max laughed. 'You're going to be sick.'

'I'm actually feeling okay this afternoon so I'm going to take full advantage. What do you fancy?'

'I think I'll go for pancakes with ice-cream and strawberries, along with a latte.'

They approached the counter where Becca greeted them with a wide smile. Becca, with her sun-kissed complexion dotted with freckles and a long blonde braid cascading down her back, was a familiar face on Puffin Island. She had set up her small beachside hut, which she named the Cosy Kettle, around three years ago, offering hot drinks during the late nights and early mornings. The hut quickly became a beloved spot for island workers, especially those who had to cross the causeway at odd hours when nothing else was open.

'Hey Dilly, how are you?' she asked cheerfully.

'I'm good, thanks. Looks like you've had a busy day,' Dilly observed, glancing at the multitude of people still spread out on the sand.

'Run off my feet, but no complaints here. Unfortunately, all the ice-creams are gone,' Becca replied apologetically.

'Pancakes, then?' Dilly inquired hopefully.

'Always got pancakes,' Becca assured them.

After taking their orders, Becca turned to the stove behind her and began preparing their pancakes, leaving Dilly and Max to find a table. He pulled out a chair for her.

'Thank you,' she said appreciatively.

They settled into their seats, gazing out across the bay with the lighthouse standing prominently ahead.

'How would anyone know its true value unless they work in property?' Dilly asked, her eyes fixed on the lighthouse.

'We'll have a better idea on Monday,' Max replied.

Dilly glanced at him. 'I like the way you said we.'

'You'll certainly be the envy of everyone here if you're able to buy it. It's such a beautiful spot, and I'd be happy to help restore it to its former glory at a reasonable cost, unlike some contractors. If it needs it.'

'I couldn't ask you to do that after a long day at the boat house. The last thing you need is more manual labour,' Dilly protested.

'Believe me, it would be a welcome distraction,' Max insisted. 'I've got nothing else pressing, other than thinking about what comes next, and I'd be happy to put that off a bit longer.'

'Do you need to move on?' Dilly asked, gesturing towards the bay. 'I'm not sure I could ever give this up.'

'This is just a temporary escape. I needed something different, away from the usual, just for a while,' Max explained.

Seizing the moment, Dilly inquired, 'What happened?

You were a fantastic teacher and you're still a brilliant artist, I could see that from today.'

'It's a series of events that shaped my path,' Max replied. He paused briefly. 'Sometimes life takes unexpected turns. Change is never easy, even when you know it's for the best.'

Dilly understood that sentiment all too well. Her recent personal turmoil with Giles had left her shattered, and hesitant to trust again. 'I hear you,' she said softly.

'But for now, Puffin Island is my sanctuary,' Max continued, looking up just as Becca placed a generous stack of pancakes and their drinks in front of them.

Dilly thanked Becca warmly, though her mind raced with curiosity about why Max needed a safe place.

'I'm looking forward to helping you out with the lighthouse,' Max said, picking up his knife and fork.

'I have to win the auction first,' Dilly replied, smiling.

'Your dad seems confident you'll do it. It's great he's so supportive.'

'He is. Generally, as long as I don't risk bankrupting myself, he'll support my decisions. I can't wait to see inside and explore where my mum was born. Hopefully any work needed is just cosmetic. I'm pretty handy with DIY and painting walls is easy,' she added.

'It's all so exciting. I have every faith you'll get the lighthouse,' Max encouraged.

'You make it sound simple. What are you doing tomorrow night?'

'I'll have to check my diary… Oh, absolutely nothing,' he replied with a smile. 'Why, what are you thinking? More pancakes?'

She laughed. 'I'm planning to put together a financial

plan and figure out my highest bid. I could cook you dinner, if you'd like to help?'

'That sounds lovely. What time?' Max asked.

'Seven o'clock?'

'Should I bring a bottle?'

'Perfect. I really want this. It's a once-in-a-lifetime opportunity,' Dilly admitted.

'Dinner with me, or buying the lighthouse?' Max teased, a glint in his eye.

Dilly smiled as she cut into her pancake. 'I'm not saying.' She glanced playfully at him across the table.

Chapter Five

The following morning, Dilly drew back the curtains and surveyed the coastline. Under the cloudless sky, the view over Blue Water Bay was simply breathtaking, the waves sparkling like diamonds as they rolled onto the sandy shore. The gallery was due to open in the next hour and she'd decided today was the day she was going to start a special painting that she planned to unveil at the opening of her new gallery.

After a quick shower, Dilly tied her hair up in her signature messy bun, slipped into her favourite dungarees and stepped into her Birkenstocks. The table was still cluttered with financial documents, which she quickly gathered and moved to the dresser before preparing her breakfast. Yesterday, after collecting her paints and easels from the beach, she'd settled onto the sofa and delved into researching the lighthouse, trying to estimate its true value. Knowing her budget limitations, which might disadvantage her against other bidders, she tried to stay optimistic.

Despite finding no concrete valuation online, similar lighthouses in comparable condition had sold for around three hundred thousand pounds, but who knew what was going to happen at the auction. For the rest of the evening, she'd browsed through countless recipes on TikTok and Instagram, searching for something manageable to impress Max during their dinner tomorrow night. While she could easily opt for Clemmie's homemade lasagne or pie from the tearoom, there was a part of her that craved the satisfaction of cooking herself. When she was with Giles, he'd never allowed her to cook. He preferred Michelin-star restaurants and lavish expenditure on his credit card, which she now knew was likely funded by his scams and the unsuspecting victims he'd exploited.

With her laptop still open from the night before, Dilly wiggled the mouse and the recipe she had chosen appeared on the screen. She had a soft spot for Jamie Oliver recipes, and with fresh fish abundant from the island's fishmonger, she settled on a fish pie. The recipe suggested it would be delicious to eat with baked beans in a tomato sauce, a quirky twist that the reviews insisted was a must and surprisingly delicious. Dilly decided to go for it, planning to serve it with steamed green beans tossed in lemon juice, olive oil and chopped red onion. She could pick up the ingredients during her lunch break, and with the gallery closing at four-thirty, she had ample time to prepare the meal.

After unlocking the front door of the gallery and flipping the closed sign to open, she relocated her laptop to her desk at the back of the gallery space. Her morning routine was always the same, checking and responding to important emails before setting up her paints for the day. As usual, her inbox was full to the brim; there were several website inquiries about specific paintings for sale, and interview requests, including one from the *Sunday Times* supplement, awaiting her attention. Then one email in particular caught her eye, prompting her to exclaim aloud, 'Whoa! I wasn't expecting that!', completely taken aback.

'Not expecting what?' Clemmie breezed through the door with a smile.

Dilly slammed down the laptop lid.

Clemmie narrowed her eyes. 'What's on the laptop? You're acting very suspicious. What don't you want me to see? And are you blushing? You *are* blushing! Spill it.'

'I'm not blushing!' Dilly protested. 'Well, maybe just a little, but that email should have come with a warning.'

'Show me!' Clemmie moved to the side of the table, and Dilly swivelled the laptop towards her. She lifted the lid slightly, and Clemmie tilted her head to the side.

'Jeez! I never pegged you for looking at porn this early in the morning.'

'I'd hope you wouldn't think I'd look at porn at any time of the day!'

'Are these your fans, sending you dick pics? You find that, don't you? The second you become well known people think it's okay to send you anything.'

'I don't find that,' she grinned, 'and this isn't porn. I have to choose a male model for our art class. I thought if we kicked off with a gorgeous life model in the first week, it would entice our new arty friends back.'

'You do know the majority of your friends are only coming because you've promised a nude male model, don't you? Not much goes on, on this island, and we have to embrace any chance of excitement.'

Dilly laughed. 'It all goes on, on this island and we all know who holds most of the secrets.'

'My grandmother! What she doesn't know about this island isn't worth knowing.' Clemmie's eyes twinkled. 'I can't believe the agency actually gives you a choice.' She pulled up a chair.

'What are you doing?'

'At times like this, I think you need your best friend. We need to study them and make the right decision. We don't want all the new budding artists to be disappointed, now do we?'

'Clemmie, you're terrible! Shouldn't you be opening the tearoom?'

'It's in my grandmother's capable hands for the next half-hour. I needed to run some errands and thought I would call in on my way past, and now I'm glad I did. This shouldn't be a decision you make on your own.'

Dilly gave Clemmie a mischievous smile and moved the laptop between them. She opened the lid slowly. 'Why is it I feel like a naughty schoolgirl?'

'They are professionals, and this is their job. I wonder if there are any rising stars amongst them.' Clemmie giggled. 'I'm curious to know how much they earn.'

'It's actually quite lucrative. Would you believe they can make three to four grand a month? But I wouldn't fancy it much in winter.'

'Wow! I would never have thought of that. You pick your top three, and I'll pick mine. They definitely come in all shapes and sizes. Can we zoom in?'

'Clemmie!'

'Just joking!' she replied playfully, writing her top three on a piece of paper and folding it over like she was doing a school test. 'I don't want you copying mine.'

Dilly shook her head in jest as she did the same. 'Let's compare.'

Turning over the paper they both laughed, seeing they'd selected the same models. 'Great minds!' they chorused in unison.

'I'm thinking Pierre for the first session. He's got a good pose, interesting facial features, some asymmetry in limb placement. His photo shows emotion.'

Clemmie stared at Dilly. 'Professional through and through. I would say, he has a fabulous chest, great thighs and…'

'Stop there!'

'Pierre it is!' Clemmie stood up and checked her watch. 'I'd best get these errands run.'

'You'd best. I'll see you later.'

Dilly was still laughing as Clemmie closed the door behind her. She could always rely on her friends to put a smile on her face.

After confirming Pierre with the agency, Dilly switched on the lights and slipped her painting smock over her dungarees before walking into the paint room at the back of the gallery. The long table was a riot of colour, covered in bottles of paint in every imaginable shade. Paintbrushes, their bristles stained and worn, were stored in numerous jam jars. Piled up in the sink were palettes caked with dried paint, and against the wall, blank canvases of various sizes stood in stacks. In the corner, propped up on the easel, was the blank canvas on which she was about to start. Unlike her usual whimsical landscapes filled with puffins and the seaside, this one would never be for sale. It was deeply personal to her, a portrait of her mother.

The photo she was painting from rested on the easel's ledge, a poignant reminder of a cherished moment frozen in time. It had been taken the night before Eva left Puffin Island for her holiday with Anton, captured at The Sea Glass Restaurant during their anniversary celebration. It was the last photo she ever took of her mother.

Dilly vividly recalled her mother's excitement that evening about their impending holiday. Her glowing skin, elegantly styled hair, and a stunning diamond necklace gifted by Anton. The three of them had savoured lobster and champagne, unaware it would be their final dinner together. As they left the restaurant they said goodnight, exchanging hugs and a kiss on the cheek. Little did Dilly know it was to be their last goodbye.

Dilly carefully mixed the paint colours she needed on her palette, arranging everything just right in the quiet space at the back of the gallery. Some days, she enjoyed sitting near the window, allowing tourists to observe her creative process and ask questions. But today, she wanted to immerse herself in her thoughts as she wetted her brush and began to paint.

Whenever she thought of her mother, a dull ache would grip her chest and she couldn't help remembering that fateful day when she lost her.

It had started off as one of the happiest days of her life. As part of the PR campaign for the Netflix series, she was featured in one of the national newspapers and she'd rushed to the island shop the day after the show had premiered, grabbed a copy of the newspaper and hurried to the tearoom. With Clemmie by her side, they eagerly flipped through to the lifestyle supplement, where her own face greeted them from the cover under the headline: WHERE DREAMS AND REALITY INTERTWINE. Five pages unfolded from there, detailing her journey as an artist, what inspired her paintings, and a link to her website showcasing her paintings for sale.

They hadn't even turned to page five when Dilly's emails started pinging incessantly. Within ten minutes, traffic to her website had quadrupled, and thousands of pounds' worth of original paintings had been sold along with numerous print copies. Shell-shocked, Dilly found it hard to believe. Checking her bank account confirmed a healthy balance, like nothing she had ever seen before. From that moment on, she was thrust into the limelight, her name and work catapulted to worldwide fame overnight. She vividly remembered Clemmie's embrace, her friend sharing in her excitement, knowing the years of hard work that had led to this moment. Outside the tearoom, she called her mum, but it went straight to voicemail. Her words stumbled over each other in disbelief and joy as she asked her mum to call her back. Sending a photo of the newspaper, she waited anxiously, but there was no response.

With the newspaper tucked under her arm, she'd walked home, and as she turned onto Anchor Way, her heart sank at the sight of a police car parked on the cobbled street. Two policemen stood outside the gallery, and panic surged. The thought *Have I been robbed?* raced through her mind. Had she become a target for theft so quickly after the TV show's release?

'Delilah Waters?'

'Y-yes,' she stuttered, glancing nervously toward the gallery. Everything appeared undisturbed.

'Would it be possible to go inside?'

She nodded and unlocked the door, a sinking feeling settling in her gut. As the police officers delivered the devastating news, a strangled cry escaped her and tears streamed down her cheeks. Her mother and stepfather, on their holiday, had been enjoying a stroll along a narrow, winding road when a speeding car had struck them, hurling them into the sea. The driver of the car had also been killed, having lost control of the vehicle on the bend and plunged into the water below. Despite a witness being present, the bodies had not been found, likely swept away by the sea.

Two years had passed since that tragic day, and the lack of closure had always weighed heavily on Dilly's mind. Without a body to mourn properly, she had travelled to France, standing on the very road where their lives had been taken. She still wished desperately that it was nothing more than a terrible dream.

Back in the present, the causeway opened and soon streams of tourists were meandering through the cobbled streets of Puffin Island. The morning flew by, and as lunchtime approached, she removed her smock, grabbed her bag and purse, and locked up the gallery. She strolled in a leisurely manner towards The Fisherman's Catch, a quaint fishmonger's hut nestled in the harbour. Intent on fresh haddock, she swiftly made her purchase before heading back toward Blue Water Bay, the sun's warmth kissing her face. A smile played on her lips, as she thought about spending the evening with Max. It couldn't begin soon enough.

Later that afternoon, Dilly closed the gallery and set her plan in motion. First, she needed to prepare the pie and pop it into the oven, then indulge in a quick shower with the brand-new body wash she'd ordered online. The table was already laid, though she hesitated, unsure if it was too extravagant. She had draped her favourite tablecloth over the round table in the open-plan kitchen, and brought out the posh wine glasses usually reserved for Christmas, along with her finest plates. In the centre of the table, she'd arranged a couple of wild roses that she'd picked from a bush outside the gallery, and complemented it all with a few tealights.

'It's too much,' she murmured to herself, debating whether it looked too romantic for just an evening at home. Removing the flowers and candles left the table looking bare, so, thinking she might as well go for it, she placed them back on the table before slipping her apron over her head and gathering the ingredients from the fridge.

After preheating the oven, Dilly began to follow the recipe from her laptop, which was open on the worktop. First, she boiled the potatoes in salted water, briefly cooking them before adding the eggs to boil for eight minutes until hard. Meanwhile, she steamed the spinach until it was tender. Draining the potatoes and peeling and quartering the eggs, she hummed along to the radio while preparing a creamy mixture of onion, carrot, olive oil, cream, cheese, lemon juice, mustard and parsley in a frying pan. All she had to do was add the bite-sized chunks of fish, mash the potatoes and add everything together.

Unwrapping the fish, Dilly let out a squeal as two pairs of eyes stared back at her.

'Oh my God.' She stepped back instinctively, though the fish couldn't possibly move as they were dead. She had no idea how to gut a fish. She had requested the freshest haddocks available, not expecting Bill to fetch them straight from the net on a boat that had just arrived in the harbour.

The kitchen, once comfortably warm, now felt stifling. Flustered, Dilly hurriedly opened the window, letting in a rush of fresh air. Why had she volunteered to cook tonight? She should have just made life easy and picked something up from the tearoom. Everything had been going smoothly until this moment and now it was turning into a complete disaster. Staring at the fish, she wondered what the hell she was going to do now.

Taking a deep breath, Dilly tried to compose herself. How difficult could it be to gut a fish? She tapped on the keyboard and opened up YouTube. There she watched a video of a fishmonger expertly cutting off the fins, slicing through the belly, and chopping off the head. Despite her determination, Dilly winced and instinctively brought the back of her hand up to her mouth, suddenly feeling nauseous. Closing her eyes briefly, she just couldn't bring herself to do it, so she quickly wrapped up the fish and returned them to the fridge. She wouldn't be eating fish any time soon.

With the fridge empty of any other options, Dilly

focused on finishing the meal. After mashing the potatoes, she spread them evenly over the creamy sauce in the dish, sprinkled them with cheese, and placed the whole thing in the oven. Disappointed that her planned recipe had gone awry, she resigned herself to a simpler dinner. Tonight's meal would just have to be pie.

Five minutes later she jumped in the shower and soon after, the second disaster struck. Dilly stood wrapped in a towel in front of her wardrobe, confronted by her tragic fashion sense. Jumpers were haphazardly shoved onto shelves, piles of jeans teetered precariously, dresses hung askew on their hangers, and mismatched shoes littered the floor. With a sigh, she surveyed her collection, mostly consisting of comfortable, paint-splattered clothes. She swiped up and down the hangers, but nothing seemed to stand out.

Her phone pinged.

> I hope you don't mind, but I got your phone number from your website. I'm looking forward to tonight x

The first thing Dilly noticed was the kiss at the end of the message. She tried to dismiss it as a casual gesture people often used in texts, but she couldn't ignore the goosebumps that prickled her skin at the thought of spending the evening with Max. Excitement surged through her entire body.

> I don't mind at all. See you in thirty x

As she saved his number to her phone Dilly couldn't

help but smile. Memories from college flooded back, specifically how the girls in his art class had always tried in vain to get his number – and now she had it securely stored in her phone. She found herself thinking about him more and more as she glanced at the clock. Now he was due to arrive in twenty-five minutes. Damn, time was slipping away, and she still hadn't decided what to wear. Then her eyes fell on her ditzy flower summer dress. Perfect. She pulled it off the hanger and slipped it over her head.

'Shit.'

The dress wouldn't budge past her bust. She tugged and wriggled, but the fabric gave way with a loud rip. Frustration and embarrassment flooded her as she managed to free herself from the ruined dress and stared at the gaping tear at the back.

She muttered angrily at herself, knowing she hadn't been taking care of herself since Giles. She couldn't even remember the last time she'd prepared a nutritious meal. She was furious at herself for falling into such unhealthy habits, but there was nothing to be done; there was no magic cure to lose at least half a stone in the next twenty minutes.

Now the oven started beeping, signalling that time was running out before Max arrived – and still the panicking Dilly needed to get dressed. Opting for comfort, she settled on some stretchy and forgiving cargos and a nice sweater. It wasn't quite the drop-dead-gorgeous look she had envisioned, but she made a mental promise to invest in some new clothes and start taking better care of herself, beginning right now … well, maybe tomorrow, as there was chocolate roulade for dessert and she wasn't going to let that go to waste. After running a brush through her hair, she admired her sun-kissed skin in the mirror, noticing the long line of freckles across her nose that had appeared after painting in the harbour under yesterday's sunshine. At least something was going right for her today.

With the oven still beeping, Dilly hurried to the kitchen, grabbed her oven gloves and checked on the pie. Satisfied, she lowered the temperature and quickly set to work cooking the greens and warming up a can of baked beans. Pouring herself a glass of her favourite wine, she took a quick sip, savouring the brief moment of calm, just as the doorbell rang. Setting down her glass, she hurried downstairs to the gallery and unlocked the front door.

On the other side stood Max, his smile warm and welcoming. 'Hi,' he greeted, holding up a bottle. 'I didn't know if you preferred red or white. I opted for white.'

Dilly opened the door wider and was pleasantly surprised when Max stepped inside the gallery and kissed her on both cheeks. She caught his familiar aroma immediately. It was the same aftershave he had worn all those years ago. Briefly closing her eyes, she savoured the nostalgia that washed over her. When she opened her eyes, Max had an amused look on his face.

'I'm sorry, I got lost for a moment there.' She grinned. 'That's the same aftershave you always wore in class.'

'It is. You have a very good memory. Some things never change,' Max replied. 'This is for you.'

In his other hand, he held a package wrapped in brown paper. Dilly recognised the signature wrapping and personalised sticker from The Story Shop on Lighthouse Lane.

'It's from one of my favourite shops.'

'The Story Shop is quite something. I could spend hours in there. After browsing the travel section dreaming of Italy, I ventured into the classics, but it was the art bookcase where I stumbled upon this and immediately thought of you.' Max handed her the book.

Dilly eagerly tore open the paper and let out a small gasp. 'I can't believe you remembered.' She held up Robert Henri's *The Art Spirit*, one of the most inspiring books she had ever read. '"A classic work of advice, criticism and inspiration for lovers of art,"' she read from the back cover.

'Lovers of art, indeed,' Max said warmly, gazing into her eyes. 'You probably have your own copy.'

Dilly shook her head with a smile. 'I haven't, even though it's one of my favourite books of all time.' Without thinking, she leaned in and kissed Max on the cheek, lingering for a moment to savour that all-too-familiar scent that had taken her by surprise a moment ago. Her heart fluttered slightly as she pulled away slowly. 'Such an amazing gift. Thank you.'

'I'm glad you like it.'

'I do, thank you. I'll treasure it. Come on, let me get you a drink.'

They made their way through the gallery and climbed a wrought-iron spiral staircase that led directly upstairs to Dilly's living room. Max paused in surprise. 'Woah, look at this. I wasn't expecting that.'

'It's something else, isn't it?' Dilly replied.

'Isn't it just,' Max agreed, holding Dilly's gaze before turning back to admire the view.

'There's nothing better than pulling back the curtains and seeing the beautiful turquoise sea gazing back at you.'

'This place is perfect. Gorgeous furnishings, fabulous wall art, and you get to wake up to exceptional views of the bay,' Max observed.

Dilly's open-plan living room was stylish, light and airy, decorated in sea greens and blue tones that echoed the ocean panorama beyond.

'Why would you want to give this up?' Max asked, looking out towards the lighthouse.

Pouring the wine, Dilly replied, 'I'm not giving it up, I just want a little more living space.'

'I could sit here for hours watching the waves roll in, and it must be amazing when it rains,' Max mused.

Cuddling up on the sofa with a heated throw and a good book while the rain lashed against the window was one of Dilly's favourite pastimes.

'It's very atmospheric. This place was my mum's before she married Anton. In fact, this place is the reason they met,' Dilly explained. 'There's an antique shop next door, and Anton was an antique dealer. One afternoon, during a thunderstorm, he had an appointment at the shop but arrived early, only to find it closed. At the time, Mum's shop had just opened – Waggy Tails, a classy boutique for lovable pets. He stepped inside to take shelter from the rain, and the rest is history, as they say. Let me get you a drink.'

Dilly placed the book gently on the coffee table and poured Max a glass of wine, taking it to him where he was standing in front of the window.

'Cheers,' she said, clinking her glass against his. 'It's really lovely to see you again.'

'And you,' Max replied, his eyes lingering on hers before taking a sip. 'What will you do with this place? If you buy the lighthouse.'

'I was originally thinking of using it for storage...'

Max looked horrified. 'You can't use a place like this for storage.'

She smiled. 'Of course I'm not using it for storage! I'm going to use it for art classes!' She stretched her arm towards the magnificent view. 'I want to give back to the local creative community by making this a community gallery that nurtures new talent in the area and showcases their work. That view would inspire many.'

'Without a doubt, it would. You are amazing and I think that's a perfect idea.' Max smiled. 'There was a lot of talent around when I worked at the college but no outside art community as such. To showcase their work in a space like this would be incredible for them.'

'It would. Dinner is ready, if you'd like to take a seat?'

'I have to say I'm absolutely starving. What are we eating?' Max asked eagerly, peering towards the oven before pulling out a chair at the table.

'It's a surprise pie,' Dilly revealed with a smile, as she plated up the greens and placed the baked beans in a separate dish.

'This looks interesting. Baked beans and green beans.'

'Jamie Oliver said the baked beans are a must,' Dilly remarked, moving aside the vase of roses to place the pie dish in the centre of the table.

'Dil, that looks amazing and smells...' Max leaned forward to inhale deeply. 'What does it smell like? What kind of pie do we have here?'

'It's a simple fish pie,' she explained, scrunching her face in thought. 'I went down to the fishmongers…'

'Fish pie? Excellent! I love fish pie and it's been a while since I've made it. Since being on my own, I don't seem to cook very often. In fact, I can't even remember the last time I ate greens. Lately, I find myself at Beachcomber Bakery every lunchtime,' Max admitted with a chuckle.

'Robin's sausage rolls and pasties are to die for, though,' Dilly said with a grin. 'But not good on the waistline.'

'Thank you for this.' Max looked genuinely appreciative.

'It's my pleasure. I'm the same, to be honest, I've not been looking after myself since…' Dilly paused, stopping the name Giles from slipping out. The last thing she wanted was to start the night with a conversation about a man whom she held in such contempt.

'Your mum?' Max gently prompted.

Dilly nodded. 'You need to look after yourself.'

'And you, too. Maybe we could look after each other for the better while I'm around for the next six months.'

'I'd like that,' replied Dilly, meaning every word. She couldn't look away as she passed him the dish of greens. 'Now, about the pie. There's something I need to tell you.'

'Sounds intriguing.'

'Like I said, I went to the fishmongers and asked Bill for his freshest haddock…'

Max scooped the pie onto his plate.

'He gave me the freshest haddock you could have possibly wished for. He literally disappeared out the back and… I have a confession to make.' Dilly took a sip of her wine. 'He gave me whole fish, with their heads still on, which I didn't know until I unwrapped them about an hour ago... They were looking at me, and I couldn't bear to chop their heads off or cut off their gills, so,' she screwed up her face, 'they're still in the fridge. So, now we have cheesy mash in a creamy sauce with baked beans and greens. I'm not sure I'm going to appear on *MasterChef* anytime soon, or win a Michelin star... Sorry! It's not one of my finest moments.'

Max laughed. 'That is too funny. We just have pie but I bet it's the best pie.'

They began to tuck in, and despite the lack of fish, it was surprisingly tasty. Soon their plates were empty, and Max topped up their wine. 'I really did enjoy that.'

'You don't have to say that.'

'Maybe I do, if I want to come again.'

'And do you want to come again?'

'I'm enjoying myself so far.' Again, he gave her a smile that made her heart skip a beat, the same feeling she'd had all those years ago. 'And potato pie is much better than a ready meal for one. I think I still have one left in the bottom drawer of the freezer.'

'No one ever goes in the bottom drawer of the freezer.'

'Which means you'll have to invite me more often, otherwise I'll have no choice but to dive into my freezer's depths.'

Dilly laughed softly. 'I think I can manage that. After all, we have a lighthouse to buy.' She paused, still feeling curious about what had transpired in Max's life since her college days and how he'd ended up working for her father. Taking a breath, she asked the burning question.

'What have you been doing since I left college? I was surprised to see you working for my father. As much as I love him and the boat house, you were a brilliant teacher. It's such a shame you've walked away from it.' As soon as she asked, Dilly noticed a flicker of emotion pass over Max's face.

'Divorce happened, and I lost my zest for life,' Max began quietly. 'If I was going to survive, I had to walk away from everything I knew, and the only way I could move forward was to make a completely fresh start. During that time, I lost my love for painting and teaching. I prefer my own company these days, and I'm still figuring out what my next steps are.'

'I'm really sorry to hear that,' Dilly replied. She understood that people needed to turn in on themselves during difficult times. She had been lucky that when Giles knocked the stuffing out of her, painting had provided her with an escape.

'Puffin Island has a certain magic about it. It's a special place with wonderful people and I think it's going to do me the world of good, being here.'

'It's the best place with the best people.'

'I got that impression right from the start. Your dad was very kind and showed me empathy. I really appreciate everything he's done for me in such a short space of time, with the flat and the job. I didn't think I'd get the job because I was somewhat over-qualified and why would a man who was a teacher and an artist want to be painting boats? But it's exactly what I need at the moment. It's given me purpose.' His voice cracked.

'It sounds like you've had a difficult time.'

'Waking up to the view of the sea and the sound of the

waves rolling in definitely makes mornings easier. Now, let's talk about this lighthouse.'

'I'm incredibly excited about it and can't wait for the open day. Firstly, it will give us an opportunity to scope out the competition, as I'm sure they'll be checking it out too. Secondly, we can assess how much work might be needed. Come and have a look at this.' Dilly picked up both wine glasses and settled on the rug opposite the coffee table, gesturing for Max to join her. As he sat across from her on the settee, Dilly reached under the table and retrieved a large round tube. She took out, and carefully unrolled, a detailed plan, which she laid out on the table. To keep it from rolling back up, she used a book and her laptop to weigh down the edges. The plan illustrated the interior layout of the lighthouse, offering a glimpse of its potential.

'Wow! This looks amazing,' said Max with admiration. 'You've been working hard.'

'This is the layout of the lighthouse interior according to the auctioneer's website. It shows the dimensions of every room, and I've already mapped out what I'd like to do with them once I win the bid, which I fully intend to do.'

'I can see that.'

Dilly picked up a pencil and pointed to the plan. 'The ground floor, currently a living room, will transform into the gallery space. I have so many ideas swirling around in my head, especially about the lighting and layout. What do you think?'

'I think you could easily double as an interior designer with this level of detail,' Max observed.

'I started painting this morning, but my mind kept drifting back to the lighthouse. I couldn't focus, so I began sketching this.' She gestured towards the window. 'Each level has these expansive windows, perfect for natural light, but I'll definitely need additional lighting for the gallery. The centrepiece will be the painting I'm currently working on, with a one-way viewing system that visitors will circle around,' she explained with a grin. 'It seems fitting for a lighthouse. The first and second floors are bedrooms, the third floor a bathroom, another bedroom on the fourth. Fifth and sixth are a dining room and kitchen. There's lots of space so there might even be a chance to expand the gallery onto the first floor.'

Max gently touched her arm. 'You really have your heart set on this, don't you?'

Dilly felt a sudden rush of warmth from his touch and wondered if he sensed the same. He gazed directly at her. 'I do,' she replied softly. 'But it all boils down to money and whether someone else has more to offer.'

'That's something we won't know until the day,' he said calmly.

'I'm planning a new collection for the new gallery,' Dilly continued, feeling emboldened. 'I want to draw everyone and everything in the past, present, and future of Puffin Island. I imagine a vibrant community atmosphere, here in this gallery, with possibly light refreshments and a feel-good ambiance.'

'How are you going to make money from a community gallery?'

'I'd take commissions from any sales and charge artists a small fee to display their work in the gallery. Exhibition fees are another possibility, as well as offering workshops and art classes. I could also host special events and private viewings for new collections. Additionally, I could sell art supplies, prints and merchandise, like postcards, posters and limited-edition prints of all the artwork, including my own. Plus, I can apply for art grants to help fund community programmes and offset the gallery's operating costs.'

'You've got it all figured out,' said Max. 'You're not just an artist but also a savvy businesswoman and soon-to-be lighthouse owner.' His gaze intensified, and Dilly found herself momentarily captivated by his dark lashes and perfect lips. They had spent three years together in art class, but Max had always been out of bounds. Now he wasn't anymore.

Dilly sensed an unspoken connection with him and wondered what it would be like to break down that barrier. He was effortlessly charming and undeniably attractive. 'Did you ever imagine our paths would cross again?' she asked, genuinely curious, moving next to him on the settee.

'I never doubted it,' Max replied, taking a sip of wine. 'I always knew I'd walk into one of your galleries and congratulate you on your success. I remember seeing you on the TV and in the Sunday newspaper, and I couldn't believe it. One day, I'll have one of your paintings hanging in my home. I just need to find a permanent place to settle.'

'You'll find it,' Dilly reassured him. 'I've heard divorce isn't easy. It must be tough.'

'It's been challenging,' Max admitted, his smile fading. 'I don't think I'll ever put myself in that position again.'

'I understand,' Dilly replied softly, thinking of her own past with Giles. She could never comprehend how someone could fake love and deceive another for financial gain.

'Shall we have a look over your figures and try and work out your maximum bid?'

The information Dilly was about to share with Max felt deeply personal, and for the past twenty-four hours she had deliberated over whether to share it. A similar scenario had unfolded with Giles, who had spun a tale about finding their dream home and convinced her to disclose details about her inheritance, all under the pretence of planning their future together. Thank God she had discovered his deceit when she did. With Max, however, the situation felt different. She trusted him. He wasn't driven by financial gain. He was here to support her, like he'd done in the past.

'I've compiled a spreadsheet,' Dilly began as they moved to the small round table in the corner of the room. 'This is the amount I can access. Do you think it's enough?'

Max took a moment to absorb the numbers spread out before him. 'You can't empty out every penny,' he replied thoughtfully. 'And you need to account for other expenses such as bills, upkeep, and the costs of converting the lighthouse into your home and the gallery. It won't come cheap. Plus, if you're keeping this place, your expenses will double unless you consider a grant. Depending on the lighthouse's heating system, upgrading or replacing it could be a significant cost.'

'That's where this spreadsheet comes in,' Dilly continued, pointing to different sections. 'I've projected potential earnings from the two galleries by calculating the space in the new gallery and estimated the number of paintings I could display, along with their potential sale prices. As you know, as well as the original artwork there's a limited edition of framed prints. I already have stock, which totals this amount.' She pointed. 'The prints fly off the website and the original paintings sell for at least seven thousand pounds each, so I believe I can achieve this total.' She indicated the final figure in the box.

Max let out a low whistle. 'By this time next year, you'll be well on your way to being a millionaire.'

'I do believe that's entirely possible,' Dilly affirmed.

'Based on these projections, you can manage both properties with your art sales, and any extra from your art classes and community gallery will be a bonus,' Max observed. 'But the big question is, how much of your inheritance do you want to set aside for emergencies? You have to plan for the worst-case scenario.'

'I think I need more wine for this,' Dilly said with a chuckle, refilling their glasses.

'If it were up to me,' Max said, picking up a pen from the nearby pad and jotting down a figure, 'I would keep at least half of your inheritance. You're young, with your whole life ahead of you. You never know what you might need in the future. So, I'd recommend bidding up to this amount…'

'But I think other bidders will have more than that.'

'It's up to you whether you want to risk more.'

Suddenly, Dilly came over all emotional. 'I hear what you're saying.'

'Hey, what's up? I didn't mean to upset you.'

Dilly looked at Max and exhaled. 'You didn't. I just feel passionate about it and I wish I had some intimation of what others might be bidding.'

'The last thing you want to do is to get yourself into any sort of financial difficulty. This is a huge commitment.'

'I've always been impulsive; the second I set my mind on something I have to have it. But it really does need a little more thought. I think I've become swept up in some sort of romantic notion of an artist living in a lighthouse where her grandfather once kept watch and where her mother was born. And yet something is telling me I *need* to do this.'

'If something is telling you to go for it, then just go for it. All you can do is see what happens.'

A tear ran down Dilly's face. 'I don't even know why I'm crying, it's ridiculous.'

Max tucked a stray hair behind her ear before passing her a tissue.

She smiled a sad smile at him. 'Every day I wish my mum was here. She would be over the moon to see how well I was doing.' She tapped the spreadsheet. 'I'd rather have her here, instead of the inheritance.'

'That goes without saying.'

'They never did find her or Anton's body,' Dilly said, dabbing at her eyes. 'And there's still a tiny part of me that thinks she'll stroll through the doors of the gallery, that this has all been a bad dream. But if she were alive, she would never stay away.' Her voice trembled with sadness as she glanced towards the lighthouse. 'I wish we could have brought her home.'

Max placed his hand over hers, giving it a gentle squeeze. She leaned her head against his shoulder, and they sat in silence, watching the waves crash against the rocks surrounding the lighthouse.

'I can't even begin to imagine what you've been through and what you're still going through,' Max said softly.

'It's hard to talk to my dad about it because they'd both moved on with their lives. My dad has never had anyone else since Mum. He says he was attached to her for so long, and now he just does what he wants, when he wants.'

'I can relate to him there.'

'I'm sorry your marriage didn't work out,' Dilly said, her voice filled with genuine sympathy.

'Thank you.'

'Even though I know a lot of the girls in your past art classes would be glad to hear that. They all thought you were hot and used to hang around outside your classroom and whisper about you.' As soon as the words left her mouth, Dilly felt a blush creep up her cheeks.

'They did, did they?' Max replied with a lopsided grin.

'Surely you must have known.' She nudged him playfully.

'I have to say, I honestly never noticed groups of girls hanging outside my classroom door or whispering as I walked past. And dare I ask, what about you?'

'I admired your intelligence, your enthusiasm for art, and the encouragement you gave me to make my dreams a reality.' Dilly purposely left out the vivid dreams she'd had about him over the years. On numerous occasions, she'd woken with a start, the dreams so real, and she'd often wondered what it would be like to wake up with him every day.

'And likewise, your passion for art was inspiring, and I admired how you stood out from the crowd,' Max replied warmly. Dilly sat up a bit straighter, intrigued.

'How so?' she asked.

'You never followed trends. You were true to yourself.

While others chased the latest fashions, you had your own unique style. Your painted dungarees, your Converse boots, and that signature messy bun secured with paintbrushes and pencils. And your genuine enthusiasm for art shone through, not to mention your infectious laugh.'

'Let's talk about my laugh,' she teased, a playful glint in her eye.

Max smiled. 'When you laughed, it was pure joy, and your smile lit up the room. So many of the other students wanted to be like you.'

'No, they didn't,' Dilly protested, though she was secretly pleased.

'Oh, they did. They'd see what art books you had sticking out of your bag and then check them out at the library, but they never dived into them like you did. When you got a new set of paintbrushes, they all bought the same ones. And all the girls tried to secure their hair with paintbrushes, but it was never quite the same.'

'It seems you noticed quite a lot about me,' she observed, her eyes sparkling.

'I did.'

They exchanged a smile, the unique bond they'd shared strengthening between them, but with a different, more charged energy this time around.

'And now, years later, you're going to help me buy a lighthouse.'

The intensity of his gaze gave her the same warm feeling she had years ago when they spent time together painting and discussing art.

'Just look at all this,' he continued, gesturing to the drawings and spreadsheets spread out before them.

Her stomach fluttered with butterflies, and her thoughts drifted back to her college days. She had dreamed of kissing him, of being wrapped in his arms, but it had always been a fantasy. Sitting here now, believing in fate, she felt their paths had crossed again for a reason. She was thrilled to be with Max in this moment.

'What are you thinking? You've gone all thoughtful,' Max asked.

'I'm thinking I'm glad you're here, and maybe we should open another bottle of wine,' she replied with a smile.

'Maybe we should,' he said, sipping the last of the wine from his glass. His eyes stayed locked on hers.

And there it was again, for the umpteenth time tonight, the race of her pulse, the thumping of her heart. She had sworn to herself after Giles that no man would take up any more of her time, yet here she was, not wanting Max to go back to his flat anytime soon. There was something about him that made her feel alive, that made her want to take a chance again.

Chapter Six

It had been a few days since Dilly had seen Max, but he had been very much on her mind. Together, they had drawn up three scenarios for the auction, each with a specific amount. The first figure was ideal, allowing Dilly to purchase the lighthouse while remaining financially comfortable. The second amount was mid-range, which would still provide a decent living but would require her to tighten her belt a little. The third was a figure that under no circumstances could be exceeded. Bidding over this amount would push Dilly to the max financially, leaving her with nothing but a lighthouse she had no means of turning into the gallery and home of her dreams.

For the next hour, Dilly busied herself tidying her already immaculate flat, trying to kill time before meeting Max at the corner of Blue Water Bay. Last night she could barely sleep, knowing today she would be stepping inside the lighthouse. She just hoped it lived up to her expectations. Her phone was fully charged and ready to take pictures, and she had a small notebook tucked into her bag to jot down any important details about the interior of the lighthouse and any upgrades or renovations that might be needed.

When it was time to leave, Dilly grabbed her sunglasses and stepped outside. The day was beautiful, bright and sunny with just enough breeze to keep the heat at bay, and she made her way down to the waterfront to pick up two teas from the Cosy Kettle before strolling along the path at the edge of the sand. As she approached the meeting spot, she couldn't help but feel a flutter of anticipation. She was looking forward to spending time with Max and viewing the lighthouse. Her thoughts wandered to the possibilities that lay ahead if she managed to buy the historic site, the art classes she could offer from her original location, the second gallery she could open, a new home she could make her own. The lighthouse was more than just a building, it was a chance to create something truly special while also giving back to the community she loved.

She arrived at the corner of Blue Water Bay, polystyrene cups in hand, and admired the spectacular view of the lighthouse against the glistening sea, gulls soaring high above. But she stopped dead in her tracks as she looked towards the jetty, where a long line of people, stretching back along the road, were waiting to view the lighthouse. Her smile faded as despair rose within her. All these people had come to view the property? Damn. She had anticipated some interest, of course, but not this much.

Max was still nowhere in sight but she was relieved he would be joining her, and hoped he might have some reassuring words in the face of the enormous queue. It was always good to have a friend in uncertain times. She wished she'd had more chances to chat with him since their last meeting, but the gallery had been busier than usual, and she knew the boat house had been extremely busy, trying to get the boats back out on the water after their repairs and upgrades.

Settling on a nearby rock, she placed one tea on the ground and sipped the other. An official-looking person stood at the lighthouse door, checking his watch. Right on time, he opened the door and people began to file inside, the potential buyers beginning their tours. Dilly willed Max to hurry, eager to get inside. Glancing to her right, she finally spotted him further up at the harbour, but he wasn't walking her way. Instead, he was deep in conversation with someone she didn't recognise.

Max looked as handsome as ever, with the sleeves of his painting overalls tied around his waist and his T-shirt hugging his body in a way that accentuated his physique. The woman stood very close to him – too close for Dilly's comfort, if she was honest – wearing a power suit with very high heels, which seemed impractical for navigating the sand and the jetty. She didn't seem the usual type of customer that frequented the boat house. She was around five foot five, slim, and as she turned around, Dilly saw she had sunglasses hiding her eyes. Her blonde hair was tied up in a ponytail that swished from side to side, and she carried a very expensive-looking handbag.

Max leaned towards her, speaking earnestly, and from where Dilly was sitting their conversation seemed serious.

Max checked his watch as the woman opened her bag. She gestured towards an envelope he was holding, which he promptly dropped into her bag. Dilly heard the woman laugh as she stepped away, heading towards a top-of-the-range sports car parked on the road. Within seconds, she had driven out of sight and Max was walking towards Dilly.

She gave him a smile. 'There you are, I was beginning to think you'd stood me up.'

'Sorry I'm a few minutes late.' He looked flustered.

'You okay?'

'I am now.'

'Got you a tea.'

'You are a keeper.' Max took the cup from her and immediately took a sip.

'Hopefully soon to be the lighthouse keeper!'

'I see what you did there.' He grinned.

'But judging by that queue, I've got a feeling there will be quite a few bidders at the auction.'

'Most of the people in the queue will have no intention of bidding on the lighthouse,' Max reassured her. 'It's the first time in years that the public can look around inside and I'll bet most of the island will be taking a peek today, just because they can. Don't let all these people put you off.'

He pointed to a man standing a little further up in the line, dressed in a tweed suit, complete with a bow tie, Homburg hat and patent leather shoes. 'He looks like he should be a detective on a cosy murder mystery show,' Max observed.

Dilly leaned in. 'That's Henry Snyder. He's a local historian and journalist. Lived on the island for years. He's obviously here for the history.'

They began to walk across the sand toward the jetty, soon joining the back of the queue.

Dilly's phone pinged. 'It's a text from my dad,' she said, glancing at the screen. 'He hopes the viewing goes well and can't wait to hear all about it.' She slipped her phone back into her bag. 'This jetty and road weren't always here,' Dilly pointed out. 'Before they were put in, the only way to the lighthouse was by boat.'

'It's a good thing there's a road now,' Max replied. 'Otherwise, I'd be rowing across to see you, and I have to admit, I'm not very good on the water.'

'You work in a boat house!' Dilly laughed.

'That doesn't mean I have to get in the boats!'

The queue had picked up pace, and visitors were already trickling out of the lighthouse, some pausing on the jetty to snap photos with their phones. Dilly glanced up, almost giving herself whiplash. 'It's quite tall, isn't it?' She had never truly considered its height until now, when she was up close.

'I think that's the whole point of a lighthouse.' He nudged her with his elbow. 'Are you ready to take a look around?'

'Ready,' she replied eagerly.

They stepped through the heavy oak door into the first room. 'Oh my gosh, I wasn't expecting this. It's just gorgeous and perfect for a gallery,' Dilly exclaimed.

'It's very quirky,' added Max. 'And very cool.'

The round room, eighteen feet in diameter, was lined with about a foot of brick, providing excellent insulation. Two windows allowed natural light to flood the space, and several alcoves set into the brick provided space for shelves and storage. Some of the shelves were lined with books, adding a cosy touch. A charming stove stood against one wall, with a small farmhouse table and chairs snugly arranged nearby, and a staircase leading to the upper levels. The stove's exhaust pipe was cleverly concealed behind a central column that extended from the basement and through the upper floors. The column was hollow and, according to a leaflet Dilly had just picked up, housed a large weight that powered the clockwork motor turning the lantern. The combination of practical design and historical charm left them both in awe.

'There's actually a floor below this one,' Dilly noted, her eyes scanning the room in admiration.

Max glanced at the leaflet. 'It says here that the basement was originally for the coal furnace, and there's now a cistern for the water.'

'What do you think of this room?' Dilly asked, sweeping her gaze around the space.

Max took a moment to absorb the details. 'As far as I can see, there's plenty of light, those alcoves will be perfect for hanging paintings, there's electricity, a stove to heat the space in winter, and the walls are in very good condition.'

Dilly squealed in delight, linking her arm through Max's. He smiled warmly at her. 'I think it's just perfect. Let's check out the next level.'

He gestured for Dilly to go first and they made their way to the winding steps.

The staircase was narrow and steep, but it only added to the lighthouse's charm. As they ascended, the walls seemed to close in slightly, creating a cosy, intimate atmosphere. Max admired the craftsmanship of the spiral stairs, the wood polished smooth by years of use. 'It's amazing how well preserved everything is,' he stated, his voice low in the confined space.

Dilly nodded, her hand trailing along the railing. 'I can already imagine the gallery here. The history of this place adds so much character. Max! Look!' Her voice echoed all around as she paused, staring at a picture on the wall. The staircase was lined with framed photos of every lighthouse keeper who had served at the Puffin Island Lighthouse, including Dilly's grandfather, Mack Sinton. 'I don't believe it.'

'He looks so young,' Max commented, peering over her shoulder.

'He does,' Dilly agreed, her voice tinged with awe and emotion. 'And handsome. I can't believe the responsibility of the lighthouse fell on his shoulders at such a young age. He looks younger than I am now. It's hard not to wonder what his life would have been like if it hadn't been tragically cut short. But my grandmother always took comfort in knowing he loved his job. It was in his blood, and he knew the risks. He died doing what he loved best.'

She was aware of the people waiting behind her on the stairs and quickly moved past the photographs, though her mind lingered on the image of her grandfather. 'If I could purchase those photos, I could create a gallery exhibition centred around all the lighthouse keepers.' Dilly was filled with excitement and determination. In her mind, she had already won the lighthouse at auction and had started moving in, despite having only seen some of it.

As they continued their ascent, the narrow stairs creaked underfoot, adding to the historic ambiance of the place. The walls were adorned with more mementos of the lighthouse's past – old maps, nautical charts and vintage tools used by keepers over the years – and the air was filled with the faint scent of salt and aged wood, evoking a sense of timelessness. Finally, they reached the next floor, which opened into another round room, slightly smaller than the first but equally charming. The walls here were painted a soft seafoam green, and the large window offered an even more breathtaking view of the ocean. The sunlight streamed in, casting a warm, golden glow that made the room feel both comfy and roomy.

Max walked over to the window, admiring the panoramic view. 'This place just keeps getting better. Imagine the sunsets you'll see from here.'

Dilly joined him, her eyes sparkling with excitement. 'I can picture it already; this room could be a private studio, filled with easels and canvases. The light here is perfect for painting.'

Max turned to her, his smile reflecting her enthusiasm. 'You've really thought this through. I'm looking forward to seeing your incredible vision for this place come to life.'

They continued up the spiral staircase, eager to explore every inch of the lighthouse that Dilly was already beginning to think of as her future home.

The second floor of the Puffin Island Lighthouse housed a large bedroom. The circular room, fifteen feet in diameter, was also brick-lined, with two windows providing ample natural light and a wardrobe against one wall.

'This must be the master bedroom, where the main lighthouse keeper slept, which means this is likely the room where my mother was born,' Dilly mused.

'Quite possibly,' Max replied, nodding.

'I could make this so homely,' Dilly continued, her imagination taking flight. 'Quilted floral duvets with matching curtains, a plush rug and an embroidered wall hanging would finish this room off beautifully.' She opened one of the doors of the wardrobe and looked back at Max, her eyes widening. 'You are not going to believe this.' She opened the door wider, allowing him to peer over her shoulder.

'What am I looking at?' he asked, puzzled.

'The semaphore flags! These are the flags my grandmother used to communicate with my grandfather when he was on duty here at the lighthouse.' Dilly pulled out the bag and placed it on the bed. 'These have got to be the originals. I could decorate the gallery with these!' She held up the two poles and stretched her arms, explaining, 'The letters of the alphabet have different positions.' Inside the bag was a set of instructions showing all the positions. She thrust the booklet into Max's hand.

'What are you doing?' he whispered. 'There are lots of other viewers milling around.'

But Dilly wasn't perturbed. 'Guess what I'm saying,' she demanded, waving wildly.

'How do you know what the positions are?' asked Max as he paged through the booklet, trying to figure out what Dilly was spelling.

'My grandmother taught me when I was little. She made some flags, and we used to take turns guessing what the message was. Let's see if I can remember.'

While other viewers of the lighthouse popped their heads into the room for a quick look, Dilly stood in the middle of the room, assuming various positions with the flags. Max perched on the end of the bed, watching with a mix of amusement and curiosity.

M-Y N-E-W H-O-M-E, she spelled out with the flags.

'I feel like a cheerleader but without the pom-poms!'

Max laughed. 'You're doing great! And you're right, this place is perfect for you.'

Dilly beamed, lowering the flags and packing them back into their bag. 'I can already see it all coming together. Let's check out the next level.'

As they continued their exploration, Dilly's mind buzzed with ideas and possibilities, her excitement growing with each step.

The third floor held a bathroom, the fourth another bedroom and the fifth and sixth the dining room and kitchen. In these rooms, the walls were lined with rich, warm wood, and a ring of small portholes allowed natural light to stream in. A final spiral staircase led up to the Watch Deck at the top of the lighthouse.

'Shall we go up?' Max suggested.

'I think we should,' Dilly replied, unable to hide her excitement.

'I have to say, all the work needed inside is mainly cosmetic. I really can't see any major problems or the need for costly renovations,' Max said, looking around as they ascended.

'I know I should be happy about that,' Dilly said with a playful smile, 'but I was quite looking forward to you coming around every night to help me work on the lighthouse.'

'Is that so?' Max's eyes twinkled.

'It is,' Dilly admitted in a flirty tone.

Above the door leading out to the Watch Deck, a weathered steel plate bore the builder's name and the date of construction, telling them that the lighthouse had been erected in the early 1880s. The plate was a testament to the enduring craftsmanship of a bygone era. Stepping through the doorway, they emerged onto a canopied walkway supported by intricate cast-iron posts adorned with delicate scrollwork. The canopy provided some shade, casting shadows on the wooden deck beneath their feet.

The view was breathtaking, with Puffin Island stretched out before them. The surrounding cliffs, jagged and majestic, framed the skyline, while the distant town of Sea's End was nestled in the landscape, its rooftops gleaming in the afternoon sun.

Dilly gestured excitedly towards the panoramic view. 'Look at Cliff Top Cottage over there. It seems so tiny from up here, doesn't it? And there's The Sea Glass Restaurant. I can even spot the boat house.' She turned towards Max with a mischievous grin. 'You could have your own set of semaphore flags, and we could communicate with each other.'

Max chuckled, shaking his head. 'You do know they've invented a new type of technology called the mobile phone, right?'

Dilly laughed along with him. 'But that won't be nearly as much fun!'

Their banter echoed against the backdrop of the expansive seascape, the sunlight danced on the waves below, and the distant landmarks of Puffin Island seemed almost miniature from where they were standing at the top of the lighthouse.

'Can you imagine sitting up here on a summer's evening with a glass of wine?' she murmured, her voice filled with wonder.

Max followed her gaze, nodding appreciatively. 'Oh, I can! And if this view doesn't give you inspiration for your paintings, nothing will. It's the perfect place to paint.'

'I've got to get this place,' Dilly declared with determination, her eyes still fixed on the stunning view.

'I hope you do,' Max replied sincerely.

As they queued at the top of the stairs, preparing to descend, Dilly paused, taking a moment to catch her breath.

'You okay? It's very overwhelming, isn't it?' Max asked.

'I've just gone a little light-headed again. It might be the stairs, but that's something I'm hopefully going to get used to,' Dilly admitted, steadying herself.

'It is warm in here with all these people,' Max agreed, casting a glance around at the other visitors.

Once back at ground level and out on the jetty, Dilly took some deep breaths. 'That feels better. I think I was just feeling a little hot and claustrophobic with all those people.' They stood side by side. Dilly looked up again at the towering structure and then out to sea. 'Just think, I may become the owner of all this, and very soon.'

'The auction will be here soon enough. You need to try not to worry too much about this place in the meantime though,' Max said, checking his watch. 'As much as I wish I could stay longer, I need to get back to the boat house. I don't want to get the sack.'

'My dad wouldn't sack you,' Dilly reassured him with a smile, 'otherwise he'd have me to deal with!'

'I'm not taking that chance.' He grinned, taking her hands in his. 'Thank you again for letting me tag along.' He slowly dropped her hands and stepped back. 'I really do have to go, but I can't wait to hear whether you are the new keeper.'

'You can come with me to the auction, if you want,' she offered.

Max's face lit up with surprise and delight. 'Really? You want me to come with you?'

'I do, I feel like we're in this together now.'

'It would be my pleasure, but I'll have to clear it with your dad first.'

Max gave a farewell wave and hurried towards the harbour as Dilly turned back towards the lighthouse, her gaze drifting towards the rocks where her grandfather had lost his life, the sight a poignant reminder of the lighthouse's history.

'We wondered if we'd bump into you,' came Clemmie's voice, drawing Dilly's attention. She turned to find Clemmie and Betty walking towards her. 'We couldn't miss out on taking a look inside.'

'It is absolutely amazing,' Dilly enthused. 'And would you believe there's a photo of my grandfather on the wall? All the chief lighthouse keepers are up there. I felt so proud seeing it.'

Betty touched her arm gently. 'And so you should be. Mack was not only one of my dearest friends but a very brave man who would be proud of you.'

'Thank you.'

'We'd best hurry inside; we've left the staff in charge while we nip out of the tearoom for ten minutes. I'm sure we'll see you before the auction but just in case we don't, know that we're rooting for you,' said Clemmie.

'And I'm really looking forward to the art class,' added Betty with a mischievous glint in her eye, chuckling as she walked towards the lighthouse.

With a spring in her step Dilly set off towards Lighthouse Lane, stealing one last glance towards the harbour. She noticed Max had paused further along, engrossed in conversation once more with the woman in the suit. They exchanged another envelope and she pointed towards the lighthouse, and Dilly couldn't help but notice that Max looked agitated. The woman leaned into him and pressed a hand on his chest before she walked away for the second time today. Max's gaze lingered on the envelope, and then he scanned the beach, as if hoping no one had witnessed their exchange.

A wave of unease swept over Dilly, a familiar sense of anxiety creeping up, reminiscent of when she'd uncovered Giles's deceit. She battled against the unsettling thoughts flooding her mind but couldn't help it. What if Max was somehow entangled in something dubious? Was it possible he had ulterior motives and his popping back up in her life wasn't a coincidence? Had he planned it? Was it possible he … wanted the lighthouse for himself? *No, that's not possible*, she thought, forcing her mind to calm.

'Urgh,' Dilly muttered in frustration, quickening her pace towards the gallery. She scolded herself for doubting Max, knowing she was only feeling triggered because of her past situation. Giles was a different kind of person altogether, and besides, not everyone operated with ulterior motives. Max was a good person, and he'd never intentionally hurt her. But as she kept walking, a feeling deep in her gut persisted that something wasn't quite right. She paused at the end of the lane and looked back. The woman was standing on the edge of the sand looking straight at the lighthouse. It felt like a bad omen and Dilly couldn't help but shiver.

Chapter Seven

It had felt like an eternity since Dilly had viewed the lighthouse but for the past couple of weeks, she'd kept herself occupied by immersing herself in painting more pieces for the gallery.

'Today is the day!' she trilled to herself as she stepped out of the shower, a towel wrapped around her. Standing before the mirror, she gazed at her reflection with a determined expression. There were still a couple of hours before she needed to head over to the auction house in Sea's End. Then, suddenly, she panicked; she hadn't even thought about checking the tide times! Grabbing her phone, she checked the local residents' private Facebook group and was relieved to find that the tide was out.

Next on her mind was the age-old question: what does one wear to an auction? Should she go for a businesslike look, or opt for something more casual to avoid giving off overly eager 'I'm going to bid' vibes? Dilly decided on smart attire. She recalled a suit she had worn a few years back to an artist event, where she had felt overdressed amongst the painters in their work gear. She laid out the navy A-line skirt, pairing it with a white blouse and draping a gauzy pink scarf around her neck. She chose pink ballet shoes to complete the outfit.

After slipping into her underwear, Dilly glanced down, noticing her breasts spilling over the top of her bra. She frowned in dismay, acknowledging that she had continued to overindulge in Nutella pancakes from the Cosy Kettle even after swearing she'd take more care in what she ate. She really needed to rein in her constant cravings. Pulling on the skirt, she stared at her expanded waistline. It just about fitted over her thighs ... barely ... but there was no way it was ever going to fasten.

'What the hell?' Dilly muttered, frustrated as the blouse also refused to fasten around her chest.

Suddenly, a thought hit her and Dilly's heart raced with panic. She grabbed her phone again, fingers trembling, scrolled to her menstrual app and stared at the date. It had been four months since her last period. She slumped on the bed, still staring at the app.

'Shit, shit, double shit. Don't panic,' she muttered to herself, though her pulse had quickened uncontrollably. She tried to convince herself that her periods had been delayed due to stress – after all, she had endured the worst couple of years of her life – but as the image of Giles flashed vividly in her mind she shuddered, recalling his smirk as he exited her life ... or so she had thought. The idea of an unplanned pregnancy was daunting enough, but the thought of Giles as the father was unbearable.

Dilly knew she would have some explaining to do. Both

Clemmie and her dad believed that Giles had been out of the picture for at least eight months and everyone on the island believed Dilly had uncovered his deceit sooner than she actually had, since she had started downplaying the relationship in the hope that her dad would eventually warm to him. But Clemmie and her dad had been right all along. When Giles suddenly encountered financial difficulties with a property deal in St. Tropez, one that he claimed had been in the works before he even met Dilly, his behaviour became increasingly erratic. He claimed he needed cash immediately to prevent the sellers from pulling out, and put pressure on her to cash out her inheritance and lend him the money. That's when Dilly's alarm bells had started ringing. After a heated argument, Giles stormed out for a walk, and Dilly had done a bit of digging, finding the folded article in his suit pocket from a national newspaper detailing her mother's tragic accident. Giles had highlighted the bit explaining that she had been married to one of the wealthiest antique dealers in the country, and was leaving Dilly a hefty inheritance.

She couldn't even entertain the possibility of being pregnant right now, let alone pregnant with Giles's baby. Yes, she had been a bit reckless with contraception, but she had been influenced by their discussions about children and the fact that Giles had sold her a fairytale dream of a family together. A fairytale that was now spiralling into a nightmare.

Right now all Dilly could do was try and push it out of her mind until after the auction. But that was easier said than done. Tears welled up as she told herself not to overthink things because it would all be okay, but she wasn't convincing herself.

All she could do was wait until all the facts were known, then she could make any decisions she needed to. Trying to calm her rapidly beating heart, Dilly tossed her phone into her bag. She needed to focus on the auction, and push aside the looming uncertainty for the next few hours at least.

Grabbing an oversized T-shirt and her trusty dungarees, Dilly hastily got dressed. Then, standing sideways in front of the mirror, she cupped her hands around her stomach, mimicking a pose she had seen pregnant celebrities do in glossy magazines. Dilly had always envisioned becoming a mother, but not like this. She had imagined it happening in a loving relationship, perhaps even marriage, with a lovely family home filled with anticipation and joy upon sharing the news with her partner.

As soon as the auction was over, Dilly planned to drop Max back on the island before driving swiftly back to Sea's End to visit the pharmacy. There was a pharmacy on the island, but Dilly was determined to keep her visit discreet. Living in a small community like Puffin Island meant that everyone knew everyone's business, and this was something she didn't want spreading around until she was ready, especially if it turned out she *was* pregnant.

Just as she finished putting on her shoes, a knock echoed through the gallery. Dilly hurried down the stairs. Through the gallery's window, she saw Clemmie smiling back at her and opened the door. In one hand, Clemmie gripped a newspaper, in the other, a white paper bag that bulged with the promise of breakfast. 'I thought you'd be rushing around this morning, so I've popped over with a bacon cob with brown sauce.'

'That's why I have friends like you! Thank you,' Dilly said, accepting the bag and peeking inside.

'How are you feeling about the auction?'

'Excited, nervous,' Dilly admitted, the mix of anticipation and apprehension evident in her voice. She pulled out the bacon cob and took a satisfying bite. Swallowing, she added. 'This is good! I needed this.'

'My grandmother is at the tearoom so I'm available if you need someone holding your hand, but I know your dad is probably going with you.'

Dilly shook her head. 'My dad is away on business.'

'I'm your girl then…' Clemmie interjected eagerly, ready to offer her support.

Dilly hesitated for a moment before admitting, 'I actually do have someone holding my hand.'

Clemmie's curiosity spiked, and she narrowed her eyes playfully. 'You look very cagey. Who?'

'Max.'

'Max? Who is Max?'

'Max Harrington.'

Clemmie's eyebrows shot up in surprise. 'Woah! How did that come about?'

'I wanted an independent opinion on buying the lighthouse and he's helped me work out my financials. He's also familiar with building work and he's working at the boat house with Dad.'

Taken aback, Clemmie leaned against the desk. 'Since when has Mr Harrington been familiar with building work? He's an art teacher.'

'Not anymore, and we don't need to call him Mr

Harrington any longer. It's Max. He's not our teacher and he's only a few years older than us.'

'Oh my gosh.' Clemmie's eyes widened with realisation.

'What?' Dilly asked, sensing Clemmie's scrutiny.

'You fancy Max Harrington.'

'Don't be ridiculous!'

'You do! I can see that glint in your eye. There's something going on between you.'

'There isn't.'

'But you want there to be.'

Dilly smiled. 'I can't deny I had a crush on him at college.'

'Didn't we all?'

'Yes, but I don't think your crush was like my crush…'

Clemmie's eyes widened. 'You didn't have an affair with the teacher? Tell me you didn't. In fact, tell me you did. It's always the quiet ones.'

Dilly rolled her eyes. 'Of course I didn't have an affair with the teacher. Max would have never crossed that line. He was always professional … and also very married.'

'Did you try?'

'No, of course not, but he was one of my inspirations.' She gestured around the gallery. 'He believed in me and encouraged me to paint for a living.'

'And now … you want him to cross that line, don't you? I can tell by that smitten look on your face.'

'You are like a dog with a bone.' Dilly wasn't going to admit that, after Max had left on the night they'd shared food and wine, she had lain in bed, wondering if she could have – should have, even – persuaded him to stay. 'I think after Giles, I need to stay away from men,' she added, playing things down. She knew that if the pregnancy test confirmed she was expecting Giles's baby, then being wrapped up in Max's arms was only ever going to be an unfulfilled dream.

'Except Max.'

Dilly gave her friend an exasperated look.

'I knew it!'

'But there's nothing going on.'

'Yet!'

Suddenly, Clemmie's demeanour shifted from jovial to serious as she set the newspaper down on Dilly's desk. Even though the morning sunlight filtered through the gallery window, casting a soft glow over the room, the atmosphere had suddenly grown tense.

'What is it?' Dilly asked.

'I know you never look at the news on your phone.'

'Way too depressing for my liking.'

'So I wasn't sure if you knew or had seen this.' Clemmie opened the newspaper and turned to page four.

Dilly's eyes immediately fell upon the photograph of Giles staring back at her, before turning to the bold headline blared across the page.

FAKE CELEBRITY BODYGUARD SWINDLES
MILLIONS FROM VULNERABLE WOMEN.

Dilly's heart raced as she read the damning article. She sank into the chair behind her desk, clutching the bacon cob in one hand while she absorbed the shocking revelations. Clemmie stood silently beside her, giving her the space to process it all.

'He's been very busy! According to this he was seeing multiple women at the same time he was living here with me. I suppose I shouldn't be surprised.' Her voice was tinged with disbelief mixed with a hint of lingering hurt. She rubbed her hand protectively over her stomach, a subconscious gesture. 'It says here that over the last five years he's swindled hundreds of women out of their inheritance,' she continued, her eyes flitting up and down the article, grasping the magnitude of Giles's deceit. 'He had it all worked out in my case,' she said.

'But thankfully he's been caught and sentenced,' said Clemmie gently, attempting to offer some reassurance amongst the turmoil.

Dilly remained in shock. While part of her felt a grim satisfaction that Giles had been brought to justice, seeing the scale of his deception was staggering. 'How would you even manage that? Remembering which lies you told to whom, which house you were supposed to be at each night… It's exhausting just thinking about it.'

Clemmie placed a comforting hand on Dilly's shoulder, offering silent support as her friend grappled with the aftermath of his betrayal and deception. The weight of Giles's actions had shaken Dilly's trust and left her questioning not just him but perhaps her own judgment as well. 'How are you feeling about it?' Clemmie asked gently.

'A mixture of relief and disbelief. How must all those other women feel? And how did he get away with so much money?'

'Because he's a professional, it's what he does. But not anymore. He's been caught and thankfully is now going to be serving time,' Clemmie stated solemnly, her voice carrying a note of finality.

Dilly took a deep breath, trying to reconcile her emotions. 'I actually thought I was the only one. That he'd just targeted me because he'd read about my mother's death and saw my rising success as an artist. I thought he was a chancer, and there was still a part of me, which I know is daft, that thought he actually liked me. But according to this...' She trailed off, her finger tracing the damning words in the newspaper.

'He's been at it for years,' Clemmie said, nodding her understanding. 'They've caught him now though and hopefully he won't be out of prison anytime soon,' she added, trying to inject some optimism into the conversation.

'At least I'll never have to set eyes on him again.'

'You won't,' Clemmie affirmed, her voice filled with reassurance. 'I'd better get back to the tearoom now but I wish you all the luck in the world today. Hopefully, in a few hours' time, you will be the proud owner of the Puffin Island Lighthouse!' Clemmie opened her arms wide, and Dilly stood up and they hugged tightly.

'Let me know the news as soon as you have any, and we will all see you tomorrow night for our first art class,' Clemmie added with a smile.

'I will, I promise.'

As soon as Clemmie left, Dilly locked the door behind her and placed a sign on the window announcing the closure of the gallery for the day. She returned to her desk and reread the newspaper article, the reality of Giles's betrayal sinking in deeper.

'How did I ever fall for you?' Dilly muttered to herself.

Tears welled up in her eyes and blurred the words on the page as she swallowed a lump in her throat. The weight of possibly carrying Giles's child felt like a heavy burden, tying her to him in ways she'd never imagined.

Swamped with a thousand thoughts, Dilly tried to calm herself, but one fear persisted. *If I'm pregnant and Giles is the father… What if the baby takes after him?* Her mind raced with worries about the future, imagining the challenges of raising a child of a conman.

That fear overwhelmed her. Dilly lunged for the wastepaper bin beneath her desk and promptly threw up.

After wiping her mouth with a tissue, she felt utterly drained. Despite the support of her community on Puffin Island, Dilly knew the road ahead would be fraught with challenges. But in that moment, she clung to the hope that she would find the strength, somehow, to navigate this unexpected chapter of her life if the pregnancy test showed a positive result.

Chapter Eight

Dilly sat and waited in her car at the bottom of Lighthouse Lane. She stared at the Post-it note stuck to her dashboard. It boldly displayed the highest bid she could afford without risking financial ruin. Inside her bag were all the necessary documents, should she emerge victorious in today's auction. Her stomach somersaulted with a mix of excitement and anxiety.

As she waited, lost in her thoughts, the sudden opening of the car door made her jump out of her seat.

'Sorry, I didn't mean to make you jump,' Max said, sliding into the passenger seat and pulling the seat belt across his body. He looked at her. 'You look green.'

'And it's not because I've tried a new brand of make-up. I'm actually really nervous.'

'Just try and stay calm. You do remember your highest bid?'

Dilly pointed to the Post-it on the dashboard. 'It's there to remind me.'

'I can't believe you still have your bright blue panda car. Fame hasn't changed you at all,' Max teased lightly.

'Some things you can never part with,' said Dilly, defending her beloved car. 'She's been a constant in my life since I was nineteen years old. Many many miles under her belt but still going strong. Now, let's go and win a lighthouse!'

As they set off across the causeway toward the town of Sea's End, Dilly didn't know what to expect. 'I've never actually been to an auction before,' she confessed, turning towards Max for a moment before looking back at the road ahead.

'I've been to a couple, but those were mainly poultry auctions,' Max chuckled. 'I had a neighbour who started breeding chickens and soon found herself overrun. The local farmer suggested she take them to auction, but she had this romanticised vision of her chickens being given lovely country homes where they could frolic in idyllic farmyards. In reality, it was local restaurateurs looking for quality meat.'

'Oh no!' Dilly gasped, imagining the scene.

'Oh yes,' Max confirmed with a grin. 'There was no way she was going to let them end up as Tikka Masala so you'll never believe what she did. She bid on all her chickens and won them back!'

Dilly burst out laughing, the tension of the day momentarily forgotten. 'That's brilliant!'

Dilly began to feel a little more at ease as they approached Sea's End, Max's unexpected anecdotes and the shared laughter having helped. His presence in general provided a comforting distraction from the myriad thoughts that threatened to overwhelm her. Today's auction would decide the fate of the Puffin Island Lighthouse, and the result of the pregnancy test would decide the rest of her life.

What if the test was positive? Could she really raise a child in a lighthouse? The romantic notion of living in such an iconic place battled with practical concerns. Would it be too dangerous living so close to the water? Would she be able to provide a stable environment for a child? Each question felt like a tidal wave crashing over her, making it hard to decipher what was best to do. She had tried to calm her thoughts but the concern still gnawed at her insides. Everything was happening so fast, and she felt caught in a current that she couldn't escape. It didn't help that, deep down, she already knew the result of the pregnancy test. The signs were all too obvious now she knew to look for them: the dizziness, the sickness and the fact that she could no longer stomach the smell of coffee, which she used to adore. How could she have been so stupid?

Max's voice broke through her thoughts. 'You okay?'

Dilly nodded, but her heart and head were still pounding. She had two choices: bid on the lighthouse and see what happens, or turn around now and explain why she had suddenly changed her mind. The pressure was immense, but turning back felt like giving up on a dream she had only just realised she'd always held.

'We've got this,' Max said, his voice steady and reassuring.

Dilly forced a smile, appreciative of his support. They

parked the car and stepped out, the fresh air doing little to calm her jitters. It didn't help that the crowd outside the town hall was larger than she had expected.

Dilly spotted Sam Wilson and Pete Fenwick standing near the entrance. Sam waved energetically, while Pete gave a nod.

'What are you two doing here? Please tell me you aren't bidding!' Dilly called out, trying to keep her tone light.

'Of course not,' Sam replied, immediately easing Dilly's worries. 'We've just come for a nosey. Hopefully it isn't developers who win. We're counting on you to keep the lighthouse in the Puffin Island family, Dilly!'

'The pressure!' Dilly laughed. 'I'll do my best, but I'm not sure if it will be enough…' she said, looking around them all, and then realising that Max was standing a bit apart from the group. 'Sorry, I don't know whether you've all met? This is Max Harrington; he's working with my dad at the boat house for the next few months. Max, this is Sam, owner of The Sea Glass Restaurant, and partner of Verity, who is the local Veterinary Assistant. And this is Pete, the island's retired vet. He lives up at Cliff Top Cottage, the cottage we could see from the top of the lighthouse.'

'I used to own the vet's before I retired and still try to keep my hand in,' Pete added with a grin as they all shook hands. 'Pleased to meet you.'

'We were lucky with the tide today,' added Sam as he also shook Max's hand. 'It only cleared a couple of hours ago.'

'I forgot to check the tide times until this morning and I tell you now, I'd have been lifting up those emergency barriers to wade across the causeway if necessary!' Dilly turned towards Max. 'The barriers were only installed recently, and all thanks to Sam and Pete. In the past, cars have got stuck on the causeway when drivers have misjudged the tide times, but now the barriers remain down if it's unsafe to cross.'

'Thankfully they're doing their job and we've had no incidents since they've been installed.' Sam pointed towards the building. 'We should probably head in soon. Looks like the auction room is already packed.'

'We're going to take a seat near the back so we can watch.' Pete touched Dilly's arm. 'Good luck. We hope you win. It will be good for the island.'

As they hovered near the door, Dilly's heart raced some more, if that was even possible. 'Are you ready to go in?' Max asked.

Dilly held out her trembling hand. 'I can't stop shaking.'

Offering reassurance, Max took her hands in his, giving them a squeeze. His smile was warm. 'Come on, let's go buy you a lighthouse.'

Following the signs, he led her down a corridor towards the auction room. The atmosphere was electric, the crowd's energy buzzing around them. With each step closer to the door, Dilly felt a mixture of fear and determination. The lighthouse was more than just a property, it was a beacon of hope and a potential new beginning for her and possibly her unborn child.

As they walked into the room she saw it was packed with people huddled in groups, armed with folders and clipboards. The noise was deafening as Dilly scanned the crowd, noticing it seemed dominated by men. In fact, as she took another swift look around, she couldn't spot another female in the room.

'It's so loud,' Dilly exclaimed, following Max through the throng of people. Rows and rows of chairs were laid out, and they managed to grab two seats in the third row.

'It won't be for long. As soon as the auctioneer bangs his hammer, the whole room will fall silent. I'll go and get the auction list so we can see what lot the lighthouse is,' said Max, disappearing towards a table at the back of the room. He soon returned, handing Dilly a brochure. 'Here you go, these are all the properties going up for auction today.'

Dilly flipped through the brochure, trying to calm her nerves as the stage in front of them came to life with movement, the atmosphere in the room growing more intense.

'We're lot number five,' Dilly noted, her eyes scanning the list.

'That's good – we don't have to wait long. Means it'll all be over before you know it. The next few minutes will go so quickly.'

Dilly wasn't sure if she wanted it to be over quickly. Once it was over, her fate would be sealed.

The auctioneer strolled onto the stage, commanding immediate attention. He was a tall man with a robust frame, dressed in a tailored grey suit that gave him a distinguished air. His hair was silver, combed neatly to the side, and he wore glasses perched on the end of his nose, giving him a scholarly appearance. His presence exuded authority and experience, suggesting he had conducted countless auctions in his time.

Dilly peeked at the Post-it note that was now inside her bag. 'Do not bid over this amount,' she murmured to herself.

The auctioneer switched on the microphone and stood behind the podium. He struck his gavel three times. Just as Max had predicted, the room, which had been full of chaotic chatter, fell silent instantly.

'Ladies and gentlemen, welcome to today's auction,' the auctioneer began, his voice clear and authoritative. 'We have a number of exciting properties for you today, so let's get started.'

Dilly's heart raced as the first few lots were called out and quickly bid upon. The speed of the process took her breath away. She clutched the leaflet, feeling the pressure mounting as the next lot approached.

Everyone's heads moved in unison, swivelling between the auctioneer and the bidders. Hands shot up, heads nodded, and to the side of the stage, several people were busy taking telephone bids.

'Going once, going twice, any more bids?… Sold!' The auctioneer's gavel came down with a decisive thud, and an official handed a document to the winning bidder. The process was swift, almost dizzyingly so, and within minutes, the first four lots had flown by. Three of the lots hadn't reached their reserve price, while one had exceeded it, leaving her with no hint as to how the lighthouse sale might go.

Dilly's anxiety spiked as she watched the rapid pace of the proceedings. She glanced around the room and locked eyes with Sam and Pete, who both gave her enthusiastic thumbs-ups. Their support was comforting, but it did little to quell the panic rising inside her.

'What if the lighthouse goes beyond my budget?' she whispered to Max, her voice barely audible over the murmur of the crowd.

Max leaned in closer. 'Stick to your limit, Dilly. If it goes beyond your budget, it wasn't meant to be.'

Dilly nodded, trying to absorb his words.

'And now, lot number five,' the auctioneer announced. Dilly tried not to hyperventilate. 'The Puffin Island Lighthouse. This is a very unique opportunity.'

Dilly's gaze was firmly fixed on the auctioneer as he reeled off the property's stats, thoughts of her grandparents and her mum flashing through her mind. She *really* wanted to win this.

The auctioneer started the bidding at the reserve price, which was immediately met.

'When do I bid?' Dilly whispered to Max, itching to put her hand up.

'Don't drive the price up or show anyone you're interested just yet, wait until the end,' Max advised, his voice calm and steady.

'One bid at the back, one on the right, one on the left.' The auctioneer was waving his gavel in the direction of the bidders. The price had already been driven up past the lowest amount that would have given Dilly a comfortable living and was rapidly heading for the mid-range price she'd mapped out.

At the side of the room, two bidders were in fierce competition. Back and forth the auctioneer went as the price rose rapidly, just like Dilly's heartbeat. Her head spun between the bidders and the auctioneer, trying to keep up with the escalating numbers. The price was still within her budget, but it was getting dangerously close to her limit.

'Any advance on three hundred thousand pounds?' The auctioneer looked towards the two bidders who were going head-to-head. One of them shook his head, signalling he was out.

This is it, it's my turn, Dilly thought, feeling a surge of adrenalin.

'Any more bids? Any more bids?' The auctioneer lifted his gavel, preparing to close the bidding.

'Now!' ordered Max, his voice urgent.

Catapulting her arm into the air, Dilly caught the attention of the auctioneer. 'Lady in the third row.'

The auctioneer looked back towards the man standing at the back of the room, but he shook his head. Then he looked towards the woman handling the phone bids. She, too, shook her head.

'Oh my gosh, I think it's mine,' Dilly whispered, her heart pounding.

'Last bids for Puffin Island Lighthouse. Going once...'

Dilly gripped Max's arm.

'Going twice... New bidder, woman in red at the back of the room.'

'No!' Dilly spun around to see the same woman she had seen Max talking to at the harbour. Without her sunglasses, Dilly recognised the woman who was now staring straight at her – Lydia Harrington. Dilly's pulse raced for all the wrong reasons and she looked at Max, her eyes narrowing. 'Have you set me up?'

Max's smile dropped as he looked over his shoulder.

Dilly thrust her arm in the air, determined not to let Lydia win. She gave Max a scathing look. 'You want the lighthouse. That's it, isn't it? Somehow you knew it was coming up for sale, so you got yourself a job on the island so you could scope out the competition. I opened up to you about my finances and now you're going to take my dream away from me. Are you still married? Did you take off your wedding ring as part of your scheme?'

'Do you know how ridiculous that sounds?' Max replied, his voice edged with frustration.

But to Dilly, it wasn't ridiculous. Because it was the exact same tactic that Giles had used to get close to her and to get her to trust him with important information before trying to take everything away from her. Dilly had never been more determined to win anything in her life. Her hand was still in the air but she barely heard the numbers the auctioneer was calling out as he looked between Dilly and Lydia. 'I saw you at the harbour, swapping envelopes the day we viewed the lighthouse,' she hissed, her voice louder than she'd anticipated. 'What was in that envelope, my highest bid?'

'What are you doing? You're going over your agreed budget. You can't afford to go any higher,' Max warned.

'This no longer has anything to do with you.' She stared at Max, then looked over his shoulder. Lydia gave them a smug smile then had the audacity to wink.

Dilly watched as Max slid from his chair and walked to the back of the room. What would he and Lydia even want with a lighthouse? Then the penny dropped. Did Lydia want to expand her cosmetic surgery business onto the island? Surely not.

'Over my dead body,' mumbled Dilly, bidding again, taking her firmly over her budget limit.

'Any more bids? Going once…'

Dilly dared to glance behind her. Max and his wife were no longer standing there. She quickly scanned the room but couldn't see them.

'Going twice…' Dilly froze like a rabbit in the headlights.

'SOLD!' The auctioneer pointed his gavel at Dilly.

The room erupted in applause. Dilly's heart was a confusion of relief, triumph and anger. She had won. She had won despite Max's betrayal, despite the odds stacked against her. What the hell had just happened?

As with the winning bidders before her, an official came over and handed her a document. It felt like she was holding a golden ticket to Willy Wonka's chocolate factory.

'Yes!' Dilly exclaimed, barely able to believe it. She had done it. She had won the lighthouse. Bursting with joy, she leaped from her chair and made her way over to Sam and Pete, enveloping them both in a triumphant hug. A sudden surge of emotion overwhelmed her, and tears began to spill from her eyes.

'Happy tears,' she explained, wafting her hand in front of her face, trying to stop herself from crying some more.

'And breathe,' said Sam with a smile. 'You've done it! Wait till everyone hears about this on the island. They're going to be so happy. But it was close there for a second, and that was a hefty sum it got driven up to in the end.'

'I'd better get busy selling a few more paintings!'

'Who was that woman?' asked Pete. 'We were on the edge of our seats, not knowing who was going to win.'

'I've no idea,' replied Dilly, not wanting to even think of Max and Lydia in this happy moment. 'I need to go into the office and fill out all the legal stuff. I can't quite believe it… I'm the owner of the lighthouse!'

Dilly said goodbye and navigated her way through the crowd to a small office at the back of the auction house, clutching the golden ticket that signified her victory. The office was just how she'd imagined it. The air was thick and stuffy, carrying the faint mustiness of aged paper. The walls, most probably once a crisp white, were now yellowed with time and adorned with framed certificates and photographs that chronicled the town's history.

The receptionist – a woman in her late fifties, who wore her silver hair in a tight, no-nonsense bun – sat behind the large wooden desk that dominated the room. Her glasses were perched precariously on the bridge of her nose and were attached to a beaded chain that jingled softly whenever she moved. Her desk was meticulously organised, with a computer, stacks of neatly filed paperwork and an old-fashioned telephone that looked like something from the 1980s. Dressed in a sensible cardigan and a floral blouse, she had an air of stern efficiency about her but gave Dilly a smile. 'Can I help you?'

'Yes!' Dilly couldn't hide her excitement. 'I've just won the lighthouse. Well, not won, as winning would suggest it's free. I'm about to buy it. I'm babbling, aren't I?'

'It's most definitely not free!' the receptionist said, clearly not one for jokes. She took the document from Dilly, looked over it, then picked up the telephone, using the rotary dial to dial an unknown number.

'The new owner of Puffin Island Lighthouse is here,' the

receptionist announced before hanging up and asking Dilly to take a seat on a nearby chair.

Dilly liked the sound of that. She quickly punched a text to her dad.

I won!

Almost immediately, her phone pinged with a reply.

Brilliant news!

She planned to catch up with her dad later, and though she would have to share what Max had done, she wasn't going to let anything spoil this moment. She had just bought her new home – her dream home! – and was eager to move in and get her second gallery up and running. Everything was coming together!

As she sat in a chair in the waiting room, Dilly logged into her banking app. She had gone a few thousand over her budget, but it wasn't entirely unmanageable, and she still had some funds left over in her savings. It just meant she would have to tighten her belt a little more than planned, a sacrifice that felt worth it.

Dilly swung a glance out of the reception window and watched the comings and goings in the car park. Her gaze wandered idly until she spotted Max and his wife. She sat up straight, tracking them as they walked across the lot to the same car she'd seen Lydia get into at the harbour. They were deep in conversation and stopped at the back of the car, gesturing animatedly.

Dilly wanted to believe that Max hadn't used her to get

information, but as he climbed into the passenger seat, that familiar sinking ache settled in the pit of her stomach. She wished he would have come and found her, to tell her she had misunderstood everything. Yet, as they drove off together, she couldn't shake the feeling that she had misjudged him entirely.

Despite her disappointment, she took some solace in the fact that whatever game Max and Lydia had been playing, they hadn't won. They might have driven up the price, but *she* was now the proud owner of the lighthouse, and she wasn't going to let them spoil her moment.

The office door opened and Dilly looked over to find a smiley woman who took the document off the receptionist then glanced towards Dilly. 'You must be the new owner of Puffin Lighthouse.' She extended her hand. 'I'm Evelyn Haye. Let's get the paperwork filled in.'

Thirty minutes later, everything had been signed and sealed and Dilly left the auction house feeling like she was walking on air. Sliding into the driver's seat of her car, she started the engine and glanced at her phone. Word had evidently already made its way back to the island, and text messages were pinging in rapid succession, congratulating her on the win. She knew she should be feeling overjoyed, but the next stop was the pharmacy, and the gravity of what the pregnancy test would undoubtedly confirm overshadowed her recent triumph. She dialled Clemmie's number, her fingers trembling slightly.

Clemmie picked up immediately. 'You have excellent

timing as I'm just on my break. I've heard the news! Congratulations! You are the new lighthouse keeper of Puffin Island. How blooming cool is that?'

'Thank you. Are you free at lunchtime?'

'Woah! You don't sound too happy. I thought you'd be jumping for joy. Is something wrong? You *have* got the lighthouse, haven't you?'

'I have but I can't talk right now, I'll see you at lunchtime.'

'Of course. Twelvish?'

'Perfect,' Dilly replied before hanging up. She knew Clemmie would be wondering what the hell was going on but she didn't want to talk about it over the phone. The adrenalin of the morning had got her through the auction but now all she wanted to do was burst into tears.

———

Five minutes later, she pulled up outside the pharmacy. The bell sounded as she pushed open the door and walked inside. Thankfully there were no other customers. Her eyes quickly darted to the pregnancy tests on the shelf behind the counter and her stomach flipped as she approached, trying to keep her composure.

The assistant smiled warmly. 'Can I help you?'

Dilly could never have anticipated that buying a pregnancy test would be on her to-do list today, but it was, so she took a deep breath and plunged ahead. 'Yes, I need a pregnancy test, please.'

The assistant nodded, reaching for one of the boxes and

popping it into a white paper bag. 'Is there anything else you need today?'

Dilly shook her head. 'No, that's all, thank you.' As she held her debit card against the card machine, she could see her hand was shaking. The transaction completed, she slipped her card back into her purse. She clutched the white paper bag tightly as she left the pharmacy, and when she got back into her car she placed it on the passenger seat and stared at it for a moment, trying to gather her thoughts.

It didn't take long to drive back to the island, and though she wasn't sure she was ready to face a positive result, she couldn't put it off any longer. She parked the car at the side of the gallery, preparing herself for the conversation she was about to have with Clemmie and the reality she soon might have to face. Walking to the front of the gallery, she spotted her dad waiting on the doorstep. Ralph was beaming, trying to control a handful of colourful balloons that had a mind of their own. Dilly quickly slid the pregnancy test inside her bag, not wanting to broach that conversation until she had concrete evidence.

'What are you doing here?' Dilly put on her chirpiest voice.

'Congratulations, Dilly! You did it!' Ralph's voice was full of pride as he opened his arms and hugged her. 'These are for you! I've just got back so I was going to let myself into the gallery and leave them by your desk. Not only a new home and gallery, but the lighthouse! You must be so happy!'

'Have you got time to talk?' Dilly asked, her voice wavering slightly despite her best efforts. She wanted to put him straight about Max's antics before Max had a chance to tell him otherwise.

'I thought you'd be over the moon. What's wrong?'

Dilly unlocked the gallery door, and they stepped inside. She locked it again behind her, the sign on the back of the door remaining set to 'Closed'.

'Have you enough money to pay for it? Did you overbid? I can help you out if needs must. I don't want you to worry.' Ralph's voice was gentle as he followed Dilly up the stairs, concern etched on his face.

Dilly took a deep breath, trying to find the right words. 'It's not that, Dad. I mean, yes, I went a bit over budget, but it's manageable. It's just…'

Filled with fatherly concern, Ralph placed a hand on her arm and asked, 'Just what, sweetheart?'

'You need to fire Max, I don't want him working at the boat house.'

Ralph looked puzzled. 'I wasn't expecting that. Where has this come from?'

'I overbid, but I think the price was driven up on purpose,' Dilly said, switching on the kettle and taking two mugs out of the cupboard. As she made two cups of tea, she continued. 'I think, for whatever reason, I've been played.'

Ralph tied the balloons to the back of a chair and sat down, his expression turning serious. 'Played? Who has played you?'

Sitting opposite her dad, Dilly took a deep breath. 'Max.'

Ralph laughed, a mix of disbelief and amusement in his eyes. 'Sorry, I don't mean to laugh, but Max? How?'

'I think he was working with his wife to drive the price up on the lighthouse for some reason, though I can't figure out why. They eventually stopped bidding and then disappeared outside and he left with her, leaving me with no clue as to what had just happened or why.'

'Max was bidding against you for the lighthouse?' Ralph's face showed confusion.

'Not exactly. But he knew what my highest bid was, and suddenly I was up against his wife—'

'Ex-wife, or soon to be ex-wife, I believe,' Ralph interrupted. 'She was bidding on the lighthouse?'

'Did Max mention anything to you or give you any indication that she, or they, wanted the lighthouse?'

Ralph shook his head. 'Absolutely not. I really don't think this has anything to do with Max.'

'He abandoned me at the auction and went home with her. And that's not all. The day we went to look at the lighthouse together, I saw them exchanging an envelope on the beach. I didn't realise it was her at the time, but I think he was handing over information on my highest bid.'

Ralph leaned back, frowning. 'I wouldn't have thought so. There had to be numerous people bidding on that lighthouse. What has he done, befriended all of them?'

Dilly blew out a breath. She knew her dad was right but something wasn't sitting quite right with her.

'You've won and that's all that matters. If they really wanted it, they would have kept going.'

'They weren't expecting me to go higher than what Max thought I could,' Dilly explained. 'I bid above my budget, taking them by surprise … and myself, too. Maybe they didn't have the funds to go higher.'

Ralph shook his head, processing the information. 'So, you're saying Max knew your highest bid, and they tried to push you to your limit?'

'Exactly that,' Dilly replied. 'I just don't understand why.'

'I do hear you,' Ralph said, his brow furrowed. 'Max and…'

'Lydia,' Dilly filled in the blank.

'Lydia, yes… From what I gather, Lydia is a highly successful businesswoman from an extremely wealthy family. If they wanted that lighthouse, they could have had it. And Max seems like a genuine guy to me. I honestly think you've got this wrong and there is some sort of explanation.'

'I don't agree. Why has he arrived on Puffin Island out of the blue? Why is he working for you? He's an art teacher, not a boat repairer. Something doesn't feel right to me. Why did you give him the job? You must have asked why his last job ended and what brought him here during his interview.'

Ralph fell silent, a pensive look crossing his face.

'What aren't you telling me?' Dilly pressed. 'I know there's something.'

'I can't tell you anything about that,' Ralph said reluctantly.

'Why not? He must have said something.'

'I'm afraid it's confidential.'

'Dad!' Dilly's voice rose in frustration.

'I can't discuss it with you,' Ralph reiterated, looking uncomfortable. 'Sorry, Dilly, but he's a member of staff and anything he's said to me is in confidence.'

'But it's okay that he pushed up the price of the

lighthouse? For what gain? To put me in a difficult financial situation? To take the lighthouse from me?' Dilly's voice was incredulous.

Ralph exhaled deeply. 'You know I love you, and I know it's been a very difficult time for you lately … but I do think Max is a good guy and I'm sure there's an explanation. Talk to him.'

'Difficult time? Please don't tell me you think I'm just stressed and overreacting.'

'You've been having dizzy spells lately, and I've noticed you haven't been your usual self. Not everyone is out to get you,' Ralph said gently.

'What is that supposed to mean?' Dilly demanded, though she had an inkling of where the conversation was heading.

'I know it was over eight months ago now…'

Dilly felt a familiar pang of anxiety in her chest. She knew exactly where this conversation was heading: back to Giles. But the truth was, it hadn't been eight months since his betrayal. She'd actually been seeing Giles right up until four months ago, when she'd discovered he was a romance scammer. She hadn't been ready to face her father with that truth, so she'd told him the breakup had happened earlier in the year, making him believe they weren't as serious as they truly were, and that she'd just needed time to process it all before telling him about Giles's scheme. It was easier that way, less painful than admitting she'd been so deeply fooled.

'Do you think this suspicion is a result of your experience with Giles? It's understandable that his behaviour has had a huge impact on you,' Ralph said softly. 'I think his behaviour may have triggered you today.'

Dilly knew he was right, Giles's betrayal had left deep scars, but she didn't want to hear her dad's logic right now. Before Giles, she had seen the good in everyone and everything. Now, she questioned everything and was wary of any new situation, especially when it involved people outside her inner circle of friends, the few people whom she knew she could trust implicitly.

'Of course Giles's behaviour has affected me deeply,' Dilly admitted, 'but this feels different. There's something off about Max and Lydia, and I can't ignore it.'

Ralph reached across the table and took her hand. 'I understand, but I think we are going to have to agree to disagree on this one. Just be careful not to let past hurts cloud your judgment. Sometimes, things aren't as sinister as they seem.'

'The point is that they tried to stitch me up for whatever reason and I think you should sack him.' Dilly knew she was being unreasonable, but she wanted answers and consequences.

'I can't go around sacking members of staff just because their ex-wife bid against you on a lighthouse that is now yours,' Ralph said firmly, though his tone remained gentle.

Dilly sighed, feeling helpless. 'I know, I'm just frustrated. I don't understand why she drove the price up.'

'I think the best thing is to talk to Max about it. For the record, I really like him. So far, I've had no complaints, he's trustworthy, reliable and a perfectionist. If there was any way I could extend his contract, I wouldn't hesitate.'

Dilly knew her dad was right. She needed to talk to Max

directly and ask what had happened in the auction room. But she hated confrontation, and if Max declared he was back with his ex-wife, she wasn't sure how she would feel about that. He'd brought a spring back into her step, and she really enjoyed his company. All her old feelings for him had resurfaced, which had taken her by surprise, especially after Giles, but his behaviour this morning had completely thrown her. The fact that he never came back to her, that he walked out with Lydia and never looked back or gave her an explanation, hurt deeply.

'Today is a good day, Dilly. It's the start of a new chapter for you. Focus on you and your new lighthouse and I promise the right guy will walk into your life when you least expect it.'

Dilly wanted to say, *And I probably won't even notice as I'll be up to my eyes in caring for a baby.*

'I saw the newspaper this morning. I assume you did too, and that's maybe why your emotions are all over the place? It's a good thing he's been caught and can't target any other vulnerable women. You had a lucky escape, and now you never have to think about that man again.'

How wrong her dad was. If the pregnancy test was positive, there were several decisions she needed to make quickly.

'Focus on what you have: a brand-new gallery to open, turning this place into a community art space, and a new home to move into, which I can't wait to see inside of, by the way. For now, I'd best get back to the boat house.' He stood up and kissed his daughter on the cheek. 'Your grandmother and mum would be so proud of you.'

Dilly walked down the stairs with her dad then watched

him walk out of the gallery door. He gave her a wave through the window.

This morning was not exactly going to plan. She'd thought she would be celebrating her new home and popping the cork off the champagne bottle that was chilling in the fridge, with Max by her side.

Instead, she was alone, a pregnancy test hidden in her bag, and a head full of worries about Max and Lydia. The lighthouse was hers, but she wanted answers, and knew she needed to face Max. But first, she needed to know if her life was about to change in an even bigger way.

Chapter Nine

Dilly spent the rest of the morning watching the clock, each tick seeming to echo louder in the quiet gallery. She tried to keep busy, rearranging the paintings, dusting the shelves and triple-checking her emails, but her mind kept wandering back to the unopened pregnancy test in her bag. Customers drifted in and out and the locals popped in to congratulate her on her fabulous news but all she could think about was the pregnancy test. Midday couldn't come fast enough and as it approached Dilly glanced at the door, eagerly waiting for Clemmie to arrive and help her face whatever news awaited.

Just past midday, Clemmie breezed into the gallery like a ray of sunshine, her face alight with joy. 'Dilly Waters, the new lighthouse keeper!' she exclaimed, throwing her arms wide for a celebratory hug. 'You're going to be the queen of Puffin Island! Imagine the views, the inspiration for your paintings! This is incredible!' But her exuberant smile faltered as she noticed Dilly's anxious expression. 'What's wrong?'

Clemmie asked. 'You didn't sound happy on the phone and judging by the look on your face, something is wrong…'

Dilly locked the gallery door then ushered Clemmie upstairs where she silently handed over the small white paper bag. Clemmie's eyes widened as she peeked inside and saw the pregnancy test.

'Oh, shit,' she exclaimed. 'But who? I didn't even know you've been seeing someone.'

'I've kind've got a confession to make… It's Giles.'

'Giles? But he hasn't been around for what … over eight months now, right?' Clemmie glanced at Dilly's stomach. 'And you definitely don't look eight months pregnant.'

Dilly looked sheepish. 'We were still together up until about four months ago, but I played it down because Dad wasn't a fan, and I know you and the rest of the gang didn't like him much either. So, when I told you all that I'd discovered he was a romance scammer, it actually happened right then, not months before like I let on. I pretended it had taken me a few months to process and get over it when, in reality, I was still right in the middle of it.'

'Oh Dilly! I'm so sorry we made you feel like that.' She hugged her friend. 'And you dealt with this all by yourself. I'm so sorry for being a rubbish friend.'

'You weren't, I just took a step back as I knew you all weren't keen on him. I just wish I'd seen sooner what you saw.'

'Do you know the result?'

'Not yet, that's why you're here. I'm actually scared.'

'Okay, let's not panic… Actually, I'm panicking a bit.'

'That's exactly how I'm feeling.'

'And if you *are* pregnant, let's remember you can do this. Look at what you've accomplished with this place, and your business is still growing! And, of course, all of the island will support you.'

Dilly knew all that, but it helped to hear her friend say it aloud. 'Here goes.'

Clemmie hugged her tight before ushering her towards the bathroom.

Dilly closed the door behind her and took a nervous breath.

'I'm waiting here. I won't move,' Clemmie called from the other side of the door.

'There's a possibility I'm about to become a mother.'

'And you'll be a brilliant one at that.'

Dilly sat on the toilet in the tiny gallery bathroom as she opened the box and stared at it before reading the instructions. Two minutes was all it would take to give her the result. She knew the second she took the test her whole life would change. The word 'baby' was pounding in her head and if this test was positive, she would be a single mother going it alone.

Just as she had positioned the stick, Clemmie's voice rang out from the other side of the door. 'Are you weeing yet?'

'Clemmie, I can't pee with you talking!'

There was a moment of silence before Clemmie chimed in again. 'Will you hurry up? The suspense is killing me.'

'Clemmie! In the nicest possible way, shut up! I swear if you don't stop talking, I won't be able to—'

'Sorry, sorry,' she interrupted.

Dilly thought this was going to be the longest two minutes of her life but it wasn't.

It turned out there was no need to hold the stick up to the light or even wait the two minutes because there was no mistaking the dark blue text that was screaming PREGNANT at her from the second she looked at the stick. It was too bold and too blue for there to be any kind of mistake.

Now, sitting on the edge of the bath, she stared at the no-question-about-it-I-am-pregnant stick, her emotions mixed. She was shocked but there was also a part of her that was excited. She didn't know whether to laugh or cry. She had never envisioned when she got up this morning that by lunchtime she was going to be a mum. There was a baby growing inside her and she couldn't quite believe it.

Dilly opened the bathroom door.

'Finally! Well?'

'I'm pregnant.'

Without hesitation, Clemmie congratulated her. 'But I'm not sure if that's what you want to hear. How are you feeling?'

'Excited, nervous, scared…'

They moved to the living room, and Dilly sank into the couch. 'But the father, what am I going to do about that?'

Clemmie sat next to her. 'There's nothing you can do about that?' she offered gently.

'Do I contact him, tell him? I've got all these questions swirling around in my head. But being honest, I don't want him to be back in my life.'

'Whether you contact him is entirely your choice, and you don't have to make your mind up this second.'

'But what if...' Dilly's voice broke, 'the baby ends up like him? And can I actually do this alone?'

Clemmie, ever the optimist, said, 'Of course you can. Who needs a man? If anyone can rock the single mum life, it's you. You'll be like one of those chic, independent heroines in a romcom! I can picture it now: you, baby strapped to your chest, running this fabulous gallery. In fact, two fabulous galleries and a lighthouse! And babies are a great excuse for everything! Late to a meeting? Baby. Messy hair? Baby. Ate an entire cake? Baby cravings!' She grinned. 'And you know what? This kid will be the envy of all its friends because it'll have the best art supplies in town, thanks to their super-talented mum. Plus, when they're old enough, we can tell them their dad is in jail because he's a secret agent undercover in a maximum-security mission. Instant cool points!' Clemmie's infectious laughter filled the room, lifting Dilly's spirits and making the daunting prospect of motherhood seem a little brighter, even with its unusual circumstances.

'I love you. You are simply my best friend.'

'And Auntie Clemmie has a fantastic ring to it!' Clemmie beamed, her eyes sparkling with excitement. 'Just think about it, a babysitter on tap! I'll teach the little one all the best pranks, show them how to bake the perfect chocolate chip cookies, and we can have endless fun adventures. And you will never have to worry about finding someone trustworthy to watch the baby. We've got this!'

'Can we keep this just to ourselves for a while? I need to get used to the idea and make a doctor's appointment. I also need to tell my dad at some point.'

'My lips are sealed, I won't breathe a word. Auntie Clemmie! I can't wait!'

Dilly couldn't help but smile at her friend's enthusiasm, feeling a wave of relief wash over her. Despite the unexpected news and all its complications, with Clemmie by her side, everything seemed a bit more manageable and even a little bit fun.

'Now get that kettle boiling and tell me all about the auction and the gorgeous Max Harrington.'

'You aren't going to believe what I'm going to tell you,' Dilly began, switching on the kettle. 'Get yourself comfortable, it's been a hell of a morning.'

'Intriguing!' shouted Clemmie from the settee.

Chapter Ten

D illy flitted around the gallery with a spring in her step, setting the stage for her first art class. She arranged the easels in a welcoming semicircle, ensuring each student would have a perfect view of the charismatic life model, Pierre. With a beaming smile, she popped the cork on a bottle of Prosecco, filling each glass, its effervescence matching her own jittery energy. The Prosecco would hopefully help everyone relax and embrace their inner artist. Dilly was looking forward to tonight; it was just what she needed, the perfect blend of creativity, friends, laughter, and a bit of bubbly magic.

After laying out sketch pads and charcoals by the easels, she carefully moved the couch at the back of the gallery to the centre of the semicircle. With a playful touch, she draped a dressing gown over the back of the couch, envisioning the artistic charm it would add.

To ensure a blend of modesty and creativity, she placed a bowl of vibrant fruit on the side table, its colourful array promising both visual delight and a tasteful cover for the model. The setup was perfect, brimming with artistic flair and a touch of fun, ready to inspire everyone in the class.

Sitting on the couch and waiting for the first guests to arrive, Dilly's thoughts turned to Max. Even though she hadn't seen him since he'd left the auction with his wife – ex-wife? – he was still on her mind. She felt a pang of disappointment that he hadn't come to see her or explain what exactly went on yesterday. She had hoped for some clarity, but instead she was left with lingering questions and a sense of unfinished business.

Determined not to let thoughts of Max spoil her girly fun, she stood up and checked everything was ready. She looked at the glasses of Prosecco and wondered how many bottles they would get through tonight. She also wondered if anyone would notice she wasn't drinking. She did have the perfect excuse, given that she was hosting the event and it wouldn't be at all professional if she was drunk on the job. Still, she knew the girls would try to persuade her to have at least one, so she discreetly poured herself a wine glass of sparkling water, determined to keep her pregnancy a secret for now. The bubbles mimicked the Prosecco everyone else would be drinking. She sipped it with a smile, happy to have found a way to keep her unexpected news under wraps.

Ten minutes later the gallery was filled with laughter and chatter, as it had been from the moment the door swung open and her first students arrived. Dilly could hardly contain her amusement, knowing full well that the source of their giddiness was the naked man they were about to draw. Clemmie and Amelia had been first to burst through the door and had immediately enveloped Dilly in a bear hug.

'Congratulations on winning the lighthouse, Dilly! You really are the queen of auctions, art and Prosecco!' Amelia exclaimed, releasing her and making a beeline for the tray of drinks.

Next came Betty, Verity and Robin, who squealed in unison as they spotted Dilly. 'You did it! The lighthouse is yours!' Betty squeezed her before picking up a drink then kissed her on the cheek. 'This is my kind of night. Good friends and—'

'And a naked man,' Cora – the co-owner of The Olde Ship Inn – finished Betty's sentence as she was next through the door, along with Becca. 'I have to say, it's good to take a night off from working at the pub and relax with friends.' She smiled.

'I never realised I was so interested in art until tonight,' said Becca, giving Dilly a hug.

'I thought you'd be working the Cosy Kettle tonight,' said Dilly. 'I'm glad you're here instead though.'

'I've got the night off. You didn't think I was going to miss this, did you?'

Once everyone had their bubbly in hand, they began to settle behind their easels. The sight of the semicircle of eager faces, all peering expectantly at the empty couch, made Clemmie nudge Dilly. 'You'd think they'd never seen a naked man before! How are you doing, by the way?' she whispered.

Dilly did a quick scan of the room to make sure no one was in earshot. 'I can't quite believe I've got another human growing inside me. It doesn't feel real to me but I know it is, and as far as Giles goes, I'm looking at the positives. He might have come into my life to take everything I owned, but I stopped him and he was the one who ended up forfeiting something precious. He left me with the greatest gift of all and it's going to be me and her against the world.'

'Her?'

'Just a figure of speech.'

'You are the most amazing person I know, Dilly Waters. Have you heard anything from Max?'

Dilly shook her head. 'No and that tells me the type of person he is, if he's not even come to explain. When you think you know someone...'

'So, when does the star of the show arrive?' Betty chimed in, sitting impatiently behind her easel, looking towards the clock on the wall.

'Patience, Betty!' Dilly replied. 'Pierre will make his grand entrance soon enough.'

The room hummed with excitement as they waited and chatted amongst themselves whilst sipping Prosecco, their anticipation building. Dilly took a moment to soak it all in, feeling thankful her friends were here to support her new venture – though there was no doubt that what they were really here for was to see Pierre get his kit off. Even so, this was going to be a night to remember, filled with laughter, creativity and perhaps a few blushes when Pierre finally made his appearance.

Just as the room reached a peak of giggly expectation, the door swung open. All heads turned and though Dilly was expecting to see Pierre, in walked Max instead, looking slightly out of breath and holding a bunch of flowers. Dilly's heart skipped a beat. Was he here to apologise and give her clarity about what had happened yesterday?

Before she could say a word, Betty gasped dramatically. 'Oh my God, Dilly, is this our model?' she exclaimed, her eyes wide with excitement. 'He's gorgeous!'

Max's eyes widened in sheer terror as he took in the semicircle of eager faces, all of the women grinning mischievously from behind their glasses of Prosecco. He looked towards the couch and the bowl of fruit then took an instinctive step back, colliding with the door he had just walked through.

Robin and Becca burst into laughter. 'Oh, he's brought his own prop!' trilled Robin, pointing at the flowers. 'To cover up his modesty.'

Dilly stepped forward, trying to contain her own laughter. 'Max, what are you doing here?' she asked, though she couldn't help but smirk at the situation.

Max cleared his throat, still looking around like a deer caught in headlights. 'I, uh, wanted to come and put things right between us. Here, these are for you, a peace offering.' He held up the flowers like a white flag.

Still feeling mischievous, Betty chimed in, 'Let's get this show on the road. We are *very* eager to begin.'

Clemmie's eyebrows shot up. 'Granny, you need to behave. That's…'

Dilly smiled and shook her head. 'Ladies, this is Max, not Pierre. He's not the model for tonight. He's currently working at the boat house with my dad. How you've missed him coming into the tearoom, Betty, I will never know. Usually, you don't miss a trick.'

Betty held her hands to her chest, pretending to look hurt, as a collective 'Aww!' of disappointment echoed around the room and Max visibly relaxed, though still looking slightly bewildered. He gave Dilly a sheepish smile. 'Well, I'm glad that's cleared up. I almost thought I was going to have to strip down for art's sake.'

Betty patted the seat next to her. 'You're welcome to join us and keep your clothes on, Max. But be warned, we might still draw you if Pierre doesn't show up!'

Max chuckled nervously, glancing at Dilly. 'I don't think this is the best time to talk.'

'I think you may be right. But you are more than welcome to join us.'

'I'll just stick to a night in front of the TV, but thanks for the offer.'

With that, Max, made his escape with a quick wave and slipped out the door before any more surprises could be sprung on him.

Dilly placed the flowers in the sink at the back of the studio. It seemed the night was off to an even more memorable start than she had anticipated. No sooner had the door clicked shut behind Max than it swung open again, this time revealing the true star of the evening.

Pierre waltzed in with all the flair and drama of a seasoned performer, a confident grin spreading across his face. Without a moment's hesitation, he began stripping off his clothes, each item discarded with a flourish, until he stood in all his glory, not even attempting to cover his manhood.

The room fell into a stunned silence, the women frozen in various states of surprise. Betty turned an alarming shade of crimson and fanned herself vigorously, muttering, 'Oh my stars!' before teetering dangerously in her seat.

Verity, ever the cheeky one, leaned over to Amelia and whispered loudly, 'Just remember, nice gentle strokes … with that paintbrush … it's all in the detail.'

Amelia stifled a giggle and replied, 'I'm pretty sure no one will miss that detail.'

Dilly clapped to get everyone's attention. 'Ladies, let's welcome Pierre and focus! Let the painting begin.'

Pierre, unfazed by the commotion he had caused, struck a dramatic pose on the couch, his every movement exuding confidence. The bowl of fruit sat neglected and forgotten on the side table. It seemed they wouldn't be needing it this evening…

Betty, thankfully, regained her composure somewhat, adjusted her glasses and peered at her sketch pad as the room was suddenly filled with silence, the only sounds pencils scratching against the paper and paintbrushes sloshing in their water pots, interspersed with occasional giggles and whispered comments. Pierre remained perfectly still as the women did their best to capture the spirit of their unexpectedly bold model.

As the evening was coming to an end, and just as everyone thought that Betty had tamed her excitement, she called out to Pierre, who was just about to move from the couch, to pause. 'Can you hold that pose for just a few more minutes? I promise, I'm almost done … with my Prosecco,' she piped up.

Dilly glanced around the room, unable to suppress a

smile. This was definitely an art class she wouldn't forget. Yet, as the clock ticked on, her mind kept drifting back to Max, wondering what he had to say for himself about yesterday. The flowers he'd brought were beautiful, but they reminded her too much of Giles's tricks. After all, hindsight had shown her that he'd always bought her flowers when he had something to hide.

Chapter Eleven

The next morning, Dilly woke up to soft light filtering through her curtains, and the gentle sound of seagulls calling outside. She stretched, feeling the warmth of her cosy bed, and reluctantly pushed herself up. With a yawn, she put on her slippers and padded into the kitchen. After grabbing her favourite mug, she made herself a cup of tea and settled on the settee, tucking her legs underneath her. Looking out at the view never failed to take her breath away. The sea sparkled and her eyes followed the line of boats moored at the jetty towards the lighthouse. Her new home.

Hearing her phone ping, she looked and found there was a text from Clemmie.

> Last night was a blast and we need to do it again soon! We just need to keep my grandmother away from the Prosecco!

Dilly could hardly keep herself from chuckling as she

recalled Betty's astonished face when the model had dramatically whipped off his clothes.

Clemmie's second text landed.

And don't forget to ring the doctors.

Before she could start her day, Dilly knew she had to make an appointment. Usually, she didn't care what anyone thought about her, but she was worried about what people would say about the pregnancy. Living on a small island had its charms, but privacy wasn't one of them. Gossip had a way of travelling faster than the island's sea breezes.

The looming doctor's appointment brought with it another worry: the inevitable questions about the father of her baby. She was certain that, despite the doctor's professional discretion, the island's residents would start wondering and speculating as soon as they found out she was pregnant. She knew she had to prepare herself for curious glances and to craft a narrative, a story she could stick to consistently, no matter who asked. It had to be believable and simple, something that would quell the gossip before it had a chance to take root. She didn't want anyone knowing the father was Giles.

She considered her options carefully, knowing that whatever story she invented would become an integral part of her life for a very long time. It needed to be something she could live with, something that wouldn't contradict itself over time. Everyone on the island knew about her relationship with Giles but they also thought he'd been out of the picture a lot longer than he had, and they all undoubtedly knew by now that he'd been sentenced. Dilly decided then and there that she wouldn't admit Giles was the father. She wanted to protect her child from the stigma and judgment that could possibly follow that revelation. If she acknowledged Giles as the father, there was also a risk that as her baby grew up, word would get to them about who their father was and what he had done, before she was ready to share the information herself. Dilly definitely didn't want that. That would be her story to tell, on her terms, and when the time was right.

Her mind raced as she pieced together the story she would tell the islanders. The tale she created revolved around a one-night stand, a spontaneous, passionate encounter that no one could easily question.

She imagined herself at an art convention in Edinburgh, a trip that had actually taken place just days after she had discovered Giles's deceit. She'd stayed overnight at a fancy hotel, which would make the perfect backdrop for her story. In her fabricated narrative, she met a gorgeous man at the hotel bar. Their chemistry was off the charts, an instant and irresistible connection that led to a night of uninhibited fun. She imagined the setting vividly, the dim lighting of the bar, the clink of glasses, the buzz of conversation around them, and the magnetic pull between her and this fictional stranger ... who looked a lot like Max, if she was being honest with herself.

Dilly reasoned that no one on the island would know she hadn't met such a man. After all, she was an independent woman with no ties to anyone, free to live her life as she pleased. She could easily claim that she'd decided to indulge in a night of excitement, something entirely out of character but perfectly justifiable given the circumstances.

She was aware that some of the locals might have their opinions about this supposed one-night stand. There would be whispers and judgment from those who held more conservative views. But Dilly reckoned that enduring a bit of gossip was far better than her child discovering the truth about their father before she was ready to tell them. With the decision made, she felt a strange sense of relief wash over her. She had a plan, a way to navigate the inevitable questions and curiosity of the island's residents. She would stick to her story, repeating it with unwavering confidence until it became as real as any other memory. The only person who would know the truth was Clemmie, but Dilly trusted her not to breathe a word to anyone.

After finishing her cuppa, Dilly reached for her mobile and dialled the doctor's surgery. The appointment was made for Monday morning. The only other thing she needed to do now was decide when to tell her dad. She knew he would support her no matter what, but first she wanted just a little more time to get used to the idea of becoming a mum, especially under the not-so-normal circumstances.

Thirty minutes later, Dilly emerged from the shower, feeling refreshed. She thanked her lucky stars for her dungarees. They had always been her favourite item of clothing, but now they had the bonus of being roomy enough to hide her ever-expanding stomach for a while longer. Most mums-to-be were able to keep their pregnancy a secret for the first few months, but Dilly knew that with her first scan just around the corner, she wouldn't be able to keep the news under wraps much longer.

As she wandered downstairs, Dilly was grateful for the hour she had before the gallery opened. Last night had been a whirlwind of creativity and laughter with the best people she knew but it had left her too exhausted to tidy up. Clemmie had offered to help, and in hindsight Dilly wished she'd accepted, but as soon as everyone had left all she'd wanted to do was snuggle under the covers, so she'd made the executive decision to leave clean-up for the morning.

She looked around the gallery now. Easels were still in place, pencils scattered everywhere, and paint pots and brushes stood next to the sink, waiting to be cleaned. Despite the chaos, last night had been so much fun. Everyone had taken their paintings home, thrilled with their work, and Pierre had been an absolute sport throughout the evening. She chuckled at the memory of him completely ignoring the protective bowl of fruit. Taking an apple from said fruit bowl, she bit into it and looked across at her desk. The only task Dilly had managed before slipping into bed was to put Max's flowers in water. The blooms were utterly gorgeous, a delicate and fragrant arrangement of roses, freesias and eucalyptus, and the soft pinks and whites of the flowers contrasted beautifully with the rich green eucalyptus, their sweet scent gently filling the room. The arrangement now sat elegantly on her desk at the back of the gallery, arranged in her favourite vase, a beautifully intricate piece of glasswork that had been a birthday gift from her mum when she'd opened the gallery.

Her mum said a gallery always needed fresh flowers in a beautiful vase.

After pausing to smell the flowers, Dilly began tidying up the gallery. She laughed to herself, recalling the moment when Betty mistook Max for the life model. Despite taking over twenty-four hours to come and see her, at least he had finally shown up, and she was still curious to hear what he had to say for himself. However, it would have to wait. Saturdays were the busiest days in the gallery. Tourists flocked to Sea's End on the ferry and often walked the causeway to Puffin Island, especially when the weather was as glorious as it was today. Dilly knew there would be no chance to slip out and see him, so she decided to text him. She needed to pin him down to a time when they could talk. Her conversation with her dad was weighing heavily on her mind. Had she overreacted about the incident at the auction? Her dad seemed to think that Max was a genuinely good guy, but if that was the case, why hadn't he come back to her at the auction? He knew bidding for that lighthouse was a huge deal for her.

Before she could send the message, he beat her to it, her phone pinging with a text message.

> Good morning. I hope you survived the evening and so did Pierre! Tonight, 7pm? Let's chat. The boat house? I've moved in x

Dilly wondered whether it would be better to chat in a neutral place but then again, anywhere else they went on the island wouldn't be private. This way they could have a conversation to clear the air and she could also have a nosey around his flat. She texted back.

> See you later x

She hesitated before adding the kiss but as he'd typed one, she did the same.

As soon as there was a lull in customers, Dilly logged on to her emails and felt a flutter of excitement that the first message was from her solicitor. The paperwork for the lighthouse was all in order, and he was inviting her in on Wednesday to finalise everything. As soon as the money was transferred, she could pick up the keys. By the weekend, she would be inside her very own lighthouse! Dilly knew the first task would be to clean it from top to bottom. She quickly logged on to her Amazon account and ordered an abundance of cleaning products. She couldn't wait to get stuck in, envisioning the gleaming floors and sparkling windows. After that was done, it would be time to paint.

With the easel already set up at the back of the gallery, she slipped on her smock before setting to work on the portrait of her mother, the focal piece for the new gallery, which, if it was possible, she aimed to open by the end of the month. Carefully she sorted out her paints and a selection of favourite brushes, and as she prepared to start she felt that familiar thrill of creativity bubbling up inside her. She took a moment to absorb the image from the photograph, then, with a deep breath, she dipped her brush into the first colour and began to paint. Each stroke was filled with love and precision as she meticulously worked to capture her mother on the canvas.

As the hours passed, Dilly found herself chatting warmly with visitors as they wandered in and out, discussing her art and the gallery, and in between visitors she focused on her painting, which was gradually taking shape, her mother's likeness coming to life on the canvas in a way that felt almost magical. This portrait was more than just a painting. It was a heartfelt tribute to the woman who had been Dilly's inspiration and best friend.

Just then, the door opened, and in walked a tall, smiley man dressed in a sharp suit. He looked very distinguished, with a moustache that curled up at the ends, giving him an air of old-world charm. Dilly looked up from the easel and greeted him with a welcoming smile. He wandered through the gallery, his eyes eventually landing on the painting of a whimsical lighthouse set against rugged cliffs and surrounded by puffins in mid-flight. His face lit up with genuine admiration as he pointed to it.

'This painting is just what I need,' he said, his voice warm and enthusiastic.

Dilly's smile widened as she stepped over to him, thrilled by his interest. 'I'm glad you like it. It's one of my favourites.'

'It's perfect. I've been looking for something that captures the spirit of the sea and the beauty of the coast. This does it brilliantly. I want to take it!'

Dilly was delighted; sales today had been remarkable. She continued to chat with the distinguished man as she carefully took the painting down from the wall. Together, they moved to the desk, where Dilly began to wrap the painting.

As she wrapped, the man shared a charming story. 'Many years ago, I visited Puffin Island,' he began. 'I was on holiday with my friends at Sea's End when I met a girl who was obsessed with puffins. We clicked instantly and spent hours here on the island watching them. She was also obsessed with a local band.'

Dilly knew exactly who he was talking about. Betty's husband had been a member of that band, as was Sam's grandfather. Though both men were no longer with them, the two other band members, Pete and John, still lived on the island. 'The Men from Puffin Island,' she supplied.

'That was them.' He paused, a wistful smile. 'That girl is now my wife. We've been married for over fifty years and our first kiss happened right on that rock,' he said, pointing to the spot in the painting.

Dilly's eyes widened with delight. 'Wow! That is so romantic!' she exclaimed, genuinely touched by his story. She could feel the love and memories that the painting encapsulated for him, making the sale even more meaningful.

The man nodded, his smile broadening. 'When I saw this painting, it brought back all those wonderful memories. I knew I had to have it for my wife and the timing couldn't be more perfect as it's her birthday tomorrow.'

'Sounds like it was fate that you and this painting would find each other!'

As Dilly was taking the credit card from the man, her eyes drifted over his shoulder and locked onto a woman standing outside the window, gazing in at the paintings.

Dilly's heart pounded in her chest, and her breath caught in her throat.

It couldn't be...

No, her mother was dead, killed in the south of France.

But if that was true, how was it that Dilly was looking at her now?

The room seemed to spin, and for a moment, she felt dizzy with confusion, her mind racing with disbelief. Quickly thanking the gentleman and completing the sale, she checked to make sure the woman on the other side of the window was still standing there.

'Mum,' she whispered, the word barely audible. The woman began to walk away, and Dilly felt a surge of urgency. She bolted toward the front door, pushing it open with a sense of desperation. 'Mum!' she shouted, her voice faltering as she called out. But the woman didn't look back. She got into a car and drove off, leaving Dilly standing in the doorway, breathless and stunned. Emotions surged through her body, a mix of shock and hope that her mum was alive. But why hadn't she come inside? Suddenly Dilly was engulfed in confusion. Was she mistaken and losing a grip on reality? She stood there, her heart aching, a million questions racing through her mind.

No, it *was* her. Dilly was certain.

Hearing someone behind her, Dilly spun around to see Clemmie walking down the street towards her. 'I'm just taking a breather. The tearoom is manic with this glorious weather. I thought I'd grab some fresh air and check you've made your doctor's appointment,' she said with a smile.

Dilly was trembling and instant concern etched itself across Clemmie's face. 'Dilly, are you okay? You look like you've seen a ghost. Oh my gosh, is it the baby? Are you feeling okay?'

'Clem, it's not the baby.' She exhaled. 'I've just seen my mum. She's alive!' Dilly blurted.

Clemmie's expression shifted to one of shock and disbelief. 'What do you mean, Dilly? Have they found her?'

'She was standing right here on the pavement, looking through the window,' Dilly explained, her words tripping over each other. 'I came out and called to her, but she got into a car and drove off. I'm not sure why she would do that.'

'Your mum was here, standing right here? On this street, on Puffin Island?' Clemmie asked, clearly confused.

'Yes, I saw her,' Dilly insisted, her eyes wide with certainty.

'But she didn't come into the gallery?' Clemmie questioned, evidently trying to make sense of it all.

'It was her, I swear! We need to go after her but I can't remember anything about the car.' Dilly shook her head, her eyes brimming with tears.

Clemmie took her hands, her grip firm and comforting. 'Dilly, are you absolutely sure? Because your mum was in a tragic accident in the south of France. It was unlikely she could have survived,' she said as gently as she could.

'Clemmie, I'm telling you, that was my mum. She had the same brown curls, the same big blue eyes. I know what my mum looks likes. It was her, I'm absolutely certain. What if she survived the accident but lost her memory? And something has brought her back here but she doesn't quite know what? You read about people losing their memory all the time and leading another life until something triggers their memory,' Dilly said, her voice rising in hope and desperation.

Clemmie's eyes softened with sympathy, yet remained cautious. 'I understand how much you want this to be true, Dilly, but honestly, I don't think it possibly could. I think this is someone that maybe just reminded you of your mum.'

Dilly shook her head adamantly, her eyes wide. 'It was her. I'm not going mad. I saw her. She was standing right there, looking at the paintings. I know what I saw.'

'Let's get you into the gallery,' Clemmie suggested gently.

Dilly hesitated, her eyes still scanning the road, hoping the car would return. But it didn't.

As soon as they were inside the gallery, Clemmie locked the door behind them. 'Let me get you a drink,' she offered.

'I don't want a drink,' Dilly snapped, her frustration bubbling over. 'You don't believe me, do you?' She sat on a chair, but her eyes kept flicking back to the window in case her mother reappeared.

'I think a couple of things may have triggered you into thinking and hoping that was your mum,' Clemmie said tentatively, her voice gentle. She perched on the edge of the desk. 'Firstly, you've just discovered you're pregnant, and I can only imagine how much you must want your mum here to share your wonderful news. It's a life-changing moment, and naturally you'd want her support and love.' Clemmie paused, her gaze drifting to the easel. 'And secondly,' she continued, her eyes now fixed on the painting, 'you're painting your mum.' She reached out and picked up the photograph propped next to it, studying it for a moment before looking back at Dilly. 'Working on this portrait must have brought back a lot of memories and emotions.'

Dilly looked at the photograph in Clemmie's hand, her eyes welling up with tears. 'I know what you're saying but it was real. *She* was real. Like I've just said, people lose their memories after a severe accident. It does happen.'

Clemmie nodded. 'It does happen, Dilly, but our minds can also sometimes play tricks on us, especially when we're dealing with so many emotions. The combination of your pregnancy and the act of painting your mum might have made you see what you desperately wanted to see.'

Dilly's hands were trembling as she wiped away her tears. 'Clemmie, she was right there, looking through the window. It's driving me crazy thinking I might have lost her again.'

Clemmie leaned forward, taking Dilly's hands in hers, offering a comforting squeeze.

'I'm not wrong, it was her,' Dilly said, her voice firm despite the tears streaming down her cheeks.

Clemmie's eyes were filled with concern and empathy. 'What do you want to do about it? Shall I call your dad? Or even the police?'

'I don't know what to do,' Dilly admitted, her voice breaking as she placed her head in her hands and sobbed. The maelstrom of hope, confusion, and fear was almost too much to bear.

Clemmie squeezed her hands a little tighter. 'It's okay, take a moment. We can figure this out together.'

Dilly lifted her head, her eyes red and swollen. Now she was starting to question herself. Was Clemmie right? Was it just someone who looked like her mother? No, deep down, her gut feeling was telling her she was right. 'It felt so real. I just… I don't want to believe it was anyone else.'

Clemmie nodded. 'How about we start by seeing if anyone else on the island saw her? Maybe someone can confirm what you saw. Every islander knows Eva so if she's back, we'll know about it soon enough.'

Dilly took a deep breath, trying to steady herself. 'Yes, that makes sense. Do you think I'm crazy? Be honest with me.'

Clemmie shook her head firmly. 'No, but I do think you're grieving and you've been through a lot. Let's just take it one step at a time. We can talk to your dad, and maybe, if you think it's necessary, we can involve the police. But talk to your dad first.'

Dilly nodded slowly, feeling a bit more grounded. 'Okay. I'll talk to Dad first. He'll know what to do.'

Clemmie smiled reassuringly. 'Exactly. And remember, you're not alone in this. I'm always here.'

Dilly hugged Clemmie, grateful for her support. 'Thank you. I just need to know if my mum is really out there.'

'I know.' They looked at each other for a moment. 'I've got to get back to the tearoom. Are you going to be okay?'

Dilly nodded. 'I have to be, I have someone else to consider now.' She placed her hands on her stomach.

Clemmie stood up. 'You have, but on this island we all look after each other. If you need me, ring me. I can always come around tonight.'

'I'm seeing Max at seven.'

'What's going to happen there?'

'I'm not sure. I need to know what the hell happened at the auction.'

'And are you going to mention the baby?'

Dilly shook her head. 'No, I need to speak to my dad first. I might call and see him afterwards. If I'm going to tell him I think I've seen Mum, I think it would be better in person than in a text.'

'That sounds like a good idea.'

Dilly watched Clemmie unlock the door and wave goodbye before walking down the street. She sighed. She knew how it must have sounded, but she saw the woman with her own two eyes. It was her mum; she just knew it.

Chapter Twelve

With her mind still filled with thoughts of her mother, Dilly made her way to the boat house to meet Max. She was early, so she perched on one of her favourite rocks just past the jetty that led to The Sea Glass Restaurant. Her plan was to call in and see her father after she'd spoken to Max, because he would be the one person that might understand the turmoil she was feeling – but now, as she thought about what Clemmie had said, doubt began to set in. What if she was wrong? What if it was just a trick of the light or a moment of wishful thinking?

The image of her mother's familiar face, those unmistakable brown curls and piercing blue eyes, had seemed so real, but now Dilly was questioning her own sanity. Telling her dad might make her look foolish and cause him to worry about her even more than he already did, but the faint hope that her mum might be alive was still tugging at her heart. After all, her and Anton's bodies were never recovered. There was a slim chance.

Dilly was torn between the fear of being dismissed as delusional and the desperate desire to believe in miracles. Her father was a fair and gentle man but also a no-nonsense character, and that was making her hesitate. As tears welled up in her eyes, she felt utterly conflicted about what to do.

She slid from the rock and decided to grab a brew at the Cosy Kettle before heading to see Max. As she walked up to the hut, the familiar aroma of freshly baked pastries and coffee enveloped her. Becca was behind the counter, her face lighting up as she spotted Dilly.

'Dilly! Loved the art class last night,' she said with a grin as Dilly ordered a cup of tea.

'Pierre was such a good sport as the life model, wasn't he? And Betty's reaction was priceless! Honestly, I thought at one point she might join him on that couch!' said Dilly.

They both laughed.

'Betty was an absolute scream. I've not laughed like that in a long time. It was definitely the highlight of my week and I can't wait for the next class.'

'I need to organise it, maybe for the start of next month. It's going to be full-on when I get the keys for the lighthouse and can start the work there, which hopefully should be this week.'

'It's all very exciting!'

They both looked towards the lighthouse before Becca handed over the tea then pointed. 'Have you seen that woman before?'

Dilly followed Becca's gaze and her heart immediately sank as her eyes landed on Lydia Harrington. She was hard to miss. Dressed in yet another killer dress that hugged her curves and accentuated her impeccable figure, Lydia looked like she had just stepped off the cover of a fashion magazine. Her hair was perfectly styled, and her makeup was flawlessly applied, making her look every bit the sophisticated city woman she was. The complete opposite of Dilly with her laid-back island lifestyle. She watched as Lydia walked with purpose, her high heels clicking against the cobblestones. It seemed she was heading straight for the boat house, which set off a wave of unease in Dilly's stomach. Her repeated appearances were raising a *lot* of questions, and Dilly couldn't help but wonder if Max and Lydia had set her up by inviting her to the boat house. Were they both going to be there?

'It's not often I get rude customers but that woman was downright hostile to me today, and for no reason! She's been to-ing and fro-ing all day to the boat house. No doubt she owns the biggest yacht in the harbour,' Becca observed.

As Lydia disappeared from view, Dilly couldn't help feeling a pang of jealousy – and some suspicion. She took a sip of tea, trying to calm her racing thoughts. In a casual tone, she replied, 'No, I don't know her.' It was a big fat lie but Dilly didn't want to delve into the details of Lydia being Max's ex-wife or the fact that she had bid against her at the auction, attempting to win the lighthouse.

Now filled with uncertainty about her impending meeting with Max, Dilly didn't know what to do.

After a day full of emotional ups and downs the last thing she wanted was any sort of confrontation, but she also wanted to know what Max was playing at. She waved goodbye to Becca and approached Max's flat, her heart beating with anticipation. As she reached the door, she paused for a moment, taking a deep breath. At the sound of a woman's voice, her hand froze in mid-air, inches from the door. She wasn't proud of herself as she leaned in closer, trying to catch the conversation. She knew it was wrong to eavesdrop, but curiosity got the better of her.

'Now that you've moved in, I wanted to see where you were living,' the voice purred.

'Why are you really here, Lydia? What are you hoping to gain?' the man – who had to be Max – asked.

Lydia's voice slithered through the crack in the door, smooth and condescending. 'You always knew divorcing me meant you'd end up with nothing. You married me with nothing, and you were never going to get your hands on any of my money.'

Dilly's heart raced as she stood still, listening to the drama unfolding inside Max's flat. She knew she shouldn't be standing there but her feet were glued to the floor.

'I don't want your money, Lydia. I never did. What's the point of this?' Max sounded weary, as if he'd had this argument a thousand times. 'Has your new relationship already run its course?'

Suddenly Lydia's tone shifted, becoming sharper, more pointed. 'Candles and flowers? Who are you expecting? It's her, isn't it? The lighthouse girl. Your pupil.'

Dilly's breath caught in her throat. She hadn't expected to be dragged into this, or that Lydia would know anything about her.

Max's voice rose in frustration. 'She isn't a pupil anymore. I no longer teach, remember? And that's because of you.'

The more Dilly listened, the more guilt she felt, but

questions were spinning around in her mind. What had Lydia done to Max to stop him from teaching?

Then Lydia's voice cut through the air like a knife. 'Does your boss know you're after his daughter?'

Dilly's heart pounded in her chest.

'You do know, when word gets out about this, it could ruin her reputation? The lighthouse girl, once your student, now your scandal. How poetic.'

Dilly's legs felt weak and she didn't want to hear any more. This wasn't her fight and she didn't want to be caught in the crossfire of Max's messy past. But just as she turned to leave, she heard something that stopped her in her tracks.

'And you can't just ignore the fact that I'm pregnant. You know you'll make a fantastic father. It's all you've ever wanted.'

Dilly's world spun. Lydia was pregnant? Max was going to be a father? The weight of it all pressed down on her chest, making it hard to breathe. Just as she was debating her next move, she heard footsteps approaching the door. Before she could react, the door swung open and Max appeared. His face was a picture of surprise. Behind him, Lydia's expression turned to smugness.

'Dil,' Max breathed, his eyes locking onto hers.

Lydia's icy voice cut through the moment like a knife. 'Well, isn't this cosy?'

Max rubbed the back of his neck. 'It's not what it looks like, Dilly. I was just—'

Dilly raised a hand, stopping him. 'She's pregnant with your baby?'

Lydia smirked, clearly enjoying the tension she was

causing. 'Lighthouse Girl, you do know he will never be yours, don't you? You're just collateral damage from his latest tantrum.'

Dilly felt like she had been punched in the gut. She stared at Max before turning and walking away.

'Dilly!' Max's voice echoed behind her but she didn't look back. She just kept walking.

She didn't want either of them to see the tears that were rolling down her cheeks. She wouldn't let herself be drawn into this mess. Not again. No man was worth this kind of trouble. Not even Max.

Chapter Thirteen

Dilly was furious as she headed back down to the harbour, but something made her stop in her tracks and turn around. She wasn't going to be talked to like that, and she deserved answers. She marched straight back to the flat, hearing raised voices as she approached the door.

'Look at what you've done. You just can't help yourself, can you? You don't want me, but you don't want anyone else to have me either, is that it? You're angry because I finally came to my senses and walked away from you. You didn't think I would choose nothing over you, but I did and I'd do it again. I would choose no money, no car, and no house over staying married to you a moment longer. I came here to get away from you, but you couldn't let me live my own life, could you? I don't *want* you, Lydia. When will you accept that?'

'But you choose *her*?' she shouted, her voice rising. 'A slip of a girl who was once in your classroom.'

'Stop right there,' Max snapped. 'Dilly is no longer in

my classroom and is very much a woman, unlike you, who gives women a bad name. You lie and cheat, and you have the evidence growing inside you.'

Dilly stopped just outside the still open door. Neither of them had noticed her but she could clearly see Lydia's face turning bright red with fury.

'I will never want you again, ever,' Max continued. 'What you did at that auction was spiteful and all just because you thought I was having a relationship with someone who was buying the lighthouse. You are unbelievable and I'm glad I have nothing to show from all those years I was unfortunately married to you, not even the job I loved, because there will at least be no reminders of you. Get out, Lydia. And as for your baby, we both know the truth. It's not mine.'

Dilly watched in horror as Lydia picked up a large, heavy candlestick and hurled it at him. Max brought his hands up to protect his face but the candlestick struck his shoulder, and soon blood was seeping through his T-shirt. Horrified, he looked at Lydia. 'I should be calling the police right now. Get out of my home and my life.'

'I'm already calling the police,' Dilly called out, beginning to dial on her phone.

Lydia began walking towards the door. 'You won't want to do that. I can ruin your reputation within seconds,' she threatened before walking out. Dilly checked she had kept going and quickly shut the front door.

'Put the phone down, Dilly. She isn't worth it.'

'But you can't let her get away with it. You're hurt.' Dilly walked to the sink and ran a clean cloth under the water. 'You're bleeding. Let me take a look.'

'This isn't the first time she's done something like this.'

Dilly took a sharp breath at the look of distress and resignation on his face. 'It's okay, you don't have to talk about this now.'

'I do,' he replied. 'There's so much to tell and I've no clue where to begin. I haven't told a soul.'

'Why?' asked Dilly, tentatively cleaning the wound.

'Because I feel humiliated and it's painful. It makes my stomach churn.'

Dilly could relate to all three. 'But surely you need to report this to someone.'

'What good will that do? Lydia's family is wealthy and has powerful connections, including a high-profile journalist working for a national newspaper. Lydia has never cared about the truth or fairness. She would not hesitate to fabricate a scandalous story about a famous artist and her former teacher. She would revel in the publicity, playing the victim and claiming that you're the reason our marriage ended, conveniently omitting the truth. The thought of her deceitful narrative taking centre stage makes my blood boil.'

'But this isn't right. Have you any antiseptic cream and dressings?'

Max pointed to a top kitchen cupboard. 'Believe me, I know it's not fair, but I have to do what's right for me, for you.'

Dilly nodded. She didn't want to push it. There was silence as she dressed the wound. 'There, it's all done now. Shall I make you a drink?'

'I'm okay, unless you want one?'

She shook her head and Max gestured towards the

settee. They sat down. 'Your dad spoke with me. He told me you thought I'd set you up at the auction. I didn't set you up, Dilly. I would never do that to you. But I did come to Puffin Island because of you, I'll admit that.'

Dilly looked puzzled. 'Because of me?'

She tucked her legs under her and hugged the nearby cushion, wanting to hear what Max meant by that. But first there was a more urgent burning question on her mind.

'Is Lydia actually pregnant?' she asked, her voice trembling with emotion.

Max nodded slowly. 'I believe so,' he said quietly. 'But it's not mine.'

He took a deep breath. 'If I hadn't discovered her lies, I might have stayed for the sake of the baby. But I'm not staying in any relationship to look after another man's child.'

The words cut through Dilly like a knife. From the minute Max had walked into her gallery, her intent to never let another man close to her had crumbled. Max was the exception, and now here he was, telling her harsh truths. She had considered telling him about her own situation, but what was the point if he never wanted to look after another man's child? Still, despite the pain his words caused, she wanted to hear his whole story.

'Tell me about it,' she said.

Max looked through the window towards the sea and focused on the lighthouse. 'I suppose I should start at the very beginning. It was September, and I had just landed a brand-new job at a college, teaching art. It was something I'd always wanted to do. I loved painting and all things creative, like galleries, museums. And then, you walked into my class, and my life changed for ever.'

Dilly's eyes widened with surprise. 'Me? How?'

A small smile tugged on Max's lips. 'Because there was something about you from the first moment I saw you. You were pure, full of laughter. You lit up my life like no one had ever done before. I never said this to anyone because, for obvious reasons, I couldn't, but you were the most beautiful girl I had ever set eyes on. You may have been the reason I loved that job so much.' He looked towards her. 'And for the record, you're still beautiful.'

Dilly felt a lump in her throat. 'I had no idea you felt that way.'

Max looked at her earnestly. 'I had to keep it professional, but you were different. Every time you spoke about art, your passion and creativity shone through. It was contagious. I started looking forward to my classes because I knew you'd be there. But I had to keep my distance, for both our sakes.'

'We were all so jealous you were married,' she shared with a smile.

Max cocked an eyebrow. 'That's good to know but no one needed to be jealous. College was my safe haven where Lydia couldn't reach me, and I could be me.'

She listened intently, her heart pounding. 'What do you mean? What happened after that?'

Max's face clouded with sadness. 'Lydia happened. I was never enough for her, and there was a part of me that liked the concept of trying to prove her wrong. I know they say opposites attract, but we were poles apart. Before I started work at the college, I was a struggling artist and I thought I'd made it when I was invited to showcase my work at a local hotel. That's where we met. Lydia was meeting a potential business customer and I was immediately intrigued by her. I overheard her making a phone call and realised she was making fun of me, calling me a halfwit painter who didn't have a cat in hell's chance of ever selling one of his paintings, never mind making a living from art.'

Dilly's eyes widened. 'She said that?'

Max nodded. 'Yes, but then I sold my highest-priced painting to a celebrity and suddenly Lydia was impressed. When she leaned into me and said that if a celebrity bought the piece, then the artist must be worth meeting, I held out my hand and introduced myself as the halfwit. By way of an apology, she offered to take me out for dinner. I should have run in the opposite direction.'

'But you didn't.'

Max sighed deeply. 'No, I didn't. I was flattered and curious. Despite everything, there was a part of me that wanted to see where it could go. We had a whirlwind romance and were married within six weeks.'

Dilly's mouth fell open. 'I didn't know that.'

'Her family had wealth, influence … everything she could want. She took me to the finest restaurants, threw extravagant parties and showered me with gifts. I was mesmerised by the world she'd introduced me to.'

He paused, a shadow of sadness passing over his face. 'Meanwhile, I was just a painter with a battered old car and shoes I'd had for years. I wasn't materialistic in the slightest. I didn't care about designer labels or luxury lifestyles. But Lydia didn't see it that way. To her, my image didn't fit the polished, glamorous look of her social circles, but I had "potential".' He rolled his eyes. 'She began dressing me in uncomfortable designer clothes, pushing me into a world that felt foreign and very suffocating.'

Dilly's eyes widened with empathy. 'That must have been hard for you.'

Max nodded. 'It was. I started saying no, insisting that it didn't matter how I dressed. I was me, and I wasn't going to change just to fit into her world. But that's when things began to unravel. Lydia's attitude shifted and her temper started to flare. The charm and grace she'd shown me initially gave way to … let's say … a more volatile side.'

His eyes were full of shame as he looked down. 'She became increasingly controlling and demanding. Every disagreement turned into a full-blown argument. She wanted everything her way and didn't care how it affected me. I felt trapped in a relationship that had become more about maintaining appearances and less about a genuine, loving connection.'

Max hesitated. 'And then … she started making snide remarks about my work, belittling my art, and my passion. It wasn't just the clothes anymore, she wanted to reshape me into someone I wasn't. I felt like I was losing myself.'

Dilly reached out and rested her hand gently on his. 'It doesn't sound a good situation to be in.'

'It wasn't. She started lashing out at me.'

'What do you mean?'

'Physically attacking me.' He pointed to the scar on his cheek. 'This was my very first war wound.'

'You mean there're more?'

Max nodded. His expression grew darker as he

continued. 'It gets worse, if that's even possible. Lydia's temper was escalating. The outbursts became more frequent and intense and were usually about me not contributing enough towards the bills. You see, she thought I was going to be another Damien Hirst when I sold that first painting, but it was one of the few paintings I ever sold. Lydia told me I needed a different job because her plan couldn't be implemented.'

'What plan?'

'Lydia had the idea that if celebrities bought my paintings, we could wine them and dine them as a thank-you and she could swoop in and talk about her cosmetic surgery business, as they would know the type of clients she was looking for. Just before the wedding she also asked me to sign a prenup.'

Dilly's eyes widened.

Max nodded. 'Yes. I had nothing to bring to the marriage financially, so the prenup mainly just meant I wouldn't gain anything if we split up. But I didn't care. I wasn't driven by money like she was, I just wanted to create art. After we were married and I wasn't as successful as she'd anticipated, she saw my painting as a hobby, not a career. That's when I took the job as an art teacher, hoping I could still paint on the side.'

Dilly interrupted, confused. 'She didn't allow you to paint at all?'

Max shook his head. 'No, she didn't. Having paints in the house wasn't allowed. Our home had to remain pristine, all white, with no trace of the artist's life I led. The furniture was too expensive, and she didn't want any potential mess.

I didn't feel in a position to disagree as she'd bought most of that furniture.'

Dilly's heart filled with sympathy. 'It all sounds so incredibly suffocating.'

Max sighed deeply. 'It was. That's why I loved staying behind at college with you. You understood what I was about. After class, I could be myself without fear of judgment or restriction. I was totally at ease with you. We both loved art and the deep discussions we had about different artists … she would never have entertained such conversations.'

He leaned towards her, his fingers trembling slightly as he entwined them with Dilly's. Dilly looked at their joined hands. 'That's something I've wanted to do from the second I set eyes on you.'

'It's the same for me. Being with you has allowed me to be me.'

Dilly squeezed his hand gently. 'Did you ever think about leaving back then?'

'Of course, but every time I plucked up the courage, something happened that meant I couldn't.'

'Like what?'

Max recalled the painful memories. 'There was one time where I'd reached breaking point. I told Lydia that enough was enough, that she needed help, and that I was leaving. It was a Friday. I didn't have anywhere else to go except to the home of a fellow teacher I was close to. He had offered me a place to stay if things ever got too rough, though I never told him the full truth about the things Lydia would hurl at me, both literally and emotionally. I think my exact words were "we're just growing in different directions".' He paused. 'I made the decision to leave that day. I was nervous when I got home, but Lydia wasn't there, which gave me a chance to start sorting through my things.'

'Did she come home before you could leave?'

'She did and was distraught. She found me in the middle of packing and immediately begged me to stay. She said she was going to get help, that she realised we had a reason to try and fix things. Then she dropped the bombshell. She told me she was pregnant.'

Dilly's eyes widened again, in shock and sympathy. 'She told you she was pregnant as a way to keep you?'

Max nodded slowly. 'Yes. I was torn. I was exhausted from the emotional turmoil and the constant strain of our relationship, and the news of the pregnancy added another layer of complexity. I stayed for a while longer, hoping her pregnancy would bring about real change. But it was just another facade. She wasn't pregnant and so she faked a miscarriage.'

Dilly couldn't even begin to imagine how all that would have affected Max's emotional state.

'It didn't stop there. We've had cancer scares, car crashes ... a suspected brain tumour.'

Dilly couldn't stop her mouth from falling wide open. She had been through her own ordeal with Giles, and as she weighed up both situations, it was impossible to determine which was worse ... someone who pretended to love you to steal your money or someone who spun every lie in the book to keep you by their side. She looked at Max, her heart aching for him. 'She must have loved you so much if she went to those lengths to keep you.'

Max shook his head. 'I don't think it was love. In fact, I

don't think she ever loved me. It was more about control and possession. I was a project. Lydia was used to getting what she wanted, and when she felt it slipping away, she did everything she could to hold on to me. I mistook her desperation for love for far too long.'

Dilly's eyes softened with understanding. 'I guess sometimes it's hard to see the truth when you're in the middle of it. I know that feeling all too well.'

'The morning of the viewing she showed up here with the excuse that some legal papers needed signing. She asked me where I was going, and it was my own fault that I actually told her. She thought we were together, which of course she didn't like, and that's why she tried to sabotage your sale. You didn't see but I literally frogmarched her out and the only way I could keep her under control was to get in the car with her. I had no clue whether you'd actually won until your dad told me. I'm so sorry for upsetting you. It's the last thing I ever wanted.'

Dilly locked eyes with Max and felt a whirlwind of feelings rising inside her. She had loved this man from the moment she'd walked into his classroom, true love at first sight. Even through her relationship with Giles, Max had often crossed her mind but she had pushed the thoughts away, assuming that he was happily married. Yet here he was, laying his heart bare, revealing the sham his marriage had been. He was still staring at her with an intensity that made her want to hug him tightly, never to let him go. At the same time, her heart was screaming that this was the perfect moment to lean in and kiss him, something she had always wanted to do.

But it didn't matter how much she wanted that kiss

because she knew she couldn't act on it. She was carrying someone else's baby, and Max had just confessed he wasn't prepared to raise another man's child. The harsh reality of her situation was eating her up inside, tearing her apart. She had waited so long for this moment, and now she had come so close – only to realise it couldn't happen.

Max's gaze softened, his fingers still intertwined with hers. 'You are the reason I came to Puffin Island, Dilly. I came looking for you.'

Dilly's heart ached, knowing she had to protect herself and her unborn child, even if it meant losing Max.

She nodded and changed the subject, trying to break the tension. 'Tell me about Lydia's pregnancy. Who is the father?'

Max exhaled heavily, his voice strained as he tried to explain. 'It's my so-called best friend's. The guy from work I stayed with when Lydia and I were having troubles. They had an affair and that betrayal was the final straw for me. I couldn't stay there, in that environment, knowing what they had done behind my back. I left that job about a year ago and took whatever work I could find just to make ends meet. At first, Lydia stayed away.'

Dilly blinked, her mind racing to process everything he was saying. 'Your best friend? Max, that's awful. But why would Lydia say the baby was yours? How did you even find out about it?'

Max shook his head, frustration evident in his eyes. 'I don't know, Dilly. Maybe things aren't going well between them, and she's trying to manipulate me again. But … I need to be honest with you. A couple of months ago, we did have a moment, and I regret it every single day. I went back to the house to collect the rest of my stuff, even though I had already been gone for a year. I know there's no excuse, but … when I arrived, she was being overly nice to me. She suggested we have a drink for old time's sake, and one bottle led to another…' He trailed off, his words hanging in the air, a confession he wished he didn't have to make. He rubbed a hand across his face, clearly ashamed. 'I should have known better. I shouldn't have let my guard down, not after everything she put me through. But I was vulnerable, and she knew exactly how to exploit that.'

Dilly felt a tiny sting of betrayal, which was daft as she hadn't even known Max then. It wasn't her place to judge him, but his revelation hurt more than she expected it to.

Max looked at her with raw vulnerability. 'She left the house early the next morning to go to work and the bathroom bin was overflowing. Just like old times I emptied it outside and that's when I saw the pregnancy test. Lydia was already pregnant by the time we slept together, but she doesn't know I know. Dilly, I know I've made mistakes. More than I can count. But what happened with Lydia… it was nothing more than a moment of weakness, and I regret it deeply. I want to be honest with you about everything because you deserve that. But I also need you to know that I'm here now, and I'm ready to move forward, if you'll let me. I promise that Lydia's games will never affect us.'

Dilly took a deep breath, trying to sort through her conflicting feelings. Max was laying it all out for her: his mistakes, his regrets and his hopes. She appreciated his honesty, but it didn't make the situation any easier.

'Even though it's been a double betrayal it's actually given me my life back and allows me a fresh start and the chance to go after the happiness I know is out there, the happiness I deserve.'

Max was looking at her in that way again. Dilly knew he meant happiness with her and wished she could wind back the clock and never have met Giles. But she had and now, despite everything he had done, she was carrying his child.

'And what about you? I thought you'd be settled down with a gorgeous man. There was never anything about your personal life online. The only thing I ever saw was the article about your mum and Anton.'

'Do you fancy that drink now? I know it's your place but I'll make us one before I dive into my personal life, because, between you, me and that lighthouse through the window, it's been an incredibly eventful day and I'm beginning to question my own sanity.'

'I have beer in the fridge.'

As Dilly went to stand up, Max gently tugged on her hand, pulling her back down beside him. She didn't resist. She didn't want to. He peered up at her from under his dark lashes. With her heart hammering against her chest, she knew he was going to kiss her. He lowered his eyes to her lips as he slowly leaned in. Dilly didn't stop him and their lips meeting for the very first time ignited a fire that had been smouldering between them for a very long time. The kiss was tender, the chemistry between them undeniable. It was the kiss Dilly had dreamed about. She knew she should pull away and be honest with him then and there, just like he'd been with her, but she couldn't bring herself to do it.

She was being selfish, aware of the fireflies fluttering wildly in her stomach as she kissed him again, this time more passionately, the kind of kiss that could lead to them ripping each other's clothes off. She gave a tiny moan, enjoying every moment yet knowing there was a huge possibility her heart was going to be broken into a thousand pieces, and maybe his too, when she shared her pregnancy news.

They pulled back and stared at each other in a contemplative silence, both smiling as he leaned forward, hooking a stray strand of hair behind her ear like it was the most natural thing in the world. Dilly didn't want his kisses to stop. She kissed him again, pulling him right on top of her, all her worries about a broken heart evaporating as her hands slid up his shirt. She gave a tiny groan as his fingers began to trace the contours of her body.

'Are you sure you want this?' he whispered.

Dilly didn't answer, only nodded. 'Can we go somewhere more comfortable?' she murmured.

Max took her hand, and led her slowly to the bedroom. 'There's always been something about you,' he whispered.

'And you,' she replied in between kisses.

Feeling her whole body trembling, Dilly looked into Max's eyes, then at the dressed wound on his shoulder. She hugged him. 'No one is ever going to hurt you again, not on my watch.'

'You're sounding like a lighthouse keeper already.'

Dilly smiled. 'I'm so sorry you've had to go through what you have with Lydia.'

'Hopefully, it's over now. Someone else has witnessed her actions so it's no longer my word against hers. Now, where were we?' He leaned in and kissed her again as Dilly pushed him gently down on the bed then pressed herself against him. She ran her hands over Max's body, his strong arms, his toned torso, whilst he kissed her neck. Every nerve in her body tingled as he lifted her top and slowly unhooked her bra. Dilly felt scared yet excited. Even though she had waited for years for this moment, something in the back of her mind was telling her she shouldn't be doing this, she hadn't been completely honest with him, and that wasn't fair … but it was too late now. She didn't want this to end. She would just have to accept that, at some point, she would have to face the consequences. With an overwhelming desire to spend the night with him burning through her, she embraced the moment, determined to banish all regrets and worries.

'I've wanted this for as long as I can remember…' she began.

Right on cue, Max took her breath away, making her feel alive and desired in a way she had never imagined.

Chapter Fourteen

Dilly woke up in Max's arms, overlooking the tranquil stretch of the sea. The sky was a brilliant blue, and boats bobbed gently on the water, creating an Instagram-worthy photograph. Max was still asleep, and as she tried to gently move from his embrace, his grip tightened, and he pulled her closer. 'Where do you think you're going?' he murmured with his eyes still closed but a smile on his face.

'Good morning,' she replied, resting her head against his chest. 'How are you feeling?' she asked.

'On top of the world,' he replied, kissing the top of her head. 'I actually feel like this was meant to be, and I know it's early days, but we can navigate this as slowly or as quickly as you want.'

Hearing his heartbeat, Dilly briefly closed her eyes, trying to savour the moment. She knew she should be feeling on top of the world too, but the secret she still kept from him was going to well and truly burst his bubble. 'Max,' she began gently, knowing she had to get this over with, even though it would spoil the magic of their night together. She could kick herself for getting carried away in the heat of the moment before telling him the truth.

Before he could answer, the alarm went off on his phone, making them jump. 'Shoot! I have to be at work in thirty minutes. It's a good job it's a short commute,' he joked.

'And I'm going to have to sneak out without my dad seeing me, otherwise we'll have some questions to answer.'

'You don't have to sneak around for me. I'm so sorry, but I've got to get a move on.' He pulled the covers back and stood up, completely naked. Dilly couldn't help but stare. He was bloody gorgeous and all she could think about was how she'd completely messed everything up.

As soon as Max was dressed, he walked over and sat on the edge of the bed, his eyes full of mischief. 'I wish I had the day off and we could just lie here all day,' he said, gently brushing a strand of hair from her face before he kissed her, making Dilly's heart flutter. All she wanted to do was pull him back under the sheets.

'Me too,' she replied, kissing him back. 'I could do this all day.'

'I think we probably did it all night. I'll be falling asleep on the job by mid-morning.'

'It's a good job you didn't fall asleep on the job last night,' she teased. 'But Max, we do need to talk,' she began, her voice a little unsteady. She reached out, taking his hand in hers.

Max's eyes sparkled. 'You have nothing to worry about, I promise. I've been upfront and honest about my situation, and I know we might have a few bumps in the road where Lydia's concerned, but it won't last for ever and as soon as she realises we're unbreakable, she'll move on. Please don't worry … about anything. Now, I have to go.' Max kissed her one last time before he walked to the bedroom door. 'The door is on the latch so it will lock when you leave.' The door shut and Dilly slumped back onto the pillow.

Staring up at the ceiling, she felt guilty. Just a week ago, if someone had told her she'd be pregnant by a romance scammer and that the love of her life would walk through the gallery door, she'd have thought they were deluded. Yet here she was, entangled in a predicament of her own making, unsure how to navigate it all. There were already two tasks on her to-do list today: the first was to attend her doctor's appointment and the second was to talk to her dad about having seen her mum. But she didn't want to do either of those things until she'd talked to Clemmie about the gigantic mess she'd got herself into. Quickly, she pulled on her clothes and slipped on her shoes. Within five minutes she was on her way back home.

She texted Clemmie.

> I've got myself into a fine mess.

Clemmie replied immediately.

> Why, what have you done now? Spent a night with an utterly gorgeous art teacher? Because if that's a fine mess, I'd say it's more like winning the lottery!

> How do you know about that?

Dilly texted back, hoping that it wasn't common

gossip around the island but knowing it was a possibility given the way things spread like wildfire. Still, she didn't want the whole island knowing just yet, not when she'd barely had time to process things herself.

> I was doing the deliveries and spotted you sneaking out of the boat house. Pretty sure you weren't just admiring the boats at this time in the morning.

Dilly couldn't help but smile at her friend's quick wit.

> I was just … uh … making sure the boats didn't float away in the middle of the night!

Clemmie responded with a laughing emoji.

> Sure, sure. And I'm guessing that includes making sure Max didn't float away too, right?

Dilly rolled her eyes, chuckling as she typed.

> What can I say? I'm just doing my civic duty, keeping Max and the boats in check. Someone's got to do it!

> Oh, the things you do for the greater good. Heroic, really. I'll make sure to nominate you for a bravery award in the next island meeting.

Dilly laughed out loud, shaking her head.

> Please do. But I am in a fine mess, can you come round?

Dilly didn't want to type out her tangled web of emotions over the phone.

> I'm on my way, I've just finished deliveries and can spare thirty minutes. Get the kettle on.

Dilly felt a wave of relief knowing her best friend would soon be there to advise her on what exactly she should do.

They arrived at the gallery only moments apart and Clemmie immediately zoned in on Dilly's dishevelled appearance. 'Look at that bed hair.' A mischievous grin spread across Clemmie's face. 'I'm hoping the sex was good because, honestly, I'd be a bit miffed trying to get those tangles out of my hair if it wasn't.'

Dilly's cheeks flamed red as she sputtered. 'Clemmie!' She laughed. 'And for your information the sex was off the scale, the best I've ever had.'

'Come on, spill the details while you make me a brew. You've got that post-romantic glow, and I need to hear all about Mr Harrington's artistic skills.'

Dilly rolled her eyes but couldn't suppress a smile as they headed up the stairs towards the kitchen.

'And what's this about a fine mess?' Clemmie asked, looking at her friend with concern. 'He's not still in a relationship, is he?'

Dilly sighed, glancing over her shoulder at her friend. 'No, he's free as a bird, but he doesn't know I'm pregnant.'

Clemmie leaned against the kitchen counter. 'If it's a

one-night stand, he doesn't have to know. It's no one else's business but yours.'

Dilly took the mugs out of the cupboard, making the tea before turning to face Clemmie. The look on her face made Clemmie's eyes widen in sudden realisation. 'Oh, you want it to be more.'

She sat down across from Dilly, her eyes locked onto her friend's.

Dilly took a deep breath. 'I know I said that after Giles I wouldn't want another man as long as I live, but I've always had feelings for Max and they're still there,' she confessed. 'If anything, they're now deeper than ever after last night. But it's not going to happen again.'

'Why can't it happen again? He's a decent, genuine guy, from what I remember.'

'Oh, he is,' Dilly agreed. 'Even my dad thinks so and we both know what he thought of Giles. Not that my dad knows anything about this,' she quickly added.

'A baby would be a bonus,' Clemmie continued, leaning forward. 'An extension of you.'

Dilly shook her head. 'The father of this baby is … scum,' she said, her voice hardening. 'I can't think of another word for him.'

Clemmie reached out, placing a comforting hand on Dilly's arm. 'If you're really serious about each other, you can work this out and become a family.'

Dilly exhaled. 'It's impossible. I'm breaking a confidence when I tell you this, but I have to share it with someone, and I know I can trust you.'

'Go on.'

Dilly hesitated. She felt a twinge of guilt for betraying

Max's trust, but she needed to confide in someone. She told Clemmie all about Lydia, from the fake pregnancy to the current real one, fathered by Max's former best friend.

'What a—'

'Cow,' interrupted Dilly 'And after he told me everything, his exact words were that he wasn't sticking around to bring up another man's child.' Dilly placed her hands on her stomach. 'And this is another man's child.'

They sat in silence for a moment before Clemmie spoke. 'This is different though, and you aren't Lydia. That sounds like quite a toxic relationship and it seems she was a compulsive liar.'

Dilly heard Clemmie's words but her mind was wandering, seeing the look on Max's face and hearing the tone of his voice when he'd declared he wasn't bringing up another man's child. She knew that he had been through the mill in his marriage, harassed by Lydia's relentless lies and her often physical temper. She could only imagine how emotionally shattered he must be. What if this pushed him over the edge?

'Is it that different though?' Dilly asked. 'I have a past, and I've not shared any of it with Max. Yet he sat there, pouring his heart out, telling me everything. He's going to think I'm as bad as Lydia, sleeping with him and not telling him the truth … that I'm pregnant.'

For a moment, Clemmie was quiet. 'You do have options,' she said cautiously.

'What do you mean?'

'It's a difficult thing to think about, but you could terminate the pregnancy. That'll mean you don't carry the stigma of Giles and you wouldn't have to tell Max anything about it. I'm not saying it's an easy decision to make, but it is an option,' Clemmie suggested.

'A termination?' Dilly repeated.

'All I'm saying is that you do have options, and no one would think any less of you. This baby is going to tie you to Giles for ever, even if you and I are the only ones who know who its father is.'

Clemmie's words lingered in the air, presenting Dilly with a stark reality she hadn't even considered.

Chapter Fifteen

Dilly sat at her desk at the back of the gallery, her thoughts churning over Clemmie's words. She had never considered an abortion. It wasn't the baby's fault who its father was. No, despite her resentment towards Giles, the new life growing inside her was all that mattered. With an hour left before her doctor's appointment, Dilly logged on to check her emails, but her concentration wavered. Each time someone walked past the gallery, she glanced up, half expecting to see her mother. She couldn't help herself.

Acknowledging that work just wasn't going to happen this morning, she opened her internet browser and searched the accident again. The image of her mother and Anton flashed on the screen, accompanied by the tragic story of their supposed death. The witness had described seeing them being thrown into the sea, vanishing within seconds. Could they have survived? Dilly revisited the details of the area where the accident occurred, something she had done hundreds of times. The terrain was rocky, with high cliffs.

Even if they'd managed to escape the water, climbing those cliffs seemed impossible. Her gaze drifted to the painting of her mother. Maybe Clemmie was right. Perhaps she was projecting her hopes onto the portrait because this was one of those times in life where she wanted her mother with her. She wanted to share her news about the baby and to ask Eva for her advice.

Dilly shut down her Google search and refocused on her emails. She noticed a couple more online print purchases, which was fantastic. She could wrap the paintings and ship them later today. As she scrolled further through her inbox, an email from her solicitor caught her eye. It had been sent early that morning and she quickly opened it, a surge of excitement making her squeal softly. The paperwork for the property had been finalised ahead of schedule and she could pick up the keys to the lighthouse anytime. She could hardly believe it. After her doctor's appointment, she knew she would be heading straight to Sea's End to collect the keys and then explore the lighthouse.

Excited, she texted Clemmie.

> I can pick up the keys to the lighthouse today!

The reply came almost instantly.

> Oh my God! Excited for you!

After logging off her emails, Dilly poured herself a cup of tea. She realised she was feeling nervous about the doctor's appointment. Dr Sandford had been the island's

GP for as long as anyone could remember and probably should have retired a long time ago, but he was so beloved he'd stayed on. He was the quintessential image of a doctor, with his silver hair neatly combed back and a pair of round spectacles perched on the bridge of his nose. His face bore the lines of age and experience, lending him an air of wisdom and authority. Despite his advancing years, his blue eyes were still sharp and observant, and often softened by a kind, reassuring smile. He always wore a crisp white coat over his neatly pressed shirt and tie, embodying a sense of professionalism and care.

Dilly's plan was to slip into the doctor's surgery quickly and quietly, aiming to avoid any questions Dr Sandford might have about the baby's father. She had crafted her story and she hoped it would be convincing enough to squash any curiosity, and that any gossip would fizzle out after the initial shock of the island discovering her pregnancy news.

She felt confident in her ability to manage the situation with Dr Sandford but what truly troubled her was the conversation she would need to have with Max. It wasn't that she felt ashamed of her pregnancy, it had just come as a shock, and she was still processing the reality of it all. The real issue was deciding how much of the truth to share with him. She deeply wanted to be honest with him, but revealing the identity of the baby's father meant another person would know, increasing the risk of the secret slipping out.

Dilly was torn between wanting to confide in him and the need to protect her privacy, fearing that the truth could eventually lead to the story spreading beyond her control.

She understood the delicate balance she needed to maintain, and because Max had already stated he wouldn't bring up another man's child, she was leaning towards not telling him the whole truth. After all, he didn't really need to know if he wasn't going to stick around.

Her phone pinged and as she looked at the screen she saw it was a text message from Max.

I'm the happiest person alive!

Immediately guilt washed over her as she thought about the inevitable heartbreak Max would face once the truth came out. And it was all her doing. She despised herself for not being honest with him before they slept together. She had kept the truth hidden because she wanted to sleep with him, to be close to him, and now the reality of her dishonesty was setting in. That conversation needed to happen *today*.

The doctor's surgery was located on the other side of the island, nestled near the picturesque Castaway Cove, so Dilly grabbed her bag, deciding that a walk through the salty sea air would help clear her mind and steady her nerves.

Fifteen minutes later, the small, charming building came into view. Its exterior was whitewashed stone, with ivy creeping up the walls, giving it an old-world charm. The thatched roof lent the building a cosy storybook appearance. A wooden sign hung above the door, gently swinging in the breeze, reading: 'Dr Sandford, General Practitioner'.

Dilly walked in and stepped up to the reception desk to check in. The interior was simple yet welcoming, with walls painted in a calming pastel blue. A few faded nautical prints had been hung up along with a pinboard and an old-fashioned clock. The seating area held a neat row of plastic chairs. The receptionist, Jan, had been here for as long as Dr Sandford. After taking Dilly's details, she assured her that Dr Sandford would see her shortly and encouraged her to take a seat.

Dilly chose a chair near the window. Staring out at the sea, she sat waiting nervously, her hands fidgeting with the strap of her bag. It wasn't long before Dr Sandford appeared in the doorway, his voice warm and welcoming as he called out Dilly's name. She stood and followed him into the consultation room, her heart pounding in her chest. The room, like the outside of the surgery, had old-world charm, blended with practical functionality. The walls were lined with wooden shelves, filled with well-worn medical textbooks, jars of herbal remedies and various instruments. A large window offered a soothing view of the rolling waves.

In one corner stood an antique wooden desk, the surface cluttered with paperwork, a vintage stethoscope and an old-fashioned brass desk lamp. A comfortable-looking leather chair sat behind the desk. The examination area was neatly arranged with a cushioned examination table covered in crisp white paper, and a few chairs for additional seating. A tall metal cabinet held a range of medical supplies, and a framed anatomical chart hung on the wall beside it, showing detailed illustrations of the human body.

He gestured towards one of the chairs and Dilly sat down. Dr Sandford settled into his chair behind the desk, his eyes crinkling at the corners as he smiled warmly at her. 'How are you, Delilah? It's been a little while since we've seen each other.'

In the past five years she'd only seen Dr Sandford twice on a professional basis: once when her mum died, and once when she'd discovered Giles's betrayal. Then it hit her. It didn't matter what story she concocted about the baby's father, Dr Sandford would undoubtedly work out for himself who the father of her baby was because she hadn't played down the relationship to him, knowing what she told him was in the strictest of confidence.

'How's the gallery doing?' he asked.

'It's going well, thank you. It's really busy at the moment, which is a good thing.'

'And I hear you're now the owner of Puffin Island Lighthouse.'

'I am. I'm actually headed to pick up the keys after I leave here.' She smiled. 'Hopefully I'll have the new gallery space there up and running very soon.'

Dr Sandford leaned back in his chair. 'That's wonderful to hear. You know, my wife has had her eye on one of your paintings for weeks now. She can't stop hinting about it every time we walk past the gallery. I think she's determined to find the perfect spot for it in our living room.'

'Then I think you should call in and put your wife out of her misery, make her day.'

'I think I may just do that.'

Dilly smiled. The conversation was bringing a much-needed lightness to the room before she dropped her bombshell.

Dr Sandford leaned forward slightly, his expression shifting to one of genuine concern. 'Now, what can I do for you today, Delilah?' he asked kindly, his tone professional.

Dilly didn't hold back. 'I'm pregnant,' she blurted and before she could even brace herself for his response, she promptly burst into tears. Having said it out loud, she couldn't help herself.

Swiftly reaching for the box of tissues on the desk, Dr Sandford handed one to her. He allowed her a few moments to compose herself, then looked at her with an encouraging smile. 'New human life is a wonderful thing,' he said, his voice filled with genuine warmth. 'It's a journey full of unexpected twists, but it's also a remarkable gift and you will make an exceptional, inspirational mother, I have no doubt, if that is the definite path you wish to go down.'

Dilly knew exactly what he was alluding to – the same option that Clemmie had put forward. But for her the choice was simple; it wasn't something she could ever do. 'I'm having the baby, Dr Sandford.'

He nodded his understanding. 'Then I just need to ask a few questions and take your blood pressure, and then we need to organise your midwife. I'm assuming you've taken a test, but would you like me to do another?'

'With the dizziness, nausea, weight gain and swollen breasts, I think it's very certain.'

'Have you got any clue when your last period was?'

Dilly had thought about that question a lot since

finding out she was pregnant and wished she'd kept better track of it. 'At a guess, a little over four months ago.'

Dr Sandford gently wrapped the blood pressure cuff around her arm, the soft rustling of the fabric momentarily distracting Dilly. As he inflated the cuff and watched the gauge, his brow furrowed slightly in concentration. The subtle beeping of the monitor filled the quiet room and when the reading was complete, he looked up at her with a reassuring expression. 'Your blood pressure is quite low,' he said. 'That's most likely the reason you've been feeling dizzy. It's not uncommon in early pregnancy, but we need to keep an eye on it.' He carefully removed the cuff and set it aside. 'It's important we manage this properly to ensure both you and the baby remain healthy. I also need to organise a scan immediately because that is overdue.' He looked towards the clock. 'That isn't going to happen today as they will no doubt be fully booked, but I can try for tomorrow?'

Dilly knew the gallery should be open tomorrow but needs must, and at least being her own boss, she didn't have to worry about taking the time off. 'Yes, thank you,' she replied.

'I'm going to get your pregnancy booklet set up, and ring through to get you an appointment. At your scan, they'll be able to give you a clear indication of a due date.'

Dr Sandford disappeared from the room but soon returned. 'It's all arranged for tomorrow at eleven o'clock. You will need to provide a urine sample –' he handed over a bottle '– and fill out this booklet with all your details. Have you got any other questions?'

She shook her head. 'I'm … not planning on telling anyone just yet,' she said hesitantly.

'I understand. Rest assured that this conversation, as with every conversation we have in this building, will remain confidential.'

'Thank you,' she said, slipping the booklet and sample bottle into her bag.

Leaving the surgery, she headed back towards the gallery. As she walked up Anchor Way and turned into Quaint Corners, her phone rang and she looked at the screen to find it was her dad.

'Hey, Dad! Guess where I'm headed in about half an hour?'

'Do tell!'

'What's that noise in the background? It sounds noisier than usual in the boat house.'

Ralph chuckled. 'You mean that awful din? That's Max belting out tunes to the radio. He hasn't stopped singing all morning. He's in a seriously happy mood, which I'm not complaining about, but I am considering running to the shop to buy myself some earplugs.'

From the background, Max's voice rose in playful protest. 'Hey! I'm just getting into the groove over here!'

Dilly laughed.

'He's been at it since breakfast. I think he's trying to turn the boat house into his personal concert hall. Anyway, where are you going?'

'To pick up the keys for the lighthouse.'

'Dilly, that's wonderful. I'm so pleased for you. What's the plan after you've picked the keys up?'

'I'm heading straight over there and am going to start

giving it a good clean, though I don't know whether to start from the top or the bottom.'

'My guess is the top and take all the cleaning stuff up with you first time, otherwise you'll be up and down those stairs.'

Dilly laughed. 'Good point. By the way, I feel like I haven't seen you properly in ages.'

'It feels like we're ships passing in the night.'

Dilly could almost picture her father chuckling on the other end of the line.

'Is that a boat pun because you own a boat house?' she teased light-heartedly. 'How about we do dinner tomorrow night? I was thinking of inviting you to the lighthouse. You'd be my very first official guest, though I have to warn you, I'm not sure what the cooking facilities are like yet. I don't even have plates or cutlery over there. So, how about we grab some fish and chips and enjoy them at the top of the tower?'

'That sounds just perfect! I can't wait to see the place.'

'Tomorrow night, seven p.m. Love you, Dad!'

After she ended the call, Dilly felt a flutter of nerves. This dinner would be the perfect chance to share her news with her dad. By then, she would have had her scan and everything would be confirmed. Her only dilemma now was whether to tell Max tonight as she had originally planned, or wait until after she had spoken to her father. She didn't want her dad to hear about the pregnancy from anyone else; it was important to her that he heard it directly from her.

Chapter Sixteen

After enjoying a quick and refreshing lunch of salad, grilled chicken and warm flatbread, Dilly felt a surge of excitement as she got into her car, eager to drive across to Sea's End and pick up the keys from the solicitor. She rubbed her stomach. 'It's me and you for ever,' she said. As she drove, she let her mind wander, imagining the lighthouse in all its seasonal glory.

In summer, just like it was now, the lighthouse would be bathed in golden sunlight, the salty sea breeze carrying the scent of wildflowers and the sound of puffins mooing from the cliffs. The warm evenings would be perfect for watching the sunset from the top of the tower, the sky ablaze with hues of orange and pink, the ocean shimmering like molten gold below. She could see herself hosting friends for drinks, thinking there was so much fun to be had high up, mingling with the distant cries of seagulls. Autumn would bring a different kind of beauty, with the surrounding landscape decked in rich tones of red, orange and yellow. She envisioned taking long walks along the beach, collecting seashells and driftwood, then returning to the lighthouse to curl up with a good book after she bathed and rocked her baby to sleep, as the shorter days faded into chilly, star-filled nights. In winter, the lighthouse would transform into a cosy refuge from the stormy seas and biting winds. She imagined the waves crashing dramatically against the rocks outside as inside she would light a fire, wrap up in a thick blanket and hear the rain lashing all around. Springtime would see the cliffs bursting into bloom with kidney vetch, clusters of small yellow flowers sitting on top of woolly cushions, along with thrift, the pink sea clover that carpeted the cliffs every year. The air would be filled with the scent of rain and blooming flowers. She imagined opening the windows to let in the fresh air, the sound of birds returning from their winter migrations, the cliffs once again filled with a puffinry of puffins.

Dilly couldn't wait to experience it all and now she would have the bonus of enjoying it with her own little human by her side. Her heart swelled with happiness at that very thought. As she pulled up outside the solicitor's office, she was filled with excitement, and it wasn't long before she was driving back over the causeway, a huge smile lighting up her face. She'd done it, she'd gone and bought a lighthouse. This wasn't just a property, it was the first true home she had bought entirely on her own. Regardless of how successful her artwork might become, the Puffin Island Lighthouse would always be her home. It was a symbol of her new beginning and she couldn't wait to get inside.

As she drove slowly along Lighthouse Lane, the narrow

road lined with quaint cottages, bespoke shops and a stream that ran at the side of the cobbles, Dilly spotted Clemmie and Amelia standing at the gate of the tearoom. She pulled up alongside them and lowered her window, shaking the set of keys triumphantly. 'Keys to the lighthouse!' she announced, unable to contain her excitement.

Amelia and Clemmie rushed over, their faces lighting up with joy. 'Congratulations!' Amelia exclaimed, clapping her hands. 'I'm so happy for you! We can't wait for the housewarming party! We were just wondering whether Pierre would get an invite!'

Before Dilly could respond, Clemmie dashed back into the tearoom, returning moments later with an oversized cake box. She handed it through the car window, grinning from ear to ear. 'What's in here?' Dilly asked, lifting the lid with curiosity.

'A homemade Victoria sponge cake with a twist,' Clemmie revealed proudly. 'It's topped with the freshest strawberries I could find, made just for you during my break. You're going to have plenty of visitors at that lighthouse in the coming days, and what better way to welcome them than with a delicious slice of cake?'

'And…' Amelia chimed in, holding up a bottle bag with a playful smile, 'I know we might have overdone it with the Prosecco at art class, but you'll need something bubbly to toast your new home. A little celebration is definitely in order!'

Dilly reached out and took the bag. 'This is the reason you're my favourite friends. Thank you both. Why don't you all come around for dinner once I get the place cleaned up and some furniture to sit on?' Dilly suggested.

Amelia's eyes sparkled. 'We thought you were never going to ask! Just let us know when, and we'll definitely be there!' She pointed towards The Story Shop. 'I need to get back to work, but huge congratulations, Dilly!'

As soon as Amelia disappeared inside the shop, Clemmie turned back towards Dilly. 'So, how did it go with Dr Sandford?'

'He was wonderful. He's arranged a scan for me tomorrow, so I'll finally find out when she's due.'

Clemmie's eyes twinkled with amusement. 'You still think it's a girl? Are you going by yourself tomorrow?'

Dilly hesitated, then nodded. 'I don't have much choice. But I'm planning on telling Dad tomorrow night after I've had the scan. He's coming around for dinner. I know it sounds daft, but I want to make sure everything is okay before I tell him.'

Clemmie reached out and squeezed her arm. 'If you want company for the scan, I can come with you.'

'Would you? I didn't really want to go alone.'

Clemmie grinned warmly. 'Did you think Auntie Clemmie would miss seeing the first glimpse of the baby? Just text me the details, and I'll pick you up. You don't have to worry about a thing.'

'Thank you,' Dilly replied. The thought of having Clemmie by her side at the scan made her less anxious. 'I'll see you tomorrow.'

Dilly drove down to Blue Water Bay and as she caught sight of the lighthouse a sense of pride and joy washed over her. As soon as she parked, she couldn't control the smile on her face as she glanced at the large, jangling bunch of keys in her hand. She climbed out of the car, and walked around the side of the lighthouse towards the front door.

'Woah! Where did you spring up from?' To her utter surprise, standing on the doorstep was Max, decked out in the shortest shorts she had ever seen, paired with a frilly apron reminiscent of that worn by Betty in the tearoom. In one hand, he brandished a feather duster with a flourish and by his feet was a bright orange bucket filled with cleaning equipment. Dilly couldn't help but raise her eyebrows, her gaze trailing from the bright pink feather duster to his pinny to his legs. 'Nice pinny,' she said, smirking as she took in the absurd sight. 'But what exactly are you doing here?'

Max grinned, striking a dramatic pose as if modelling for a 1980s cleaning advert. 'Your dad sent me over. For the next hour or two, I'm at your complete disposal, madam. Chief cobweb sweeper and spider catcher, reporting for duty!' He gave a mock salute with the feather duster, his expression full of mischief.

Dilly burst into laughter. 'Well, you certainly look the part,' she teased, still chuckling. The sight of Max in his ridiculous outfit, combined with his drop-dead gorgeous looks, made her heart leap. He leaned in and kissed her. She didn't stop him even though she knew she should.

'What have you got there?' Max asked, eyeing the cake box with an exaggeratedly curious look.

Dilly rolled her eyes playfully. 'Cake,' she stated, as if pointing out the obvious.

'And what sort of cake might that be?' Max pressed.

'Victoria sponge with added strawberries,' Dilly replied.

Max's eyes lit up. 'My favourite!' he declared.

'My guess is anything in this box would be your favourite,' she joked. 'We can't let the worker go hungry though, now can we?' He reached out eagerly, and Dilly handed him the cake box with a grin. As she turned to unlock the front door, she felt a flutter of excitement. She slid the key into the lock, looked up at the towering lighthouse and took a deep breath. 'This is it, home sweet home for us,' she murmured, turning the key and pushing the door open.

'Us?' Max quipped with a gleam in his eye. 'I think it's a bit early in the day to ask me to move in. It's been what, twenty-four hours? I know you're a fast mover, I mean you dragged me into that bedroom and kept me at your beck and call all night, but still...' He grinned mischievously.

'Any complaints?' Dilly asked, steering the conversation in a different direction, flustered by her slip-up. She couldn't be talking to the baby in front of Max when he still didn't know about it!

He put the cake box down on a nearby table then pulled her towards him. 'None whatsoever.' He wrapped his arms around her waist and pulled her closer. 'Is it a proposal next?' He shot her a playful grin, clearly enjoying himself.

Dilly burst into laughter. 'Shut up!' she exclaimed, shaking her head.

'There's only one way to shut me up.' He had that playful look in his eye as he lowered his lips to her. 'Welcome to your new home,' he said, kissing her briefly before pulling away slowly, leaving Dilly wanting more. 'I think you need to stop distracting the worker.' He bent down to the bucket and pulled out a pair of bright yellow Marigolds.

'They suit you!' she said, watching as Max put them on. 'Come on, let's explore and see where we should start with the cleaning.'

'The bedroom?' he suggested.

Grabbing the feather duster, Dilly playfully swatted him. 'You're impossible!'

Max picked her up and spun her around in the middle of the room before she chased him up the spiral staircase, their laughter echoing through the lighthouse.

———————

The next couple of hours were filled with chatter and the satisfying sound of scrubbing as Dilly and Max worked their way from the top of the lighthouse down to the third level. Max, ever the gentleman, carried bucket after bucket of soapy water up and down the narrow staircase, while Dilly diligently cleaned away years of dust and grime.

'It didn't actually look that dirty when we came to view it, did it?' she asked, taking a breather and opening the window.

'Just think of the number of dirty shoes that would have traipsed through on viewing day.'

'There were over eight hundred people according to the local newspaper.'

The pile of dirty rags and dusters grew steadily. When they reached the kitchen, Dilly's eyes landed on an old-fashioned radio tucked away on a dusty shelf. 'Look at this. It looks prehistoric! Do you think it still works?' She took a cloth, wiped it clean then plugged it in and fiddled with the dials. The radio crackled to life as she extended the aerial and music played. 'Wow! It actually works!'

'Let's dance!' exclaimed Max, taking hold of both her hands.

'Don't be ridiculous!'

'I'm not,' he replied, not taking no for an answer and leading her into the middle of the room. He glanced back over his shoulder at her and the way he was looking at her made a burst of adrenalin electrify her heart. The spark between them was like no other Dilly had felt, except all those years ago when she was in Max's company.

'I don't think I've danced with a man wearing yellow Marigolds before.' Her eyes quickly ran up and down his body. He was the kind of guy who would turn heads wherever he went, with a good sense of fashion – though admittedly not right now. He was the whole package, and although Dilly had told herself she never wanted another man after Giles, she couldn't deny that she wanted Max. But that wasn't surprising. It had always been Max for Dilly.

There was a sparkle in his eyes as he flashed her a gorgeous smile. 'And I don't think I've ever danced with a woman as beautiful as you.'

Sheer pleasure ran through Dilly's body. It had been a long time since she'd danced with anyone. Her pulse was racing and she thought she would either combust or melt in his arms. They moved around in circles, every inch of her tingling with desire and the intensity growing between them as he looked deep into her eyes. Max drew her in closer, and she marvelled at how safe she felt with his arms wrapped around her, a feeling she knew she could easily get used to. As the song came to an end, they stayed in each other's arms and Dilly briefly closed her eyes as Max slowly tilted her face towards his.

She couldn't stop her eyes from filling with tears.

'Hey, what's up?' he asked softly, his thumb caressing her cheek.

'I'm just happy,' she replied.

'Me too.' He kissed her softly. 'I can't believe we're here … together. It feels like I've known you for ever.'

'You have… Well, for a long time anyway.'

Max slowly dropped her hands. Then, as if on cue, Queen's 'I Want to Break Free' blasted from the radio. With a mischievous grin, Max grabbed the feather duster and began mimicking Freddie Mercury's iconic moves from the music video, pretending to clean with exaggerated flair. Dilly doubled over with laughter at the sight of Max hamming it up in his yellow Marigolds.

'This is how it's meant to be,' Max declared, pausing mid-dance. 'Full of fun and laughter.' He looked at Dilly, his eyes warm and relaxed, and she couldn't help but smile back. She felt the same – happy and at ease, except for the secret she was still keeping from him.

'It's so easy being with you,' he added, sincerity in his voice. 'I can goof around and joke and just be myself.'

Dilly grinned. 'You can, and with all that dancing, I think it's time for cake. But I've got no tea or milk.'

'I'll nip back to the boat house and grab some provisions and a couple of plates and cutlery.' He leaned in and kissed her lightly on the tip of her nose before heading toward the door.

'You'd better bring a kettle, too!' she called after him, laughing as he waved and disappeared down the spiral staircase. 'And take those gloves off!'

Through the window she watched him walk up the jetty and across the sandy shore towards the boat house. The gentle breeze ruffled his hair and Dilly smiled, a smile she couldn't suppress even if she tried. Watching the man she had loved from afar for so long, she knew she wanted him to be a constant in her life.

For the very first time, Dilly found herself questioning her decision to keep the baby. It was a choice she had made confidently, certain that it was the right path for her, regardless of the lies she'd have to tell to keep the father's identity under wraps. But now, feeling the love she felt for Max, she wasn't sure whether she was prepared to lose him. It made her wonder about the possibilities she hadn't considered, and that was something she never could have anticipated.

Chapter Seventeen

Twenty minutes later they were sitting at the top of the lighthouse, sipping tea and savouring the delicious cake that Clemmie had baked. The view was breathtaking, the ocean stretching out beneath the open sky, a gentle breeze bringing the scent of saltwater.

'This is the life,' she said contentedly, taking a bite of cake. A thick layer of cream and jam oozed out the other side, and, laughing, she quickly licked her fingers clean. Max grinned as they both stretched their feet out to rest on a nearby wicker trunk, enjoying the last of the day's sunshine as it slowly ebbed away.

'I think I'm done with cleaning for now. I'm actually feeling exhausted, and I've still got to wrap up the paintings I've sold today, though they can probably wait for tomorrow. We've made a great start. Thank you for coming to help.'

'What's the plan for moving in?' he asked, making short work of the cake and placing the empty plates on top of the wicker basket. He stretched his arm around her and Dilly snuggled into his chest.

'If I can get the rest of the lighthouse cleaned in the evenings of this week, I can hopefully start to move my stuff across this weekend. Next week I want to paint the walls of the new gallery and finish the portrait of Mum. Once that's done, I can organise the opening day. I also need to advertise for a member of staff to work in the current gallery.'

'You've got it all planned.'

'Yes, and it's going to be a busy few weeks.'

'Remember I'm here to help.' Max nudged her elbow. 'What's in there? It looks like an old fishing trunk.'

Dilly pointed towards the wicker trunk. 'That, you mean? I've not looked yet,' she said. 'There's a padlock that'll need to be cut off.'

Max leaned over to inspect the rusty lock. 'It doesn't need to be cut off, it's not actually locked,' he replied, removing the padlock and placing it on the floor next to her.

Dilly's eyes widened with anticipation. 'It might be treasure!' she exclaimed, eagerly untying the leather strap that bound the lid to the basket. 'Lighthouse treasure!' She lifted the lid, and they both peered inside.

The first item she pulled out was a pair of binoculars. With a playful grin, she immediately raised them to her eyes and focused on Max. 'I spy, with my little eye, a gorgeous man who takes my breath away every time I see him,' she teased, leaning over to place a soft kiss on his lips before setting the binoculars aside. 'What's this?' she asked, pulling out a curious-looking metal item.

Max seemed to recognise it. 'That's an oil pitcher,' he

explained. 'They used these to fill the large lamp with oil. And this,' he continued, pulling out another piece, 'is an oil drip pan. They used it to fill lamps, lanterns and smaller oil cans. The items would be placed on the tray, and the oil poured in until they were full.'

Dilly looked at him, impressed. 'How do you know so much about this stuff?'

He shrugged modestly. 'Just things I've read over the years.'

'Good-looking and intelligent, you do have it all going on, don't you, Max Harrington?' she teased.

'And this,' he said, pulling out the last item, 'is a clock!'

Dilly rolled her eyes with a smile. 'No kidding, Sherlock. Even I could have guessed that one.'

Max grinned. 'It's probably to keep track of the lamp's operation and oil consumption.'

Dilly raised an eyebrow, smirking. 'You're making this up as you go along.'

'Just an educated guess,' he admitted with a playful grin.

Dilly then picked up an old leather-bound logbook. She carefully opened it. 'Oh my, look at this…' She blew out a breath. The pages were filled with neat handwritten notes. 'It's years old. The old lighthouse keepers logged the weather and events, and there are even folded-up maps inside.' She flipped through the pages, suddenly stopping. Her face grew serious as she read a particular entry.

'What is it?' Max asked, noticing her intense expression.

Dilly looked up. 'This is a record of the night of the storm, when my mum was born and my grandad lost his life. The storm is detailed here along with the number of explosives that were set off, signed and dated by Mack Selby.' She placed a hand over her heart, visibly moved. 'This must have been the last thing he recorded before he died.'

'Your grandmother must have been such a remarkable woman, especially during such a difficult time.'

They sat in silence for a moment. Finally, Max spoke, his tone almost reverent. 'What a fantastic piece of history.'

Dilly nodded, feeling a deep connection to the past. Her thoughts drifted to her grandmother, imagining what she must have felt that fateful night. One moment, she had a loving family and was about to welcome a child into the world; the next, she faced the daunting reality of raising that child alone. But, testament to her grandmother, she brought up Dilly's mother all by herself. If it wasn't for her strength and reliance, Dilly might not be here today.

Dilly stood up and peered through the binoculars, marvelling at the panoramic view. 'I can see everything from up here: the gulls, the puffins, and even the guests sitting inside The Sea Glass Restaurant. There's a couple having seabass… Oh, and one having lobster.'

'You're kidding me. You can't see that.'

'I could be right nosy from up here,' she kidded delightedly. Feeling mischievous, she trained the binoculars on Max's flat. 'And I can spy on you. I could watch you getting changed for bed if I fancied,' she teased.

'I might need to get myself a pair,' he said with a chuckle. 'Though I'm hoping that sometime in the near future we won't need them … because we'll be in the same bed together.'

But Dilly barely heard his comment because her focus

had shifted. The binoculars were fixed on a figure standing at the end of the jetty. Her breath caught in her throat, and she gasped. 'It's her,' she whispered, her voice barely audible. 'Oh my God, it's her.' Her voice rose. 'I'm not dreaming. She's alive!' Her voice trembled with emotion. 'She's here, at the lighthouse.'

Her heart raced as she flung the binoculars toward Max, barely able to contain her shock and excitement. Her pulse was racing. 'It's my mum!' she repeated, before racing down the spiral staircase as if her life depended on it, with a speed that surprised even herself.

Max shouted after her. 'Dilly, wait!' but his words barely registered as she reached the second floor.

Chapter Eighteen

M ax sprinted after Dilly, struggling to keep up as she raced to the end of the jetty.

'Mum!' she screamed at the top of her lungs, her voice echoing all around. She spun around frantically, scanning every direction. 'She was here, standing right here! You must have seen her.'

Finally, Max caught her up. Out of breath, he placed his hands on his hips as he inhaled deeply. 'My God, you're fast.'

'Did you see her? Which way did she go?'

'See who? Dilly, what's going on?'

'My mum! She was standing here, looking straight up at me,' Dilly insisted, her voice choked with emotion. 'Which way did she go?'

'Dilly, you're not making sense, I thought your mum was dead.'

'No, she's survived. She *had* to have survived because

I've seen her twice this week. Once at the gallery and just now,' Dilly argued, her words tumbling out so fast they were almost incomprehensible. Her eyes were still darting around, searching for any sign of the woman she had seen through the binoculars.

'Dilly, breathe,' Max urged, lightly gripping her arms. 'You aren't making any sense.'

'Which bit don't you understand? She must have survived the accident. My guess is she has amnesia and can't remember who she is, but somehow she's found her way back here. Tell me you saw her.'

Max shook his head slowly, his heart aching for her. 'I'm sorry, I didn't see anyone.' He kept his hands on her shoulders as Dilly's eyes searched his, looking for confirmation. But all she found was concern and confusion.

'Let's get you back inside.'

'I don't want to go back inside. We need to find her.'

Max looked all around. All they could see were dog walkers, a couple holding hands walking towards the bay and a group of fishermen loading up the lobster cages ready for the morning.

Dilly felt a surge of helplessness wash over her. She was utterly convinced that she'd seen her mum, despite Max's certainty that no one had been near the jetty. Once again, she wrestled with her own doubts. Was her mind playing tricks on her? Were these sightings driven by stress or possibly unresolved grief?

Max gently probed, 'What does your dad say about this?'

Dilly remained silent, her eyes unfocused. She suddenly felt herself swaying.

Max noticed it too and reached out to steady her, but it was too late. Dilly's knees buckled, and she fainted, her body going limp in his arms. Max carefully lowered her to the ground, ensuring her head was supported.

'Dilly,' he said, his voice urgent.

Immediately he dialled the emergency services. Thankfully the causeway was open, allowing an ambulance to get through. As he hung up the call Dilly began to stir, her eyelids fluttering open. 'Don't panic,' he said softly, his voice calm and reassuring. 'You've fainted but you're going to be fine.'

Dilly looked disoriented. 'I don't feel...' she murmured, trailing off as she closed her eyes again.

Max gently squeezed her hand. 'Just stay still. You don't need to move. The ambulance is on its way, and even if you feel okay in a minute, it's better to get checked over.'

Five minutes later, Max had carefully helped Dilly move to a chair on the ground floor of the lighthouse, trying to keep her as comfortable as possible. She sat there, pale, but tried to reassure him. 'It's okay, I'm feeling okay now,' she said. But as she finished speaking, she suddenly clutched her stomach and winced with pain.

Max's eyes widened. 'Do you think it's something you've eaten? Food poisoning?' he asked.

This was the moment Dilly had been dreading but had known was inevitable. But she didn't want to tell him like this. She took a deep breath. 'Max,' she said, looking into his eyes. But before she could say any more the distant sounds of sirens cut through the air, growing louder as the ambulance approached the lighthouse.

'The ambulance is here. Do you want me to call your

dad?' he asked, already reaching for his phone. The question hung in the air, heavy with implications. Dilly hesitated, torn between the need to share her secret and the fear of how he would react. 'Yes,' she said. 'But Max…'

'It's okay, just try and stay calm,' he said, squeezing her hand. But Dilly shook her head, tears welling up. 'It's not okay, Max. I'm sorry.' Her voice cracked with emotion. She couldn't look him in the eye.

'Sorry about what? You don't need to apologise for fainting on me.' He leaned down and kissed the top of her head gently. 'The ambulance is here now. Let's get you checked out, just to be safe.'

The piercing siren had stopped, and Max moved to the doorway as the paramedics arrived. He watched as one of them went to the back of the ambulance and retrieved a wheelchair, whilst the other approached him carrying a medical bag. She smiled. 'Hi, I'm Polly.'

'Dilly's in here,' Max said, stepping aside to let them in.

The paramedic immediately set to work, asking Dilly a series of questions as she prepared her equipment. 'Can you tell me where you're feeling pain?' she asked.

'Stomach.'

The paramedic nodded, taking out a blood pressure cuff. She wrapped it around Dilly's arm and began to inflate it. 'Your blood pressure is very low.'

'What would normally cause that?' asked Max.

'There's a number of possible scenarios, emotional stress, fear, pain.'

'Pregnancy,' replied Dilly, closing her eyes.

'Are you pregnant?' asked Polly.

Dilly nodded.

'How many months?'

Dilly briefly closed her eyes. 'At a guess around four months. I've only just found out. Will everything be okay?'

'Let's get to the hospital and get a scan sorted and then the doctors will be able to tell you more.'

Dilly nodded, her eyes finally meeting Max's. The shock was written all over his face. 'I'm sorry,' she mouthed, feeling the weight of the unspoken words between them. She knew he must have plenty of questions. Even though they needed to have that conversation, right now wasn't the moment … again. She watched Max gather her things, including the bunch of keys and her bag.

'Is there anything I can bring along for you?' he asked. His voice was steady but he didn't look directly at her.

'You want to come with me?' Dilly asked, surprised.

'I'm not going to leave you on your own.'

'Thank you.'

The paramedics helped Dilly into the wheelchair, and Max locked up the lighthouse behind them. As they reached the ambulance, he climbed in and sat next to her, holding her hand tightly. The gesture meant the world to Dilly, especially after the bombshell she'd just dropped.

'I wanted to tell you,' she whispered, her voice cracked. 'I'm so sorry.'

Max squeezed her hand. 'Don't worry about that right now. You and the baby are the priority. Everything else can wait.'

As the ambulance sped towards the hospital, Dilly felt a flurry of emotions. Guilt gnawed at her, not just for hiding her pregnancy but also for the thoughts she had entertained earlier that day. The idea of a termination had crossed her mind, but now, knowing there could be a possibility of losing the baby, she knew for certain she would never have been able to go through with it. She wanted this baby, no matter what challenges lay ahead, and all she could do was pray that everything would be okay.

Chapter Nineteen

As soon as they arrived at the hospital Dilly was whisked up the corridor and into a private room where she was transferred to the bed. They were left alone for a brief moment. 'How are you feeling? Has the pain subsided?' asked Max.

'It just feels like an uncomfortable niggle,' replied Dilly.

'Your dad is on the way. Does he know about the pregnancy?'

Dilly shook her head.

'Have you said anything about us?'

She shook her head again. 'I only found out yesterday, just before... I know I should have told you before I dragged you into the bedroom. I know it sounds so wrong when I say this but I just wanted you. I've always wanted you and now I've...' A tear rolled down her cheek.

Max briefly closed his eyes. 'Concentrate on you. We can talk later.'

The conversation was cut short as the doctor walked

into the room with a cheery 'Hello'. He introduced himself and checked through her personal details. 'I believe you are pregnant, is that correct?'

Dilly nodded. 'I don't know how many months exactly, possibly four,' she replied.

'And how's the pain?'

'A dull ache and a tiny niggle but bearable.'

The doctor nodded, consulting the documentation filled out by the paramedics. 'Your blood pressure is low, which likely caused the dizziness and fainting. But let's get you in for a scan to see what's going on. The nurse will take you down now. And you can come too, Dad,' he said, glancing at Max.

'Oh, he's not—' Dilly started to explain, but Max interrupted, his gaze steady on hers.

'I'll come if you want me to,' he offered, his voice gentle but firm.

Dilly looked at him, her eyes searching his face. She hadn't thought for a moment that he would want to. She nodded, grateful he was still sitting here with her. 'Yes, please,' she whispered.

Dilly reached out for his hand and he took it and gave her a reassuring smile, before she was wheeled down the corridor into a tiny room. The sonographer introduced herself as Grace and helped Dilly settle on the bed before she set up the equipment. Dilly felt nervous. She didn't know what to expect. Seeing your baby for the first time should be a joyous occasion but she was more scared than excited. What if something was wrong? Grace picked up the information on the clipboard and checked everything over with Dilly.

'When was the last time you ate and drank anything?' Grace asked.

'Cake and a cup of tea, about an hour ago now,' replied Dilly, looking up at the clock on the wall. Time seemed to have slowed right down. She just wanted the scan to be over and done with and for Grace to tell her everything was going to be okay.

'What type of cake?'

'Victoria Sponge with strawberries.'

'My favourite! Now you're making me hungry; I've not eaten since eleven this morning.'

'I'm surprised you aren't feeling just as dizzy as me.'

Grace smiled. 'And when was the last time you went to the toilet?'

'A while ago. I'm bursting!'

'Then we'd better get on with this scan as quickly as possible. I'm going to take your blood pressure again quickly just to see if things have settled down a little.'

Dilly nodded.

'It's still a little on the low side,' Grace confirmed two minutes later, turning the monitor towards herself and preparing for the scan. 'We're ready to begin though. Just try and relax. Is this your first baby?'

'Yes,' replied Dilly.

Grace took a large paper blanket from the shelf. 'If you could just pull down your trousers a bit, I'll tuck this into the top of your knickers.' The dry crackling sound of the paper blanket contrasted sharply with the soft hum of the ultrasound machine. Dilly lay back and Max took hold of her hand as she tried to calm her racing heart.

'I'm going to put this jelly onto your stomach. It may

feel a little cold.' Grace smiled encouragingly. 'And I may need to press down at times, which can be uncomfortable, especially if you need the toilet, but the scan itself won't hurt. Do you have any questions before we start?'

Dilly shook her head. This was the moment she would see her baby for the first time, and she felt a surge of emotions – nervousness, joy and an almost overwhelming sense of reality. Her thoughts raced; she wanted to know that the baby was healthy and she wondered if Grace would be able to tell whether it was a boy or a girl. As the cool gel touched her skin, she jumped slightly, causing Grace to give her another gentle smile. 'It can be a bit of a shock, I know.'

Grace moved the probe slowly, her eyes focused on the screen. The anticipation was almost unbearable.

'Is everything okay?' asked Dilly, seeking some reassurance.

Grace finally looked up, her gaze moving between Dilly and Max. 'I just need to get the doctor,' she said, her voice calm but firm. 'Please excuse me for a moment.' She quickly left the room and the door clicked shut behind her, leaving a suffocating silence behind.

Dilly's panic surged. 'There's something wrong, I can feel it…' Her voice faltered and tears welled up.

'Just try and stay calm.'

Grace walked back in with the doctor, who took the probe and gently ran it over Dilly's stomach, his eyes focused intently on the monitor. Dilly couldn't hold back her anxiety any longer. 'Please tell me everything is okay.'

The doctor looked up and met her gaze, a warm smile spreading across his face. 'Everything looks just as it should,' he reassured her, turning the monitor towards Dilly and Max.

The doctor turned up the sound on the monitor and a rapid, rhythmic thumping filled the room, resonating with a steady, reassuring beat. 'This,' he said, 'is the sound of your baby's heartbeat.'

'Oh my gosh!' The relief was instant as she stared at the monitor. The sound was mesmerising, like a tiny train chugging along its tracks, strong and regular. But the doctor wasn't finished. He moved the probe slightly and pointed to another spot on the screen. 'And this,' he said with a grin as the sound coming from the monitor changed ever so slightly, 'is the sound of your second baby's heartbeat.'

Dilly's eyes widened, and her mouth fell open. 'What do you mean, my second baby's heartbeat?'

'Twins!' the doctor confirmed, his smile growing even wider. 'You're expecting twins. Congratulations, Mum and Dad! You are certainly going to have your work cut out! Both are looking very healthy with very strong heartbeats.'

'Twins!' Dilly repeated, putting a hand on her own heart. The news took her breath away. She turned to Max who was grinning from ear to ear, his eyes shining with amazement. He squeezed her hand tightly, leaning in to kiss her forehead.

'Twins! Just look at them!' said Max.

'I'm actually lost for words!'

'There's always a first time for everything,' he teased.

'Do you have twins in your family?' the doctor asked.

Dilly racked her brain then shook her head. 'Not to my knowledge.'

'The measurements suggest you are around four months pregnant, as you suspected.'

Dilly looked down at her stomach. 'I would have been expecting to be the size of a whale with two babies in there, but instead I just thought I'd eaten too many pancakes.'

'You have a very neat, tiny bump now, but my guess is that it won't stay like that for much longer. At this stage I can tell the sex of the babies. Would you like to know?'

Immediately Dilly looked towards Max. 'What do you think, should we find out?'

Max's grin widened, his eyes sparkling with excitement. 'It's up to you,' he said, his voice filled with anticipation.

Dilly hesitated for a moment, the enormity of the news still sinking in. 'I'm not sure,' she began, her words tumbling out in a rush. 'I would love for it to be a surprise, but the main surprise is that I'm four months pregnant! In just five months, I'll have two babies! I haven't got long to set up the new gallery, decorate the nursery, and make sure I'm ready. And names… I need to think of names! Yes! Tell me … before I change my mind!'

The doctor smiled warmly, clearly enjoying the moment. 'Girls!' he announced. 'You are expecting twin girls! Congratulations!'

Dilly's eyes widened in delight, and she immediately leaned over to hug Max tightly. 'Girls!' she repeated. The thought of having twin daughters filled her heart with a warmth and excitement she had never felt before.

'I feel it's going to be a very pink lighthouse!' added Max, squeezing her hand.

'I think the discomfort you felt earlier might have been

your stomach expanding. Have you felt any kicking?' the doctor continued.

Dilly shook her head, still processing the news.

'Well, it won't be long now,' the doctor reassured her. 'As for the low blood pressure, you need to take it easy. Move slowly when getting up, avoid overexertion, drink plenty of water and rest often. We don't think you need to stay overnight, but we would like you to rest here for a few hours to ensure you're pain-free before heading home.'

Dilly nodded, her mind already racing with plans and ideas. 'Yes, of course.'

As the doctor left the room, Grace stepped forward to gently wipe the excess gel from Dilly's stomach. Dilly looked at Max, her eyes bright with happiness. 'Twin girls!' Without thinking she leaned across and planted a kiss on his lips. 'I still can't believe it!'

Chapter Twenty

D illy settled onto the hospital bed, the reality of expecting twin girls still sinking in. There was a long list of things she needed to prepare. There would be cots to organise, prams, car seats, clothes and more. It was overwhelming, but in the best possible way. The sight and sounds of their tiny beating hearts had made everything feel real, and the thought of Giles was far from her mind. These were *her* babies, and she was determined to do everything in her power to give them the best start in life.

She glanced over at Max, who was standing by the window, opening it to let in some fresh air. He paused for a moment, staring out, lost in thought. Dilly felt a pang of guilt. Caught up in her whirlwind of emotions, she realised she hadn't even considered how he might be feeling. Just twenty-four hours ago, they had been blissfully exploring the possibilities of their new relationship, filled with excitement and hope for the future. Now, the revelation of her pregnancy with twins had completely upset his world.

Despite her own happiness, she knew the news must have been a shock to him, and she hadn't taken a moment to check how he was processing it all.

She watched as he pulled out a chair beside her bed and sat down. 'How are you feeling about all this?' she asked.

'I can see how happy you are, and I'm really happy for you ... honestly I am,' he replied.

Dilly knew that was the kind of person Max was, always supportive and caring. But she also knew she had let him down. This was as much of a shock for him as it was for her, and she could tell he was struggling to find the right words.

'This is a lot for me to process, too,' she admitted. 'I know you must have a lot of questions, and I want to be honest with you.'

'I'm actually not quite sure what to say,' he began. 'Twenty-four hours ago, I was finally in the arms of the woman I had always admired and... I'm going to be honest with you, Dil, even though I know it sounds daft, but you were always the one for me; it was just the wrong time, wrong place. I knew from the first moment I saw you ... but now, it seems it's the wrong time again. I know you and the father of your babies have a lot to talk about, and I don't want you feeling guilty about me. I had the best night of my life, and having had the chance to spend that time with you will always be something I will cherish. This might be a chance for you to start a family, to make things work with him. You've got so much on your plate right now ... the babies, your mother... You don't need me complicating things.'

Dilly could see from the look in Max's eyes that she'd

broken his heart, but still he was trying to be strong, to say the right things.

She knew there was a place for Max in their lives but that was a decision he would have to make. She came as a package now and if she was in his shoes, she would have no clue what to do. All she knew was that she didn't want to lose him when she'd only just found him again.

She opened her mouth to explain the truth about Giles, how he wasn't a factor to worry about, and the story she had concocted to tell the islanders, but just then, she heard her father's voice echoing down the corridor. 'Delilah Waters? She was brought in by ambulance with abdominal pain. I'm her father.' The door swung open a moment later, and her father rushed in, enveloping her in a warm, protective hug.

'Dilly, what's happened? Are you okay?' he asked, his voice filled with worry. For a moment, the room felt like it was spinning with emotions.

Max stood up. 'I'm going to leave you to it. Are you okay to take Dilly home?' Max looked at Ralph.

'Yes, of course.' Ralph extended his hand. 'Thank you for getting her here and staying with her.'

'That's no problem at all. I'll see you in the morning at work.'

Max hesitated by the door. His eyes locked on Dilly's and he looked like he wanted to say something, but he simply gave her a slight smile and let the door shut behind him. She could see his feelings were in turmoil, and she didn't like that she had been the cause of that.

Chapter Twenty-One

'What's been happening? Has the pain subsided?' Ralph asked sitting down in the seat. 'Max said something about abdominal pain.'

Dilly smiled reassuringly, trying to put him at ease. 'Dad, the pain has subsided. They did a scan to check everything,' she said, feeling her heart race with the excitement of the news she was about to share.

'I thought it might be your appendix – they grumble you know, sometimes for months. Did they find anything?'

'They found a heartbeat,' she began, watching her father's puzzled expression.

'A heartbeat?' Ralph repeated, still not fully grasping what she meant.

Dilly nodded, unable to contain her joy. 'Actually, they found two heartbeats!'

She waited for the penny to drop. It didn't take long before the puzzled look on Ralph's face morphed into a full-on beaming smile. 'You're not…?'

'I am! I'm pregnant!'

'Two heartbeats? You mean … twins?' he asked.

'Twins!' Dilly confirmed, her smile widening.

Ralph's face lit up as surprise and happiness flooded over him. 'Twins! Oh my God, Dilly, that's incredible!' he exclaimed, hugging her. 'This is such amazing news!'

Dilly laughed, knowing the joy in her heart was likely mirrored on her face. 'It's the reason I've been feeling dizzy and nauseous, and why I've been getting a little chubby around the middle,' she said, placing a hand on her slightly rounded stomach.

Ralph pulled back to look at her, his eyes shining with pride and love. 'This is such wonderful news,' he said. Then his smile slipped. 'But who's the father? It's been eight months since Giles left.'

'I've not been quite truthful with you,' Dilly admitted. 'He was still very much around four months ago. When I told you I'd discovered his deceit, it was happening there and then, not months earlier, like I said. I didn't want you to worry about me.'

'Oh Dilly.' Ralph reached for his daughter's hand.

Just at that moment the nurse breezed into the room and checked the notes attached to the clipboard at the end of the bed. 'Can I get you both a drink?' she asked. 'The coffee machine at the end of the corridor isn't working, and we've got the most damn awful coffee in the staffroom, but it's probably better than nothing.'

'I'm okay, but thank you,' replied Ralph.

'And I'm okay too.'

As soon as the nurse left the room Ralph turned towards his daughter. 'So, Giles is the father.' He blew out a breath.

'It's not ideal, is it?'

'I thought we were well and truly shot of him.'

'We are. I haven't had much time to think about this, but as far as I'm concerned, he's not going to be a part of their lives. He's in prison, and he's not the kind of person I want around my children. The twins will have nothing to do with him. He won't even know they exist. I don't want to expose my children to someone like him. But be honest, do you think I'm being out of order? Should he know about the twins?'

'Absolutely not,' Ralph replied firmly. 'I agree with you totally and I'm relieved that you've already come to this decision on your own.'

'I've thought it all through, and I have a plan,' she said, looking her dad straight in the eye. 'I'm going to tell everyone I had a one-night stand. No names, just an intense, fleeting attraction. People might feel sorry that I got caught out and am now pregnant, but I'll make everyone see I'm thrilled about it, and squash any gossip. I can do this.'

Ralph squeezed her hand. 'I don't think anyone who knows you would doubt that,' he said reassuringly. 'But I think you're wrong.'

'Wrong?'

Ralph nodded. 'This is Puffin Island we're talking about. I know gossip spreads like wildfire but what's the reason we all stay on the island? Because this is a community where we all look out for each other. No one on this island is going to judge you, Dilly. They know what Giles did and if he ever set foot on this island again, I wouldn't like to be him. I think the twins would be safer with everyone knowing, but it's your call.'

'I'm worried about the press as well. Can you imagine the headline? "The romance scammer and the artist..."'

'No resident would ever speak to the press, Dilly, they will all have *your* back. You need to remember how incredible you are and how important you are to the island and its community. Those kids are going to be lucky to have you and to grow up on Puffin Island. I still can't believe I'm going to be a grandad!'

'Two girls!'

'Girls!'

As they held each other, Dilly felt a surge of strength. She knew the road ahead wouldn't be easy, but with her father's support and her own fierce determination, she was ready to face it all. She took another deep breath. 'There's something else I need to talk to you about.'

'Sounds serious.'

'Mum.'

'She would have been over the moon about this news.'

Dilly took a deep breath, bracing herself for the conversation. 'Dad, what do you think the chances are that Mum and Anton survived that crash?' she asked.

Ralph looked at her with a perplexed expression. 'Absolutely zero,' he replied firmly. 'Not only were they both hit by a car, but they also could never have survived the icy cold sea. There was nowhere for them to escape to, and there was a witness that—'

'But we know Mum was a good swimmer,' Dilly interrupted, her eyes searching his face for any sign of hope.

'Yes, she was,' Ralph acknowledged, his tone softening. 'And that was all thanks to Selby. She knew how dangerous the water is, especially after watching your grandad save so many lives at the lighthouse. It was important to her that your mum should be a strong swimmer. But, Dilly, it's not just the fact that they were tossed into the water. The current was too strong, and no one could have swum to safety in those conditions. It was like the rip currents we have here on the island … impossible to fight against. And I know this is hard to hear, but the car hit them with some force, so it's likely the impact killed them instantly before they ever entered the water.'

Dilly watched her father closely. 'I disagree,' she said, her voice trembling slightly.

Ralph looked at her, confusion etched on his face. 'Disagree about what?' he asked.

'I've seen her twice,' Dilly said, letting the words hang in the air. She watched as Ralph's expression turned to disbelief. He shook his head slowly.

'How? When? You can't have. Have you spoken to her?'

Dilly took a deep breath. 'I saw her outside the gallery, looking through the window. I was serving a customer, and at first I thought I was imagining things. But then, this evening, she was standing at the end of the jetty, looking up at the lighthouse. Unfortunately, by the time I got down there, she was gone. It was like she'd vanished into thin air. I think she might have lost her memory and doesn't even know who she is. Somehow, she survived being thrown into the sea, and something must have triggered a memory of living on Puffin Island.'

She could tell from her father's face that he was sceptical.

'Dilly, I really think you're mistaken. It's easy to mistake someone who looks like your mum for her, especially with the stress you've been under. Think about it – if your mum was actually walking around the island, don't you think people would have noticed? Someone would have seen her, and we'd all know about it.'

Dilly's heart sank at his words. It was exactly what Clemmie had said. She glanced down, feeling a wave of frustration. 'I walk past people on the street without recognising them sometimes,' she said quietly, feeling desperate. 'But how could I mistake my own mother? It felt so real, Dad. I'm telling you, she was there. I truly believe that she's somehow out there, trying to find her way back to me.'

Chapter Twenty-Two

The next morning, Dilly sat in her living room overlooking Blue Water Bay. When she had arrived back from the hospital, the sky had turned a threatening shade of charcoal and crackled with the energy of an impending storm, which arrived soon after with a ferocity that the island hadn't seen in a while. It had raged through the night, jagged streaks of lightning splitting the sky, illuminating the landscape with brief, blinding flashes.

The thunder had rolled in, each rumble sounding like a distant drum, and the rain had poured down, hammering against the windows, which was mesmerising. Dilly had watched the storm for hours before finally falling into a restless sleep. By morning, the storm had passed, and as she opened the window and breathed in the fresh air, she thought about the conversation she'd had with her dad. He hadn't believed she'd seen her mum. He was confident that there was no way she could have survived. Dilly might have agreed with him if she'd only seen her mum once –

that, of course, could have been a case of mistaken identity – but not now that she'd seen her twice.

She'd showered and had breakfast. The gallery should be open today but she had more pressing things on her mind. She wanted to chat with Max, sooner rather than later, even though he would be busy at work and not expecting her. She needed to have an honest conversation with him about Giles. All night, she had wrestled with the dilemma: should she tell him the truth or stick to the fabricated story of a one-night stand? Her dad thought she should be open with the whole island, but she still hadn't made her mind up about that.

No, Max deserved the whole truth and she trusted him with the detail. And if he didn't want a relationship, she fully understood. Things had changed. She knew she could go it alone as a single mum, but there was a huge part of her that hoped Max would see the bigger picture of the future.

Hearing a knock at the gallery door, she glanced at the clock and realised it was already past nine, but she didn't move. She didn't want to see anyone until she'd spoken to Max. She knew the community would be concerned, as an ambulance on the island was a rare occurrence. Everyone would want to know what had happened and why she'd been taken to hospital. But she wanted to enjoy that little bit of information on her own for just a while longer.

The knock sounded again but Dilly stayed seated. She switched on her phone and immediately it burst into life. Last night she'd switched it off, not wanting to talk to anyone, but now there were umpteen messages from her friends, all concerned about how she was. It made her feel a little guilty that people had been worrying about her.

Immediately her phone began to ring. It was Clemmie. Dilly picked it up.

'It's me, are you home? I'm at the gallery door.'

Dilly hurried down the stairs and quickly ushered Clemmie through the gallery and up the stairs. 'What's going on?' Clemmie asked, her eyes wide with concern. 'There are rumours circulating that you were in the hospital, and everyone's been speculating about what's happened.'

'You haven't said anything, have you?' Dilly asked.

'Of course not,' Clemmie reassured her. 'I didn't know what to do or say, so I kept quiet. Is the baby okay?'

A huge smile spread across Dilly's face as she grabbed hold of Clemmie's arm. '*Babies!* I'm having twins!'

Clemmie's mouth dropped wide open.

'You're catching flies,' Dilly teased, laughing.

'Oh my God, twins?' Clemmie squealed, her excitement infectious. 'That's amazing! How far along are you?'

'I'm nearly five months. The doctors think I was just experiencing some normal stretching pains. And now, my father knows … and, of course, Max.'

'Yikes, how did that go down?' Clemmie asked.

'That's the reason the gallery isn't open. I need to go and see Max. Have you got time for a brew?'

'Of course.'

Dilly made two cups of tea and filled Clemmie in about the second sighting of her mum. 'And then that's when the pain started. Max was brilliant and he called the ambulance, but of course I had to tell the paramedics I was pregnant. He was understandably shocked but still came with me in the ambulance, holding my hand the whole time. When we got to the hospital, the doctor mistakenly assumed Max was the father and invited him in for the scan. Max didn't correct him, and honestly, I was secretly thrilled. I didn't want to go through it alone, and having him there made everything feel a little less scary.'

'And what happened when you discovered it was twins?'

'I was completely shocked! Judging by the look on Max's face he was happy for me but he evidently decided there and then that this was a good opportunity for me to get back with the father.'

'And does he know who the father is?'

Dilly shook her head. 'I didn't have a chance to chat with him because as soon as the scan was over my dad turned up and Max promptly left to give us time alone. That's why I want to go now and explain everything.'

'Is that a good thing? I thought you were sticking to the story of a one-night stand? I know I've said it before but does he need to know the truth?'

Dilly exhaled. 'Dad seems to think that it's better to be open and honest with everyone in the community.'

'Everyone will have your back, I'm sure of that, but this isn't something they all need to know. You have the right to a private life and so what you choose to say about the twins and their conception is your choice. Do what you feel is right.'

'I know, but I do feel Max deserves the truth.'

Judging by the look on her face, Clemmie disagreed. 'Just remember this is someone who has turned up in your life again. I know you think you know him—'

'I do,' interrupted Dilly.

'But if he disappears out of your life that's another

person who knows the truth and secrets will always come out when you least expect it. I wouldn't be your best friend if I didn't warn you to be careful and not to rush into anything.'

Dilly knew exactly what Clemmie was saying because the very same thoughts had been turning over and over in her mind all night. 'But what if we do have a chance together?' As soon as the words left her mouth, she knew that was unlikely. He didn't want to bring up another man's child, let alone two of them. She pressed on anyway. 'And one day the truth comes out and I've been lying to him all this time.'

'Only you will know when you talk to him whether there's any chance of that happening, but does that conversation need to take place before you've had time to think about it a little more? And what did your dad say about the situation with your mum?'

Dilly exhaled. 'He thinks I'm deluded and have mistaken her for someone who looks like her. He thinks it's impossible that they could have survived the accident, and he said that even if she had lost her memory and come back to the island, everyone would know about it because everyone would recognise her.'

'I don't like to say it, but I agree with him.'

'I know, but there's still a tiny part of me that wants to believe it's her. But what can I do unless I happen to see her again?'

'Let's focus on the positives … my best friend is not only uber talented, a gorgeous person inside and out, but she is also the keeper of a lighthouse and is expecting twins! What I want to know is: when can we start shopping for the babies? And what's the plan about moving across to the lighthouse?'

'We can go shopping any time and as far as the lighthouse goes, I need the move across to be as soon as possible because I'm going to have to make one of the rooms a nursery for two and I need to get it all finished before I'm too fat to move.'

Clemmie laughed. 'Well, I'm free on Sunday and most evenings. I don't want you carrying anything heavy, and that's an order from Auntie Clemmie!'

'I won't, I promise, and thank you.' Dilly looked at her watch. 'I'm going to go and see Max now as otherwise it's going to be on my mind all day.'

'Good luck. You should also prepare yourself – our friends are already asking questions about why you were in hospital and it won't take long before word gets around.'

'I'm sure my dad will have told half the island by now. I'm not ready to talk about it but it's no secret now I know everything is okay, which is such a relief.'

Clemmie stood up and gave another squeal. 'Twins! Yikes!' They hugged before they walked down the stairs and Dilly locked the gallery door behind her.

Ten minutes later, Dilly set off for the boat house. The recent storm had left the air crisp and cool, and the bay, usually bustling with activity, was quiet for once. Dilly felt nervous about the conversation she was going to have with Max. She was still unsure whether to reveal the whole truth or hide the fact that Giles was the father.

As she approached the weathered wooden boat house, the conversation she'd had earlier with Clemmie was replaying in her thoughts. She knew Clemmie was right: the fewer people that knew, the better. But then her dad was right too; the islanders were family. She was still torn but decided that, when they came face to face, she would go with her gut. Taking a deep breath, she walked into the boat house. She couldn't see Max but noticed her dad was talking animatedly on the phone and looking stressed. As he hung up his call and spotted Dilly, his face softened.

'How are you feeling this morning?' he asked, giving her a hug.

'We are all doing just fine.' She patted her belly and smiled. 'But you look like you have the weight of the world on your shoulders.'

'I do,' he sighed. 'I have a big job coming in at the end of the week and now I'm a man down.'

'What do you mean? Where's Max?'

'He's gone without giving me any warning. I'm not happy about being left in the lurch. I thought he was a decent bloke, and only yesterday he was happy the job was coming in, as we talked through the restoration. I've no clue what the hell has changed overnight but I woke up to a garbled voicemail and all his things have gone from the flat.'

Dilly couldn't believe what her dad was telling her. The shock of hearing that Max had left hit her hard, especially as she knew it must be because of her and the revelation of her pregnancy. He likely couldn't bear the thought of her possibly reconciling with the twins' father. What he didn't know was that such a reconciliation would never happen.

'Do you know what time he left?' Dilly asked, trying to gauge how far he might have gone. She quickly dialled his number, but it went straight to voicemail. 'Damn,' she muttered.

'I've tried calling him too,' said Ralph. 'I just don't understand what happened in the last few hours to make him leave, especially when he felt so happy and safe here after...' Ralph stopped in his tracks.

'Lydia,' Dilly finished. 'I know all about her and how she's treated him.'

Ralph nodded. 'Yes, after Lydia, I thought he was finally starting to find some peace here, but then she tracked him down. Modern technology has a lot to answer for. I saw them last night when I got back. They were arguing on the harbourfront. I went over to make sure everything was okay and I heard Max tell her that it was the last chance for her to disappear from his life, otherwise he would take out a harassment order – and how would that look to her celebrity clients? I could see he was at his wits' end, but he was firm. He shot her down in flames and it was obvious she doesn't have a place in his life. I think it's possible he's moved on to get some peace and yet another fresh start, somewhere where she can't find him.'

Dilly took a deep breath. 'Actually, I suspect he's left ... because of me.'

Ralph raised an eyebrow. 'Why would he leave because of you?'

'Because we had a ... moment ... but now he knows I'm pregnant with another man's child.'

'A moment?'

Dilly didn't want to spell it out but there was no getting

away from it. 'We slept together. There's always been something between us, but we never crossed that line,' she quickly added, 'until a couple of nights ago. And I wasn't honest with him about the pregnancy.' She could feel herself getting emotional. 'And then he found out when the ambulance turned up.'

'Don't go getting upset. Things have a way of working themselves out.'

But Dilly didn't know how that was even possible if Max wouldn't pick up his phone.

Chapter Twenty-Three

Feeling heartbroken, Dilly decided against opening the gallery. She needed time to gather her thoughts and wanted the morning to herself. Instead, she headed towards the lighthouse and, as she opened the door, noticed a handwritten letter on the mat, addressed to her. As soon as she shut the door behind her, she ripped it open, her heart beating nineteen to the dozen. It was from Max.

Dear Dil,

I'm sorry to leave without saying goodbye. This is a conversation I know I should have faced in person but I'm not sure I could cope, with my heart already breaking. I wish you'd been honest with me before we slept together.
The short time we spent together will always hold a very special place in my heart and I'm truly happy for your pregnancy and the new adventure ahead of you. I've always wanted you to be happy and that will never change, but I

couldn't face seeing you with another man and making a life with someone else when my feelings for you are so strong. They always have been and always will be.

Love always
Max x

The words 'I wish you'd been honest with me' cut straight through her. She wished the same. If only Max had stuck around for a while longer and let her explain... She climbed the winding staircase to the top of the tower, stepped onto the balcony and leaned against the railing, letting the cool breeze wash over her.

The two cups and plates from the night before were still there, along with the binoculars, which were lying on the floor exactly where she'd dropped them when she ran down to the jetty. Dilly gazed at the ocean. She felt like she was riding a rollercoaster; one minute she was experiencing extreme highs and the next extreme lows. She rang Max's phone again. Once more it went straight to voicemail. She took a deep breath before blurting out a message.

'Max, there is no father. Well, there *is*, obviously, as I can't make a baby on my own, but it's not what you think. I can explain. I *want* to explain, and I would have explained. I came to the boat house to see you this morning but you'd already gone. I should have been honest with you and I'm sorry. It's always been—'

The phone cut her off before she could finish her message. She sighed. It felt like the road to love was just full of the worst goddamn potholes, and the second she passed one she had another to swerve round. But this time it felt like her tyre was well and truly burst.

For the next ten minutes she watched the comings and goings of the harbour. Now the sun was shining there were more tourists setting up camp on the beach.

At the end of the jetty, a car pulled up and then started to slowly drive down the road towards the lighthouse. It was a classic cherry-red 1965 Ford Mustang, with gleaming chrome bumpers and round headlights, and it looked like it had driven straight out of a sixties feature film. The car had a distinctive elongated hood, and the polished exterior reflected the sunlight, giving it an almost cinematic glow. She knew who the car belonged to, so when it parked she wasn't surprised to see Henry Snyder, the local historian, climb out, instantly recognisable in his signature attire. Whatever the weather, he always wore a tweed suit with elbow patches, a matching bow tie, and a homburg perched neatly on his head. His silver hair peeked out from under the hat, and his wire-rimmed glasses glinted in the light. Dilly guessed he must be in his mid-seventies. Once upon a time, Henry had been a journalist, the editor of the local newspaper, his articles rich with the history of the island. Now he was about to retire and lived in one of the charming pastel-coloured rainbow cottages on Lighthouse Lane.

Dilly watched curiously as Henry walked to the boot of the car and retrieved a cardboard box. Then he placed it in front of the lighthouse door and rang the bell. She hurried down the stairs to answer.

'Hello, Henry! How are you, and what have you got there?' she greeted him warmly as she opened the door wide and let him in. He carefully placed the box on a nearby table, then removed his hat and gave her a courteous nod.

'Good morning, Miss Dilly,' he replied, his voice rich with timeless old-world charm.

Dilly couldn't help smiling. She loved the way Henry called everyone 'Miss,' regardless of their age or status. It made her feel as though she'd stepped into a historical TV drama, the kind where she'd be dressed in an elegant gown, shielding herself from the sun with a delicate lace parasol.

'As you know, I love history and it's been a significant part of my personal and professional lives. But as the years are ticking on, I've started to have a clear-out, and I stumbled across this box.' He swung a glance around the lighthouse. 'Congratulations on your new home, by the way. It's a magnificent place to live and holds so much history for your family ... which brings me to the box.' He tapped the lid. 'I thought this belonged here.'

'What is it?' asked Dilly, intrigued.

'Every article I've ever written and every photograph I've taken of the lighthouse.' He lifted the lid and Dilly peered inside.

'Henry! This is a treasure trove of history,' she exclaimed excitedly. She picked up a photograph from the top of the pile. The image was faded with age, but Dilly recognised the two people standing in front of the lighthouse.

'Oh my goodness! This is a photo of my grandmother and grandfather,' she said, turning it towards Henry.

'Yes, I took that photograph on your grandfather's first day as the lighthouse keeper. It was a momentous occasion. The islanders lined the harbour all the way down to the bay and up Lighthouse Lane. He had the best send-off. Mack was a very proud man that day and your grandmother couldn't stop smiling.'

The photograph showed her grandparents standing in front of the lighthouse. Her grandfather looked dignified in his brand-new uniform. Her grandmother, wearing a modest yet elegant dress, stood with a hand resting on his arm.

'I used to be fascinated by the lighthouse and the storms. There are many photographs just of the lighthouse and the weather. I thought some might provide inspiration for your paintings.'

'Can I make a collage with the photographs for the new gallery?'

'You can do whatever you wish. I just thought they belong here.'

'Thank you, Henry, this means so much.'

'I also have something I want to ask you.'

'This sounds intriguing.' She noticed that he looked a little emotional.

'When I was a young boy, I was absolutely fascinated by the lighthouse, and when I was growing up your grandfather was one of my best friends,' shared Henry, his voice full of fond recollection. 'Every opportunity we got we spent exploring the rock pools, crabbing and swimming off the jetty. We'd race our kites up and down Blue Water Bay. Your grandfather was obsessed with the sea and I was captivated by the history of the island.'

Dilly listened, fascinated. She loved to hear tales about her grandfather. It was a glimpse into another era, when life was filled with simple joys.

'The very first article I ever wrote that was published was about your grandfather's first day as the lighthouse keeper,' Henry continued. 'It was a big moment for both of us. Mack was starting a new chapter in his life, and having my article published began my career as a writer.'

'No way, Henry! That's incredible!' Dilly exclaimed, genuinely amazed. She could see how much that moment had meant to him, and it made her appreciate the shared history of their families even more.

Henry gestured towards the box. 'You'll find that article in the box, along with photos. I was always around this area with my camera, capturing the storms and the sunsets, so there are lots of images for you to pick through.' He paused. 'There are also photos in there of the worst storm that Puffin Island ever witnessed. It was a night of terrible loss, but also one of incredible bravery. Your grandfather was a hero, risking his life to save others.'

This was going to be emotional for Dilly. She hadn't realised that night had been captured in photographs.

'It's about time I finally retire,' he said with a little chuckle, 'and I was wondering whether I could come full circle. My first published article was about your grandfather and the lighthouse, and so I would like my last published article to be about Mack's grand-daughter, the new lighthouse keeper, if that's okay with you?'

Dilly pressed a hand to her chest. 'Henry, you're going to make me cry. Yes, of course. That would be wonderful.' It would be an experience and an honour she could treasure for ever.

'Could I take some photos of you standing in exactly the same place as your grandparents?'

Dilly nodded, not trusting herself to speak, she was so close to tears. Henry walked back to his car and returned with his camera. He snapped a few photos of Dilly standing on the doorstep, shook her hand then tipped his hat. 'It'll be something to show the children.' He winked before turning and walking back to the car. Dilly watched as he pulled away and waved as he beeped the horn, before closing the door behind her. She stared into the box. She couldn't wait to sit down and go back in time, but first she was going to try to ring Max again. She dialled the number but it went straight to voicemail. 'Please ring me,' she said before hanging up.

Chapter Twenty-Four

The afternoon sun was glorious and Dilly decided to keep the gallery shut for the rest of the day. She needed to escape her usual routine and didn't feel like making small talk with prospective buyers. With her canvas and easel under her arm and a bag full of paints in her hand, she set off for a walk along the harbour where the boats swayed gently with the tide, their colourful sails flapping in the breeze. She checked her phone every two minutes in the hope that Max would ring, but there was nothing. Heading towards the sand dunes, she took off her shoes, feeling the warmth of the sand beneath her feet for a while before putting them back on and taking the coastal path.

At the very top of the cliff, just outside Cliff Top Cottage, was a bench overlooking the water, a favourite spot for locals because not many tourists ventured this far. She set up her paints then paused, taking in the panoramic view of the sparkling water, stretching into the distance under the bright afternoon sun. Surrounded by the sounds of nature – the seagulls crying above her, the waves crashing against the rocks and the puffins with their bold, colourful beaks mooing, a sound that always made her smile – she painted solidly for the next few hours.

'It's not very often I see you up here.'

Dilly spun round to see Pete leaning on the garden gate of Cliff Top Cottage.

'I thought I'd come and see the lighthouse from a different viewpoint.'

The gate creaked as Pete opened it and walked towards her. He joined her on the bench and pointed to the lighthouse.

'Over the years, I've watched that light shine out across these waters,' he began. 'I'm quite envious that you get to live there now.'

Dilly smiled. 'Henry came over earlier and gave me a box of old photographs of the lighthouse. It's filled with history. He said it would be something to show the children.'

Pete chuckled softly. 'That sounds like Henry, always thinking ahead. And yes, the news has spread. An ambulance arriving on the island doesn't exactly go unnoticed. Congratulations, by the way. How are you feeling about it all?'

Dilly took a moment, looking out at the puffins riding the waves. 'I'm happy,' she finally said. 'It's not something I ever anticipated for myself, being a single mum of twins, but it feels like a fresh start. A new home, a second gallery… I just wish my mum was here to share this adventure with me.'

Pete nodded. 'It's heartbreaking to lose someone so close,' he agreed. 'It's not something you get over quickly, but as time passes, the pain becomes less raw. You learn to live with it, and the memories become a comfort. Sometimes they even make you smile.'

Dilly appreciated Pete's words. She knew he understood, as he had lost his best friend to a rip current when they were in their early twenties. 'You knew my grandparents and my mother well, didn't you?' she began.

'I did,' Pete replied, a fond smile spreading across his face. 'Selby Sinton, your grandmother, was a mighty fine woman. Hardworking, straightforward, but fair. And she was never without her cherry-red lipstick. Your grandfather was the same – minus the lipstick, of course – and a rock for this community. And your mother, well, she had a spirit all of her own.'

'That's what I love about being part of this community. Everyone looks after everyone. I'm never alone.'

Hearing footsteps on the gravel they both turned and saw Betty approaching. 'That cliff path gets harder by the day,' she said as she held up a white carrier bag. 'Cake and scones from the tearoom. I thought I'd call in on my oldest friend as I've got the afternoon off.' Betty locked eyes with Dilly. 'Congratulations, Dilly! I'm not sure who is most excited, the newbie grandad or the godmother. Please tell me you'll get the babies christened? You'll likely have to, as Clemmie is already picking an outfit.'

Dilly laughed. 'That sounds like Clem!'

Betty leaned across and kissed her on the cheek. 'You are going to make a brilliant mother. Shove up,' she said to Pete then sat down next to him.

'Girls, too!' exclaimed Betty. Dilly caught Pete leaning forward as he shot Betty a subtle but warning glance.

Dilly knew exactly what was on Betty's mind. She wanted to ask the burning question that all the islanders would be asking: who was the father? But Dilly decided not to entertain the question. It was nobody's business except her own so there was no need for a make-believe story of a one-night stand.

Instead, she confirmed the detail that Betty was already aware of. 'Yes! Twin girls! I'm going to have my hands full for sure.'

Dilly could see Pete smirking at how she'd handled the situation. Now she had her own burning question to ask.

'Betty, I'm going to share something with you.' Dilly hesitated, knowing that she could be opening up a can of worms and Betty and Pete might think she was completely insane. Betty sat forward eagerly, hoping – Dilly suspected – it was information about the father. 'Something strange has happened that I can't quite explain. Not just once but twice.' Dilly had their undivided attention. 'I think I've seen my mum.'

The other two stared at her.

'And I don't mean I'm seeing ghosts.'

'What exactly *do* you mean?' asked Pete.

Dilly took a deep breath and began to recount her recent experiences. 'She had the same hair, walked the same, it was her. But, every time, she disappeared before I could reach her.'

Betty and Pete exchanged a glance, their expressions both concerned and confused.

'It was her,' Dilly said again, feeling a need to convince them. 'I know it sounds impossible, but the only explanation I can think of is that she survived the accident and maybe has amnesia.'

Pete spoke softly. 'Dilly, I know you want this to be your mum, but it seems very unlikely. It's probably someone who just looks remarkably like your mum, and you're in such a state right now that you're willing it to be her.'

'But I know what I saw… Betty?'

Betty, who was usually full of opinions and quick to speak, had gone quiet, and her face had paled.

'What do you think, Betty?' Dilly pressed, wanting to hear her thoughts.

Betty hesitated, glancing briefly at Pete then back at Dilly. Dilly noticed a flicker of something, maybe uncertainty – maybe even fear – in her eyes. 'I … I second Pete,' she said finally. 'It's probably just a case of mistaken identity. Someone who resembles her.'

'Do you know something, Betty? Have you seen her, too?'

Betty was quick to shake her head. 'We would know if your mum was alive.' She stood up abruptly. 'I need to get back. I'll catch you both later.' She started walking back down the coastal path.

'I thought we were having cake and scones,' Pete shouted after her but Betty was nearly out of sight. 'I'll never understand women,' he said, taking off his cap and mopping his brow with his hanky.

'Do you think Betty was suddenly acting very weird just now?'

'The majority of women I know act weird.' Pete chuckled.

But Dilly couldn't shake the feeling that Betty knew more. Betty had looked like she wanted to say something but then changed her mind. Why?

Chapter Twenty-Five

A fter finishing her painting, Dilly made her way back from the cliffs, craving a change of scenery. She'd decided to have her first sleepover at the lighthouse so she mentally ran through the list of things she'd need: a sleeping bag and pillow, a kettle, some provisions, and her favourite book. It was a simple plan, but it felt like a small adventure, a step towards embracing the new chapter in her life.

As soon as she walked into the gallery, she locked the door behind her and turned her gaze to the portrait of her mother, still resting on the easel. The painting was finished, and Dilly felt an immense sense of pride. It was so lifelike that Eva's eyes almost sparkled and her smile seemed so real. There was only one thing left to do and that was to sign the painting. The portrait was more than just a piece of art to her and would never be for sale, but it was going to be centre stage in her brand-new gallery.

She needed to sort out a few things on the business side

of her big life-change, starting with finding a staff member to manage the community gallery. Sitting down at her computer, she began drafting the job description. The role was crucial, as the person would be responsible, along with handling day-to-day operations, for assisting customers and liaising with local artists and colleges. Dilly carefully outlined the qualifications and responsibilities, emphasising the importance of passion for art, excellent customer service skills and knowledge of the local community. When she was satisfied with the wording, she posted it on her website and local social media groups. The position was to begin in two weeks' time, which gave Dilly plenty of time to set up the new gallery.

After she had gathered the items for her night at the lighthouse, she headed back down Lighthouse Lane.

'I've been looking out for you!' Amelia was standing in the door of The Story Shop and hurried over towards Dilly, giving her a hug. 'You are such a dark horse. Congratulations!'

'Thank you!'

'How, when, where?' asked Amelia.

'I think we're of the age where I don't need to draw you a diagram!' Dilly replied with a smile.

'I knew the second that Max Harrington walked into the gallery holding flowers. That spark between you both could light up the whole of Puffin Island. I just can't believe you managed to keep your relationship a secret without any of us knowing for months. God, he's gorgeous! And how beautiful are your babies going to be?'

Realisation dawned on Dilly. Amelia believed that Max was the father of her babies and that their relationship had been going on for a while. Dilly was taken back and, though she didn't know why, she didn't correct her.

'I congratulated him only minutes ago,' added Amelia. 'He looked like a proud parent-to-be too.'

Dilly's eyes widened in surprise. 'Say that again?'

'He was walking down Lighthouse Lane just a few minutes ago. Well, maybe more like ten minutes.'

That little piece of information hit Dilly like a tidal wave. She looked towards the bottom of Lighthouse Lane but there was no sign of Max.

Hastily, Dilly took off, juggling the items in her hands as she hurried towards the bay. 'I've got to go, catch up later!' she shouted to Amelia. Her heart was pounding; Max was back and she needed to talk to him.

Her eyes darted along the golden sand then towards the tables outside the Cosy Kettle, but there was no sign of him. She quickened her pace and headed towards the boat house. As soon as she arrived she dropped everything she was carrying. Her dad looked up. 'Where's the fire?'

'Max. Have you seen him?' she asked urgently.

Ralph shook his head. 'But if you do, tell him he's welcome back to work, because I'm already behind today.'

Dilly stepped back outside, scanning the surrounding area again. Damn. Where could he have gone? She picked up her things and headed towards the lighthouse. The best place to see across the bay would be at the top of the tower and she could use the binoculars. Once inside the lighthouse she grabbed a quick drink of water then climbed the steps to the top. She welcomed the breeze as soon as she stepped outside and perched on the bench, the binoculars trained across the bay. 'Where are you?' she muttered.

About to give up, she heard a loud whistle. She spun around towards the harbour and couldn't believe her eyes. Through the binoculars, she saw Max perched on top of the largest rock, waves gently lapping around it.

'What the...' she murmured to herself. He was waving something. Oh my gosh... It was the semaphore flags! Her heart skipped a beat as she realised what he was doing. He was going to send her a message.

Max began moving the flags. Dilly watched, her breath catching in her throat, as he spelled out his first message.

I A-M S-O-R-R-Y

A smile hitched on Dilly's face. She swallowed a lump. Max had chosen the most old-fashioned, heartfelt way to express his feelings. She fixed her gaze on him as he carefully spelled out:

B-U-T T-H-A-T-S N-O-T A-L-L

I D-O-N-T W-A-N-T T-O L-I-V-E W-I-T-H-O-U-T Y-O-U

Each letter laid his heart on the line. Happy tears blurred Dilly's eyes and she quickly wiped them with the back of her hand. Max wasn't finished. He began to hold up the flags again.

L-E-T-S M-A-K-E T-H-I-S W-O-R-K

By now, a crowd had gathered on the edge of the harbour, captivated by the man standing on the rock waving flags in the air. When the last message was spelled out, Max threw his hands up, waiting for her response.

Without hesitation, Dilly cupped her hands around her mouth and shouted from the top of her lungs. 'YES!' The word echoed across the bay and the crowd that had gathered erupted into cheers and applause. Max punched the air triumphantly, his grin wide, before putting the flags away in a duffle bag.

Dilly noticed her dad had been watching with a knowing smile from the doors of the boat house, and saw him shout to Max, 'Now can you get back to work? No, I'm only joking! You can have the rest of the day off.'

With a final wave to the cheering onlookers, Max tossed the duffle bag onto the shore and dived off the rock into the sparkling blue water of the bay. The crowd erupted into a fresh round of applause as he swam confidently towards the lighthouse. Dilly hot-footed it down the stairs and flung open the front door just as Max pulled himself up onto the jetty, dripping wet but beaming with happiness.

She ran towards him. Max flung his arms open wide and Dilly jumped straight into them. 'I feel like I'm in a movie!' she exclaimed. 'Eugh! You're all wet!'

Max smiled, holding her tightly. 'Sorry-not-sorry about that!' He tilted her head towards his and kissed her. 'I got your message.'

Another round of applause could be heard from the crowd gathered on the beach. Lost in the moment, Dilly felt her heart swell with happiness. Even though they had a lot to talk about, this was the start she wanted.

Chapter Twenty-Six

A few hours later, they were wrapped in each other's arms at the top of the lighthouse under the starlit sky. Dilly couldn't stop smiling. This morning her heart had felt like it had shattered into many pieces; now, miraculously, it had been put back together. The night was clear, and the stars shimmered above them like tiny diamonds, casting a soft glow over the makeshift bed they'd set up, which was surrounded by snacks and drinks. 'This is what you call a proper sleepover,' Dilly giggled as Max pulled her in closer, squashing a bag of crisps. She still couldn't believe that just a few hours earlier he had been standing on a rock, signalling his feelings with semaphore flags.

'How did you get the flags and when did you learn to use the flags?' Dilly asked, still amazed by the effort he had put in.

Max grinned. 'As soon as we saw them in the lighthouse, I Googled away and managed to buy a set from the internet then I started learning the different letters. I planned to signal to you every morning when you moved in.'

'How romantic!' Dilly exclaimed.

'How mad do you think your dad will be at me for going AWOL today?' Max asked, sounding a little concerned.

'As long as you're back at work tomorrow, I think he'll just be relieved.'

Dilly's expression turned serious. 'We do have a lot to talk about,' she said softly.

Max nodded. 'I know, I just didn't want to spoil the moment.'

'Can we talk about it now though? I don't want to fall asleep and have the conversation still hanging over us by the time you go to work tomorrow.'

Max squeezed her tightly. 'Who is the father of the babies?'

The question hung in the air for a split second whilst Dilly considered which version of events to share with him.

'Giles Fox,' she replied, opting for the truth. She leaned over to her bag, which was resting on top of the wicker basket.

'Why do I recognise that name?'

'He's been in the news recently.' She handed Max the folded-up article that she'd torn out of the newspaper. Max slowly took his arm from around her and read it.

'And this is the father of the twins?' Max asked, still looking over the article.

'Yes, unfortunately,' Dilly replied. 'He handpicked me as a mark for one of his schemes, making me fall in love with him so I would willingly hand over my inheritance money.'

'How did he even know you had any?'

'My mother and Anton's deaths were covered in the newspaper – you saw it yourself – and the article linked them to me, an up-and-coming artist from Puffin Island. He walked into the gallery, pretending he worked for a celebrity who'd fallen in love with my art. His plan was to sweep me off my feet and make me fall in love with him, and he was convincing, let me tell you. Soon we were talking about starting a family, buying a house together… At the same time, he was in the process of buying a property in the South of France.'

Max looked thoughtful. 'Let me guess, he suddenly had a cash-flow problem … that old scam?'

Dilly nodded. 'Exactly that. He said his money was tied up in bonds and it was taking too long to release and the buyer had decided to pull out if the contracts weren't signed by the end of the week. He was pushing me and pushing me to transfer him the money, as he didn't want to lose the property. It was then I got a feeling that something wasn't right, so I hesitated and he suddenly began to get agitated, which was out of character. Up until that point, he'd been gentle, loving, caring… It was a complete 360. He tried to make me feel guilty, saying that because of me he was going to lose the house, and he walked out in a rage. Whilst he was gone, I got the strong feeling he was hiding things so I quickly checked the pockets of his suits and found the article about my mother's death and my estimated inheritance. It really hurt that someone could try to scam me that way. Using my feelings to try and manipulate me into doing what they wanted. I still can't get over how someone can sleep with someone when they actually have no feelings towards that person at all.'

'Unfortunately, it's what they do, and they are bloody good at it. We both clearly chose the wrong partners.'

'At least now he's been caught.'

'And he's in prison,' added Max.

'Thankfully, yes. And it looks like he won't be out for a very long time, which, of course, I'm pleased about.' Dilly placed her hand protectively over her belly. 'I did think about a termination, especially for our sake, but then I was in the ambulance and the thought of losing my baby nearly killed me.'

Max looked confused. 'What do you mean?'

'When you told me about Lydia…' Dilly paused. 'You said you didn't want to raise another man's child. And now I'm going to have two of those.'

Max looked towards her and pushed his fringe out of his eyes, showing more of his face, which was tanned from the sun. Shaking his head slowly in disbelief, he smiled, sending a swarm of fireflies swirling at top speed around her stomach. He reached out, gently taking her hand. 'Dilly, believe me when I say that you are *nothing* like Lydia and this is a totally different situation. She lied to me and cheated on me for years, and I'm not sure if it was ever love I felt for her. You're a kind, gentle, loving soul, whereas she was the queen of manipulation. I would never bring up another man's child *with her*.'

'And me?'

'I'm sitting here, aren't I? I've just taken my life into my own hands by jumping off a rock and swimming to the jetty. I don't even like the water!'

Dilly giggled. 'All those tourists were cheering you on.'

'I do have a question though... Are you going to tell Giles about the twins?'

'I've thought about that a lot, too, and the answer is no. I'd have concerns about the safety of my children. Our relationship was over before he went to prison and I don't think it's beneficial to the twins to know a man like him is their father. I don't want any stigma attached to them as they grow up. How do you feel about it?'

Max took a moment. 'I think you're the mother and you know what's best to do. I'll support you, whatever you decide.'

'But how do you feel knowing that I'm pregnant by another man? Will your feelings change towards me once they're here?' Dilly took a breath. 'I vowed, after Giles, that it would be a long time before I gave any man the time of day again—'

'But I'm not just any man,' Max interrupted. 'We go back a long way and I think the best relationships are those made from friendship and shared history... And the mutual love of art helps,' he added with a smile.

'I agree, but this isn't going to be an easy journey. I don't want to get close to you and then wake up to find you've gone as it's all got too much. And I know this is extremely early days, but—'

'I'm not going anywhere.' Max took hold of her hands, his thumbs brushing over her knuckles. 'We can do this ... together. I've loved you in secret for many years already and my feelings aren't going to change. I didn't run because I don't care for you, I ran because I panicked. I thought this would be your chance to start a family with the father and, as much as I want you to be happy, I couldn't have watched that happen; it would have been too painful for me. But when I received your voicemails, I knew this was our chance. I don't see this as you bringing his children into the world, I see this as you bringing our new family together. It's not about who their biological father is, it's about who loves them and is there for them. Dilly, I want to be that person, if you'll let me.'

Dilly couldn't speak through all the happy tears that were rolling down her face. His acceptance and willingness to step up and be there for her meant the world.

'Yes,' she whispered, leaning in and kissing him.

Chapter Twenty-Seven

Waking up at the top of the lighthouse, with the sound of waves crashing against the rocks, brought a smile to Dilly's face. She was still snug in Max's arms. Last night had been magical; they'd made love under the stars and she hadn't wanted the night to end. As soon as her eyes opened Max kissed her on the top of her head. 'Good morning, sleepy-head. Would you like me to make you a cup of tea?'

'That would be lovely!' She unzipped the sleeping bag to let him out then chuckled as he stood up stark naked, stretched his arms out wide and shouted, 'I'm on top of the world!'

'Max! You have no clothes on! Someone might see you!'

'Who is going to see me right up here, except you and the seagulls?'

All of a sudden, they heard a voice shout back, 'Top of the morning to you!'

Startled, they both looked up to find that a vibrant

procession of hot air balloons were drifting gracefully across the sky and the men from the nearby basket were waving at them.

'Shit!' exclaimed Max.

Dilly chuckled. 'Oh my, they've just had an eyeful,' she teased, slapping his backside then handing him a pillow to cover up his modesty. They watched as the balloons floated gracefully above the sparkling harbour and over the lighthouse tower. 'Wow! What a sight!' Dilly exclaimed. She stood and slipped her arm around Max's waist, feeling the warmth of his body as they gazed up at the sky. 'It's the annual balloon race,' she added, her voice filled with excitement, as the breeze carried the balloons higher, their reflections shimmering on the surface of the calm sea below. 'Can this sleepover get any more romantic?' she mused, her heart swelling with happiness. The beauty of the moment, combined with the lingering warmth from their night under the stars, made everything feel perfect.

'I could make you some toast, too?'

'That would be lovely but there's no toaster.'

Max looked at the leftover snacks. 'Chocolate and tea it is!' With a mischievous grin, he began inching backwards, clutching the pillow like a makeshift shield. He grabbed his trousers and, as soon as he reached the top of the stairs, tossed the pillow aside. With a wicked grin, he turned and wiggled his bum in Dilly's direction as he disappeared out of sight.

Dilly laughed, shaking her head as she slid back into the warmth of the sleeping bag. Settling in, she turned her attention back to the sky and the balloons.

Max soon reappeared, holding a tray with two mugs of tea and the newspaper.

'You've had a delivery!'

'This should be the issue with Henry's article,' Dilly said as she unfolded the newspaper, spreading it across the floor in front of them. 'Aww, look, there's pages dedicated to Henry's life and everything he's done for the local community.'

Max slid his legs back inside the sleeping bag and placed the two mugs of tea next to them.

'Look at this,' said Dilly, pointing out the feature article.

Max leaned in, examining the headline and looking at the photo of Henry. 'That's exactly how everyone imagines a historian to look!'

'I don't think he's taken that hat off in the last five decades,' Dilly chuckled.

As they turned the pages, they came across Henry's first-ever published article, which had been revisited in the special edition. 'That's my grandfather on his first day as the lighthouse keeper,' Dilly told Max. 'I love how he's standing there so proudly next to my grandmother.'

'It must have been hard being the wife of a lighthouse keeper,' Max said thoughtfully. 'They must have been away for weeks on end, facing dangerous conditions.'

Dilly nodded. 'I suppose you have to accept the risks when you marry a lighthouse keeper. The sea can be both beautiful and treacherous.'

They continued flipping through the pages, sipping their tea as they read the stories and looked at the different photographs of Puffin Island. The next write-up caught Dilly's eye and she tapped the newspaper. 'Look at this section titled "Puffin Island's Worst Storm Ever",' she said. The page was filled with dramatic photographs, a black sky swirling around the lighthouse, a boat smashed against the rocks, the waves raging in the storm.

But there was a particular photograph that made Dilly stop in her tracks.

It showed a calm sea, in stark contrast to the stormy images around it. At the foot of the lighthouse was a small rowing boat and two women. 'That's my grandmother.' She leaned in to take a closer look. 'This must have been taken after the birth of my mum. She and Betty were heading back to the island, knowing my grandfather had been killed.'

Max looked at her, understanding in his eyes. 'It's incredible that Henry captured that moment on camera,' he said softly. The image was simple yet profound.

'This is more than just a photograph, this is my family's history. Did I mention that Henry gave me a box of photographs that he said belonged to me and the lighthouse? I've not had a real chance to go through them yet.'

'Maybe it's something we can do together, if you'd like that?'

Dilly nodded. 'That would be lovely. I plan to make up a wall full of the photographs in the gallery downstairs.'

'Sounds like a wonderful plan.'

'I think for the likes of Betty and Pete it will be a trip down memory lane, which will hopefully be nice for them. Today, though, I'm going to arrange a date for opening the new gallery.'

'There's no stopping you, is there?'

Dilly shook her head. 'I need to organise as much as I can before I get too fat to even move.'

Max laughed. 'You won't be fat, you'll be pregnant!'

'And will you still like me when I'm humongous?'

'Of course. It just means there will be so much more of you to love.'

Dilly's eyes widened with joy. 'Say that again.'

'There will be so much more of you to love,' whispered Max, pulling her in for a kiss.

In the gallery, Dilly settled at her desk to look through her emails. She was pleased to see several job applications had landed in her inbox, and she began to sift through them, hoping to find a candidate worthy of an interview. But as she read them, disappointment set in. No one stood out from the crowd. No applicant seemed to match what she was looking for, bringing a true passion for art and the local community. She sighed and moved the emails into a 'No' folder. Hopefully more applicants would fall into her inbox soon.

Dilly spent the rest of the morning wrapping her sold pieces of art and carefully leaning them against the gallery wall, ready for shipping. Then she began thinking about the layout of the new gallery. She wanted customers to be wowed as they walked through the door, and she had already decided upon a nautical theme that linked her whimsical paintings of the lighthouse and puffins with the history of the space. She envisioned different wall spaces, each telling a story of the sea and the lighthouse. The photographs of the previous lighthouse keepers would be rehung in the main gallery and the portrait of her mother – the only person to have been born in the lighthouse itself – would be the centrepiece of the collection, visible from the front window. Dilly could imagine exactly how it was going to look.

That evening she planned to sift through Henry's box of photographs, looking for images that could be used in a collage celebrating Puffin Island's heritage. For now, though, she began to plan her next painting. After this morning's spectacle it was definitely going to include hot air balloons drifting past the lighthouse. The colours would be bright, and she thought she might write the names of the previous lighthouse keepers across the baskets.

The door of the gallery swung open and Dilly looked up from the computer with a smile to greet the customer. In walked Max holding a toolbox and a cardboard box.

'What are you doing here? And what have you got there?' Dilly stood up and gave him a soft kiss on the lips.

'I'm under strict instructions to make you safe!'

'And what exactly does that mean?'

'Your dad is suggesting that we put up CCTV outside the lighthouse.'

'I was only thinking about that a few days ago. It's a good idea, especially with me having no neighbours as such.'

'There's been a delay in the next boat being delivered so your dad has offered a set of cameras that he was going to put up at the boat house. He said he can order some more. So if you want to give me the keys, I can get this installed this afternoon.'

'Brilliant, thanks so much!'

Dilly opened the drawer on her desk and pulled out a bunch of keys. 'You've actually saved me a job because I have the engineer coming out this morning to install the WiFi. I was waiting for his call and was going to have to close the gallery while I nipped across the bay.'

Max smiled warmly. 'Consider it taken care of. Oh, and before I forget, I've been congratulated numerous times.'

'Congratulated?' Dilly asked, puzzled.

'On our new arrivals… Amelia and Betty, and Becca at the Cosy Kettle yesterday.'

Dilly chuckled. 'Betty was dying to ask me yesterday who the father is, but I managed to dodge the question. Amelia congratulated me and…' Dilly scrunched up her face, feeling both guilty and amused. 'I didn't correct her when she suggested you were the father. It just seemed easier not to. I'm sorry. I should have and I will.'

'Well, what if you don't?'

'I was going to spin a story about having a one-night stand…'

Max raised his eyebrows. 'I'd leave them to think what they want; it might make it easier for us in the long run.' He pulled her in for a hug.

'And you don't mind?' She looked up at him.

'Completely honoured,' he replied, kissing her. 'Now I best get on with installing the cameras.' He took the keys and kissed her one more time before disappearing out of the door.

The gallery had been unusually quiet all morning so as one o'clock approached Dilly decided to lock the gallery doors for lunch and wander down to the lighthouse to see how Max was getting on. But just before she left, she decided to move the portrait of her mum to the lighthouse. Having swathed it in layers of bubble wrap, she carried it under her arm and the easel in the other hand.

As she approached the lighthouse, she spotted Max up a ladder. He had a screwdriver in one hand and was looking at the camera attached to the lighthouse wall. He looked over his shoulder as he heard Dilly approaching.

'The WiFi is installed and so is the CCTV, so you just need to download the app and you can view it anytime on your phone. If a person is detected it will automatically record. You can also set the time you wish it to record or have it running constantly.' Max climbed down the ladder. 'What have you there?'

'It's the portrait of my mum. I wanted to bring it across and set it up.'

They walked into the gallery. Placing the easel in a prime spot, she unwrapped the portrait with care, then took a look around. 'I'm thinking maybe a fresh coat of paint is needed in here before I start to move all the paintings across. Maybe white. What do you think?'

'It would take a couple of hours. I can get that sorted for you this afternoon?'

'Are you sure you can spare the time? Dad was run off his feet at the boat house yesterday – and anyway I'll need to buy the paint first.'

'The boat that was being transported for restoration has now been delayed until tomorrow so I'm sure, if there's nothing else pressing, I can do the painting this afternoon. And we have plenty of white paint at the boat house.'

'Eek! Thank you, it's all coming together!'

'Now, if possible, could you make the worker a brew while I set you up on the app and connect the CCTV to your phone?'

'Done!' said Dilly, handing over her phone.

Twenty minutes later they were sitting on the edge of the jetty, dangling their feet into the sea as they drank their tea.

'It sounds like we've both had quite a successful morning. If I can get the gallery painted this afternoon you could have the paintings hung by the weekend and your collage made.' Max looked through the open front door, where the portrait of Eva could be seen on the easel. 'What are you going to do about the sightings of your mum?'

'Maybe my dad is right. If it was her, then surely others would have spotted her too, and we both know how quickly news spreads on this island. So, unless I see her again, I'm not sure what I can do.'

Max nodded. 'It's a tricky one,' he admitted.

'But...'

'But what?'

'I'm probably over-thinking things but when I mentioned it to Betty, she went very quiet.'

'It's probably the shock of you saying you thought your mum had been on the island.'

Dilly looked at her watch. 'Maybe, but I feel there's more to it. I know you don't know Betty as well as the rest of us, but she carries the majority of the island's secrets and can usually be found in the thick of everything. If there's something to know, she's the person to know it. Anyway, I best be heading back to the gallery, even though I've kind of got the feeling I might be distracted this afternoon.'

'Why's that?'

Dilly flicked her phone on and brought up the security app. 'There are now cameras inside and outside the gallery allowing me to watch a gorgeous sexy man hard at work all afternoon.' She leaned against his shoulder then looked up and kissed him on his lips. 'I'll meet you back here after work. Shall we grab some food together?'

'Sounds like a plan.'

Dilly stood up and dried her feet with a towel before slipping on her shoes and heading back towards her existing gallery. Her life was finally coming together. If she could finish preparing the new gallery space by the end of next week, she could start to coordinate the transformation of her current gallery into a proper community gallery and art class space. However, that would depend on finding the perfect member of staff who matched her vision.

As she walked, she noticed her father sitting with someone outside the Cosy Kettle. 'Dad!' she called out, waving.

Ralph looked up and smiled. 'Hey!'

'Thanks for loaning Max to me for the day. The CCTV is up, and he's offered to paint the gallery this afternoon. I really appreciate it.'

'The boat we're working on isn't arriving until tomorrow,' Ralph explained.

'Yes, I know. It's perfect timing for me. There's so much to do, and having Max's help will make a huge difference.'

Dilly looked at the man sitting with her father. 'Luke!

What are you doing here? I thought you'd left to go travelling. You're not due back for another six months.'

Luke shifted uncomfortably, glancing between Ralph and Dilly. 'I'm here begging for my job back. Travelling wasn't for me. I became homesick, and as much as I wanted to see a bit of the world, there's no place like Puffin Island.'

Dilly found a chair and sat down. 'It's great to see you back, but, forgive me for asking, what does this mean for Max?'

Ralph sighed, looking concerned. 'That's what I'm trying to work out. Max is on a week-by-week contract, and he's such a hard worker. But I can't afford to pay both sets of wages. I'm going to have to try and come up with a solution.'

Dilly nodded thoughtfully. 'Maybe we can find a way to make it work. I know how much you value Max, and Luke has been a part of your team for so long. There has to be a way to keep them both. You might need to find a way to get creative with your budgeting.'

Ralph rubbed his chin, and turned to Luke. 'You've definitely thrown a spanner in the works.'

'Believe me, I understand. I know how difficult it is to find even one good employee and you have two.'

'Have you not had any applicants for the job at the gallery?'

Dilly shook her head. 'All the applicants I've had so far lack that something special. No one stands out from the crowd. I want to find someone with a real passion for art, who is community driven and someone I can trust implicitly.' She paused, looking around the familiar setting of the bay before locking eyes on Max, who was moving a set of ladders inside the lighthouse. 'It's not just about managing the gallery. I want someone who understands art, and can get passionate talking about it with the local artists I'm hoping will use the community space. The right person would make all the difference…' Her sentence slowed. 'I also need peace of mind when the twins arrive.' She was still staring at Max. Her eyes widened as she turned back towards her dad and Luke. 'You know what, Dad? I think I may just have a genius solution to both our problems.'

'Are you thinking what I'm thinking?' asked Ralph, flicking a glance between the lighthouse and his daughter.

'I'm thinking so. Shall I put the idea to him later?'

Ralph nodded, a relieved smile stretching across his face.

'Why is everyone talking in riddles?' asked Luke, clearly not keeping up with the conversation. 'And twins? Whose twins?'

Dilly stood up smiling and patted her tummy. 'I'm expecting!'

'I leave the island for a month and this happens. Congratulations!'

'Thank you,' Dilly replied. 'I've got to get back to the gallery, but I'll message you later.' She kissed her dad on the cheek before waving farewell.

As she walked back to the gallery, thoughts tumbled through her mind. Max should be putting his talents to better use than painting boats in the boat house. He would be the perfect manager for the new community gallery and event space. He knew art, had a deep appreciation of it and could even return to painting himself. He had the college contacts and he was brilliant at nurturing up-and-coming talent. He could even take over the regular art classes while she was on maternity leave, something she knew he would love and excel at.

The idea excited her and she was imagining numerous possibilities, maybe even collaborating on future projects. After all, he always knew the perfect addition to make her work even better. She was keen to put her proposition to him. She hoped he would say yes.

Chapter Twenty-Eight

D illy was itching to get back to the lighthouse. The day couldn't pass quickly enough. Half an hour ago a note had been pushed through the gallery door and landed on the mat. She ripped open the blush-pink envelope and smiled widely as she pulled out a card.

Delilah Waters is invited for dinner at the lighthouse at 7 p.m.

The message was handwritten in old-fashioned ink and the cover had a sketch of the lighthouse that had been filled in with watercolour. Dilly brought the invitation to her nose and inhaled deeply. Max's familiar scent lingered. She smiled.

After she closed the gallery, Dilly had an hour to spare before she was due to meet Max, just enough time for a soak in the bath. Earlier that day a parcel had arrived with some dresses Dilly had ordered that would allow her expanding waistline to expand some more. As she pulled one of the new dresses over her head, the material floated over her bump. It fitted perfectly. She stared in the mirror and gave a twirl. Her skin was glowing. In fact, it looked better than ever before.

Just before seven p.m. she slipped on her shoes and with a fizz of excitement she followed the path at the edge of Blue Water Bay towards the lighthouse.

She couldn't wait to find out what Max thought of her plans for the gallery community space – any more than she could wait to see the ground floor of the lighthouse with a fresh coat of paint. She had been tempted to check the cameras numerous times that afternoon, to see how it was coming along, but had managed to resist.

As she approached, she saw that the lighthouse door was open, but when she stepped inside, Max was nowhere to be seen. There was, however, a trail of paper arrows leading to the door at the back of the first floor that opened on the small enclosed garden. Dilly looked around the room in astonishment. The gallery space was all painted, and looked fresh and clean. Max had placed her mother's portrait on show in the window and had painted a wooden sign that read: 'New Gallery Opening Soon'. He'd done a wonderful job.

She followed the trail of arrows and when she opened the door to the garden, she gasped in amazement. At the far end of the garden was a charming bistro table and chairs, framed by glass panels that offered a breathtaking view of the ocean. The small courtyard was a burst of colour, with flower boxes and hanging baskets overflowing with vibrant blooms. A beautiful climbing rose wound its way up the trellis, and cheerful bunting was draped along the lighthouse wall. In a corner, a potted olive tree twinkled with fairy lights, adding a magical touch to the scene.

Max had gone to so much trouble, and it was absolutely perfect. The bistro table was draped in a crisp linen cloth, and tealights flickered gently atop the whitewashed wall, casting a warm, inviting glow.

'Dinner is served.'

Dilly spun around, her heart beating nineteen to the dozen. Max looked gorgeous as he pulled a chair out for her then poured her a glass of sparkling water.

'Max! All this is just beautiful. You've had a very busy day.'

'I have.'

'What are we having for dinner?' she asked, accepting a kiss on the cheek.

Max grinned. 'Fish pie, but this time with the fish.'

Dilly burst out laughing.

'Along with fresh greens and baked beans.'

'It really worked with the baked beans though, didn't it?'

Max nodded then disappeared, returning with two steaming plates of pie.

'This is all just amazing, and the gallery... I can't thank you enough.'

'It's been my pleasure. It's certainly made a difference. Everywhere feels fresh. I can paint the next two levels for you over the weekend.'

'Are you sure?'

'Of course! Now, how's the pie?'

Dilly tucked in. 'Definitely better with the fish!'

As they began to eat, Dilly couldn't believe how Max had transformed this little space into something off Pinterest. 'The flowers and the lights … how did you fit it all in?'

'The painting didn't take long, and Betty told me there was a plant sale over at the farm so I took a stroll to the other side of the island and picked up some lights, candles and bunting from The Nautical Nook.'

'And did you stop by the tearoom for something delicious?'

Max shook his head. 'No, Betty actually came here. She was acting a bit strange and she had Henry's newspaper article in her hand.'

'Why's that strange?'

'Remember how Henry mentioned in the article that he had given you a box of photographs, including pictures of the storm and the aftermath? Betty was adamant that I let her have a look at the photographs he'd given you.'

'And did you let her?'

'No, because they aren't my photographs. They belong to you, and you haven't had a proper chance to look through them yet. I told her to come and ask you about them, but she wasn't taking no for an answer.'

'What do you mean?'

'I had moved the box and the portrait to the back of the room while I was painting the front half. She noticed the box and asked if it was the one full of photographs. She actually started making a beeline towards it, so I had to literally turn her around by her shoulders and walk her back out the door, blaming the wet paint. Then, a couple of moments later, I came out here to paint that small wall.

When I walked back into the room, I couldn't believe my eyes ... she had come back in, and the lid was off the box.'

'You're kidding me!'

'No. So, again, I guided her to the door and told her to come back when you were home. This time, I locked the door behind her.'

'How utterly strange.'

'She was on a mission to look through those photographs for some reason.'

'As soon as we've eaten, we can take a trip down memory lane. Maybe we can figure out what she was so determined to see. It'll be good to take a proper look at Henry's photographs of the island through the years. No doubt he caught my grandparents in many of them.'

Just at that moment, a trill sounded on Dilly's phone, alerting her that the CCTV camera had been activated outside. 'It's probably Betty trying a third time to look inside the box,' joked Dilly. 'I turned off the notifications whilst you were working here this afternoon, but on my way over I switched it back on.' Dilly opened up the app and saw a couple walking up the jetty. They took a look through the gallery window before turning and walking away.

'At least you know it works and the picture is very clear. You can create different motion settings and for different times of the day, because if you're sat in this gallery you probably don't want it going off all the time and causing distractions. Any luck on applicants yet?'

Dilly set down her knife and fork. 'That was delicious. About the applicants – I'm glad you asked, as there's something I wanted to talk to you about,' she said with a huge smile on her face.

'Why are you looking at me like that?' He narrowed his eyes.

'Because I think I've come up with the best plan ever and I'm hoping you are going to love it as much as I do.' Dilly had a glint in her eye.

'Go on...'

Dilly explained how none of the applicants so far appeared to have the same enthusiasm for art as she did, and she emphasised that she wanted someone she could wholeheartedly trust to manage the community gallery. 'So, I've been thinking,' she said, 'how would *you* like to become the manager of the gallery in Quaint Quarters? You could possibly start painting again, too, and maybe do what you do best ... run the art classes. You are so good at nurturing talent, and you have good community contacts in Sea's End to spread the word about the classes. How fantastic would that be?'

Max sat in silence, absorbing Dilly's unexpected proposal. 'You're ... offering me a job?' he asked, sounding surprised.

Dilly's eyes sparkled. 'Don't you think it just makes sense? I'd say it's more like a partnership, a family business even. Your skills are far too valuable to be spent painting boats, and I know I can rely on you to run the gallery. Imagine converting the upstairs into a painting studio! You can teach art up there, set up classes ... and what a view for inspiration. What do you think?'

A huge smile spread across Max's face. 'Are you actually being serious?'

'Completely serious,' Dilly confirmed. 'It struck me today that you're the perfect candidate. You can think about it, of course, but I do need an answer pretty soon as I'm keen to get both galleries up and running as soon as possible.'

Max hesitated. 'What about my job at the boat house? I don't want to let your father down.'

'I'm going to be completely honest with you. Luke has arrived back home. Travelling wasn't exactly his thing and he got a little homesick. He can start back at the boat house ASAP, so it wouldn't leave my dad in the lurch.'

Max's brow furrowed. 'Is that the reason you're offering me a job? Because I don't want you to feel you need to, just because your dad may get rid—'

'Don't be ridiculous,' she said, her tone leaving no room for doubt. 'You are the best man for the job. You love and teach art and in this role you can get back to what you do best. I really do think we can achieve so much together, in so many ways...' Dilly stopped talking and rested her hands on her stomach. The smile dropped from her face.

'What is it? Are you having pain again? Shall I get help?'

Dilly gasped and her heart skipped a beat. 'Quick, come here.' She reached out for Max's hand, urging him to join her. He stood up swiftly and Dilly placed his hand gently on her stomach. 'It's the babies, I can feel movement,' she whispered, her voice trembling.

'Oh my gosh, I felt that!' Max exclaimed, his face lighting up as he stared at her stomach. 'And again.'

Happy tears welled up in her eyes as she watched his reaction. She placed her hand over his. 'Hello, little ones, is that one of you or both of you?' she murmured. A rush of emotion flooded her, an exciting blend of delight and awe at the tiny lives growing inside her. 'They're real,' she exclaimed, pulling Max in for a heartfelt hug.

'And they'll soon be here,' he whispered. 'I don't need to think about the job, Dilly.'

Dilly pulled slowly away from the hug and met his gaze. 'Is that a yes?'

'I can't think of anything I would like better.'

Chapter Twenty-Nine

After dinner, they washed up the dishes and decided to take the box of Henry's photographs and articles to the top of the tower, where they could sift through them while watching the sunset. Max carried a tray of drinks and some biscuits, and soon they were sitting on the bench, listening to the gulls and puffins calling from the cliffs. 'So, what are we doing with the photographs?' asked Max.

'I think if there's any that stand out, showing the lighthouse or even the keepers, we should put them to one side so I can include them in the exhibition when we open up downstairs,' Dilly replied as she opened the box.

'Oh my, look at some of these,' she exclaimed. 'This is Betty … in a dress! Not something I've seen in my lifetime. Gosh, it's a classic 1950s dress with a full skirt, and she's carrying a delicate parasol. She looks stunning! And that's Eric, her husband; he's no longer with us. It looks like some dance on the beach. Doesn't she look so young? And here's my grandparents, waving from the top of the tower. It's strange to think they were standing right there.' Dilly looked to the exact spot where they were standing in the photograph. 'I know it sounds daft, but I do feel close to them whilst I'm here.'

'It doesn't sound daft at all.'

As they worked through the photographs, each one seemed to come to life. They were amazed by the clothes the islanders wore, how old-fashioned the shop-fronts on Lighthouse Lane looked compared to today, and the fact that the fishmonger's wasn't a hut near the bay; according to the photographs and articles, they used to sell the fresh fish from a boat on the harbour!

'It's fabulous to go back in time like this,' Dilly observed as they looked at each photograph in detail.

'It's such a treasure trove,' Max said.

As the sun began to set, Max extended his arm along the back of the bench and Dilly snuggled into his chest. The sky was breathtaking and the horizon ablaze with hues of fiery orange and deep crimson, gradually blending into shades of lavender and dusky blue as the first stars began to twinkle. The soft calls of the gulls quietened and the lapping of the waves gentled against the shoreline.

'I've had a lovely evening,' said Dilly.

'Me too.'

'I can't wait to move in properly.'

'I'm sure over the weekend we can get most of your things moved across and you can start to think about how you want the nursery decorated.'

'We've got loads to shop for. I'm really excited about it all.'

'Me too,' replied Max, kissing her forehead before he

bent down to tidy away the photographs. 'There's another envelope in here.' He picked it up and Dilly noticed the title on the front: *Ten Photographs from the Worst Storm to Hit Puffin Island*. He handed her the envelope and she took out the snaps.

'That's strange. There are only seven photographs in here.' They stared at the images, each one so vivid and full of life: a boat crashing against the rocks, the lighthouse's beam cutting through the dark sky, lightning forking dramatically across the bay.

'It's so sad thinking about all those people who lost their lives that night, including my grandfather,' Dilly said, swallowing a lump in her throat. 'Look at this one.' The photograph showed a light through a window, with a woman looking out. 'Wow! What a photograph. That's probably the room where my grandmother gave birth, as that looks like Betty. That's definitely one to include in the collage.'

'It's unbelievable how history has been captured on camera film,' said Max, flipping through the remaining photographs.

'I wonder where the other three photographs are. It says ten on the envelope.'

'You never know, Henry may have given a few to your grandmother.'

'I suppose that's possible,' she replied. 'These are the photographs I'm going to use for the collage,' she said, holding a few up, 'and these I'll put back in the box for now. But I do want to try and use some of these images in my future paintings.'

'Good idea.'

They were beginning to clear away the mess they'd made when they heard the screech of car tyres, an unusual sound at this time of night on the island. They exchanged puzzled looks, wondering what was going on, and Dilly stood up and looked over the balcony railing. 'It's Betty's car driving away at high speed. What is that all about?' She looked at Max. Both of them were mystified.

He gestured towards her phone. 'The cameras likely picked up something. Why don't you take a look back?'

'You're not just a handsome face, are you? Excellent idea.' She picked up her phone and opened the app. Her eyes widened as she stared at the screen. 'I wasn't going mad,' she murmured, her voice barely above a whisper.

'What is it?' asked Max, leaning in as Dilly held the phone between them. 'Who's that?' he asked.

'That's my mother,' Dilly replied, her voice trembling. 'She's staring at the portrait of herself through the lighthouse window. She recognises herself. Max, she's alive.' Dilly's heart pounded so fiercely she felt like it might burst out of her chest. Her hands were shaking, and shock and disbelief were overwhelming her. For so long, she had believed Eva was dead, and now she had CCTV footage confirming she was alive. Her mind raced with questions and emotions, joy, confusion, hope, and fear all mingling in a dizzying swirl.

'Rewind the footage a little more.'

They watched Betty's car begin to drive down the road towards the lighthouse. Betty jumped out, leaving the door wide open and the engine running. 'What's going on?' asked Dilly, as they saw a short conversation between Betty and her mother. 'Does the video have sound?'

'It should do,' replied Max.

Dilly turned up the volume on her phone but it was inaudible. 'Damn.'

Just then the two women hurried to the car, and Betty took off at high speed. Dilly held Max's gaze, her eyes wide with astonishment. 'I didn't dream that, did I?'

Max shook his head as Dilly played the video back again.

'She's alive. Oh my God, she *is* alive and you've seen it and Betty knows. I'm not going mad.' Dilly stood up abruptly.

'Where are you going?' Max asked.

'Over to Betty's. My mum is there. I need to see her,' Dilly replied, hugging Max tightly. 'She's survived. She could be traumatised. She might not remember who she is or me...'

'There's only one way to find out,' Max said, as they hotfooted it out of the lighthouse and across the bay towards the tearoom. The urgency of their steps matched the frantic beating of Dilly's heart, each step bringing her closer to a long-awaited reunion.

As they ran, Dilly dialled her dad's number. 'Dad,' she said, breathless, 'Mum's alive and she's at Betty's. Dad! I've seen her. Get over there.'

It took less than five minutes to reach the tearoom. Betty's car was parked outside. 'They're here,' said Dilly, racing around the back of the tearoom to the front door of the cottage. She rang the bell and waited eagerly.

'Are you sure you want me here? It might be better if you see your mum on your own.'

'I want you here,' Dilly replied, looking at the front door

and willing it to open. She rang the bell again. Still there was nothing. She moved towards the window. The curtains were drawn but she could see through a small gap between them. 'She's in there. Oh my God, she's actually in there. She and Betty are just sitting still. Why aren't they opening the door?'

Max took hold of her hands. 'We don't know what's going on here. Maybe your mum has lost her memory and doesn't know where she is or even who Betty is? We may have frightened her by knocking on the door.'

Dilly began to feel anxious. 'Do you think I should call Dr Sandford?'

'I think we need to see if anyone opens the door. What did your dad say?'

'He's on his way back from Sea's End. He can't quite believe it.' Dilly impatiently rang the bell once again. 'Where is Anton? Did he survive, too? Betty knows someone is at the door because she keeps looking towards the window. Mum looks well, her hair is exactly the same and she's wearing her favourite shade of lipstick.' She banged loudly on the door, her frustration getting the better of her. 'Betty! I know you're in there,' she shouted through the letterbox. 'Let me in.'

Max was still looking through the gap in the curtains. 'Betty is moving, I think she's coming to the door.'

'Finally!' murmured Dilly.

Betty opened the door and peered around it. 'Is everything okay? It's getting late.'

'Betty, you're acting like you don't have my mum sitting in your living room, very much alive,' Dilly shot back, not waiting for an answer. 'We saw you at the lighthouse.' She pushed past Betty, followed by Max, who apologised profusely.

Dilly burst into the living room. 'Mum, oh my gosh, it's you! It's really you. You're alive and home.' She launched herself at her mother, hugging her tight. Tears began falling down Dilly's cheeks, relief sweeping through her.

But her mum looked bewildered and Dilly immediately sensed that something wasn't quite right. She turned to Betty and noticed that she wasn't sharing Dilly's enthusiasm. Instead of showing joy or relief, her expression seemed tense and guarded.

Dilly's words tumbled fast as she turned back to her mother. 'Where have you been? Where's Anton? I knew you were alive, I just knew it.'

The woman was visibly upset and shaking but she didn't take her eyes off Dilly.

'Mum, please say something.'

'I'm so sorry, I'm not your mum.'

'Don't be daft, of course you are. You've just lost your memory. That's it, isn't it, Betty? We need to call the doctor.'

Betty shook her head.

'Why are you shaking your head at me? Mum's back! This is nothing short of a miracle. No one thought you'd survive the sea, but I said you were a good swimmer and would have got to safety.'

'I'm sorry, I'm not your mum,' the woman repeated. 'I'm Annie.'

'Annie? No, you're Eva, my mum. You must recognise me? I'm Dilly, your daughter.'

'Dilly, I think you'd best sit down.' Betty turned towards

Max. 'Would you go and make four cups of strong tea? I think we're going to need it.'

Bewildered, Dilly sat down, unable to stop staring at Annie. 'What is going on here? I don't understand. You look like my mum, you sound like my mum…' She was close to tears. 'Have you lost your memory? Because I'm sure we can get you help.'

'I never thought I would ever have to have this conversation. I'm so sorry,' Betty began, her voice faltering, 'but this is Annie, daughter of Frank and Violet Bettencourt. Frank was the keeper of a lighthouse on the coast of Devon before he retired.'

Max returned and carefully placed the tray, holding the teapot and mugs, in the centre of the coffee table.

'This doesn't make any sense,' said Dilly, full of anguish.

'I'm not sure where to start,' admitted Betty. 'I appreciate this is going to be difficult for both of you.'

Dilly's pulse was racing as she watched Betty walk to the dresser in the corner of the room. She opened a drawer, took out three photographs and held them against her chest as she turned around. Then she placed them in the middle of the coffee table and Dilly saw that they were photographs of the night of the storm.

'Did you get these photographs from Henry?' asked Dilly. She saw that Betty's face was drained of all colour.

She shook her head. 'I'm sorry, I stole them from the box that Henry gave to you.' Betty looked guiltily towards Max. 'When I sneaked back into the lighthouse and you were out the back.'

'Why did you want the photographs enough to steal them? Why was that even necessary? I would have given them to you if you'd only asked. I know you were close to my grandparents.'

Betty hesitated. 'Because there was something I didn't want anyone to see. I'm so sorry –' she handed one of the photographs to Dilly '– but it's time…'

Dilly stared at the photograph, which was similar to the ones she had already seen. It showed two women climbing down a ladder, and a rowing boat with a man onboard waiting for them below.

'Is that Eric?' Dilly asked.

Betty nodded.

Dilly passed the photograph to Max. 'I don't understand what you're trying to tell me. Why would you steal these, for what gain?' She looked between Annie and Betty.

Max was staring intently at the photograph. 'There's two babies,' he shared. 'Betty and Selby are each carrying a baby.'

Dilly looked at the photograph again. Max was right. Each woman was carrying a baby. The next photograph Betty handed over showed the two women sitting in the rowing boat, each cradling a baby. 'Whose babies are they?' Dilly stared at Betty.

'Selby's.'

Dilly gasped. 'My grandmother had twins?'

Betty nodded, her eyes filled with tears. 'Yes, that night Selby gave birth to twins.'

'I've only found out recently,' said Annie. 'I still live by the lighthouse, in a cottage on the coast of Devon, and something strange happened to me a short while back. I was walking my dog on the beach and someone called me Eva. They said they'd seen an article about me in the newspaper and couldn't believe I was alive. I told them I wasn't the person they took me for. I just assumed it was a case of mistaken identity and never thought anything of it again. But both of my parents have very recently passed away –' she opened her bag and pulled out another photograph '– and I discovered this in their belongings. It has the name of the lighthouse written on the back and my name and date of birth. My parents never told me I was adopted, so it came as quite a shock, but they were the loveliest of people and I've had a good life, full of love.'

Dilly's mouth fell open. She had so many questions.

'How did one twin get adopted? Who made that decision, and why would that even happen? My mum couldn't have known she had a twin because she would never have kept that information to herself.'

Betty looked distraught. She closed her eyes briefly, as if trying to summon the strength to continue. 'You have to remember, the 1950s were not like today.'

'But it wasn't as though my grandmother was an unmarried mother. Surely there was no disgrace brought on the family. Her husband was killed, and Grandad was hailed as a hero.' Dilly felt her voice rising and Max placed a supportive hand on her knee.

'No one knew there were two babies except me and Eric. Selby didn't know she was expecting twins. She gave birth to the first baby just as Eric knocked on the bedroom door. Selby, as you can imagine, was completely distraught to hear about Mack's disappearance. She began to wail instantly, and I was holding her in my arms, rocking her gently, when she suddenly pushed me off. She was screaming that she was dying and was in so much pain. I honestly thought it was the grief that was consuming her. Eric and I didn't know what to do. And then, all of a sudden, Selby wanted to push again. The contractions were coming thick and fast and to our astonishment she gave birth to a second baby.'

Dilly's mind raced, trying to absorb the magnitude of this revelation.

Betty took a tissue from the box and dabbed her tears away. 'When we got back to the mainland, Selby faced the fact she couldn't bring up two babies on her own. She had no money and nowhere to live. She was heartbroken, but she knew she had an impossible choice to make.'

Dilly looked across at Annie who was clutching her mug of tea like her life depended on it. 'This must be hard for you to hear, Annie.'

Annie nodded, silently taking it all in.

'All the lighthouse keepers' wives were in a postal group,' Betty explained. 'We would pick a wife and write her a letter once a week. It was a way to keep our morale high since it was tough with the keepers being away so much. Frank had been an assistant keeper at Puffin Island before he got promoted to principal keeper and moved to Devon, and Violet and Selby had maintained a close friendship even after Frank's transfer. But then, the day after Mack's death, right when Selby was in the midst of trying to figure out what to do, she received a letter with the sad news that Violet's baby had died during labour. Selby was the first person Violet told. Knowing that this could be the answer to her prayers, Selby made the telephone call that would change everything.'

'I can't quite believe this,' murmured Dilly.

'We met with Frank and Violet just before Mack's funeral. It was a heartbreaking decision for Selby, and believe me it completely broke her, but she felt she was doing the best thing for her twins as she couldn't afford two babies. Violet and Frank were such lovely, decent people, and Selby knew that the baby she entrusted to their care would have a good life.'

Annie's eyes were filled with tears. 'It must have been such a difficult decision. I can't even imagine what Selby was going through, losing her husband like that. It must have broken her heart.'

'It did,' confirmed Betty.

A question was burning inside Dilly, and she knew it might bring distress to Annie, but it escaped her lips before she could stop it. 'How did my grandmother decide which baby to give away?'

Betty looked pained, and placed her hand on her chest as if steadying herself. 'Selby couldn't make such a heart-wrenching choice.' Her voice faltered and she dabbed her eyes again, her lip trembling. 'She asked me and Eric to make the decision, but I couldn't do it either. We watched as Selby dressed the babies in exactly the same clothes and laid them side by side, then the doorbell rang. It was Frank and Violet. Selby turned towards Eric and asked him to take a baby and give her to her new parents. Selby went to the back room and sobbed. As soon as the front door shut behind them Eric brought Selby the remaining baby. She called her Eva, as that was her mother's name.

'The next day was Mack's funeral. Frank attended but Violet didn't. Frank shared the news that she had given birth to a baby girl they'd named Annie. It was a lovely touch,' Betty said, turning to Annie, 'because Annie was Mack's mother's name.'

The tears were streaming down everyone's face now. Dilly and Betty went over to Annie and the three women embraced.

'Please believe me when I say Selby thought it was the only way to ensure both babies had a chance of a good life. We never meant for it to become such a painful secret. It was a different time, and we were doing what we thought was right under extraordinary circumstances.'

The room was heavy with decades of revealed secrets, but a newfound warmth began to spread as Dilly spoke. 'But now we're reunited. I know my mum would have loved having a sister and now I get to have an auntie. We have so much to catch up on.'

Annie's eyes shimmered with tears as she took both of Dilly's hands in hers. 'We do. I'm sorry for your loss, and I'm so sorry I never got to meet Eva, but if you'd like, I can be a part of your life and family.'

Tears brimmed in Dilly's eyes. 'I would love that so much.' They embraced again before sitting back down.

'This is all such a shock, I don't even know where to begin. Tell me all about you. Do you have any children?' Annie asked Dilly.

Dilly grinned, patting her stomach and glancing toward Max before answering. 'We're expecting twins.'

Annie gasped, her face lighting up with joy. 'Such wonderful news! I can't believe it!'

'And,' Dilly continued, her smile growing, 'I've just bought the lighthouse and hopefully will move in this weekend. It's unbelievable that you and my mum were born there, and now my own twins will live there. It feels like my family's history is coming full circle.'

Annie's eyes sparkled with tears of happiness as she squeezed Dilly's hands. 'It's like fate has brought us back together.'

'Can I ask, how did you know to come to Puffin Island?'

'After the person had stopped me on the beach, I Googled Eva's name and was amazed to see my own face staring back at me. After a little more research, I discovered that she had once lived on Puffin Island and I came to visit, not knowing what I might find. And then, when I saw the portrait of Eva in the gallery window, I knew it definitely wasn't a coincidence. I was plucking up the courage to talk to the artist but when I discovered it was you, Eva's daughter, I didn't want to frighten you by showing up out of the blue, looking like your late mum.'

'That's when I spotted Annie, looking through the lighthouse window,' added Betty, 'and realised who she was.'

Dilly turned to Betty. 'You are definitely the keeper of secrets on this island.'

Betty raised her hands in mock surrender. 'I swear, I don't know how I always find myself in the thick of things. Wrong place, wrong time. Sometimes it feels like a talent.'

Dilly raised an eyebrow. 'But you don't know anything else … right?'

Betty paused dramatically. 'Well, except…'

Everyone held their breath, eyes wide with anticipation.

Betty smiled. 'Just kidding!'

'You had us going for a second!' admitted Dilly. Just

then they heard the front door open and Ralph's voice shouting, 'Dilly!'

'In here, Dad.'

Ralph walked through the door. He stared at Annie and his mouth fell wide open. 'Oh my gosh, Eva, you're alive. I can't believe it!'

'Dad, it's not Mum. This is Annie, Mum's twin sister.'

Ralph looked puzzled.

Betty stood up. 'I think we all need something stronger than tea. Ralph, sit yourself down. I'll get the whisky.'

Chapter Thirty

Five months later

Dilly was up with the gulls, sitting in the new gallery at the lighthouse, just a couple of hours before it was due to open. The soft light of the day was already filtering through the windows, casting a golden glow on the artwork that adorned the walls. Dilly loved this time in the morning when she could sit at her desk enjoying a cup of tea. The familiar clang of the letterbox sounded and the national Sunday newspaper landed on the mat with a thud. She hurried to pick it up, her heart racing with anticipation. She flipped through the pages, her eyes scanning for the headline she knew would be there.

TWINS BORN AT PUFFIN ISLAND LIGHTHOUSE AS HISTORY REPEATS ITSELF.

Her thoughts drifted back to a week ago, to the night the twins were born, a night marked by a storm that would go down as the second worst that Puffin Island had seen in seventy-five years.

The island had been battered by relentless winds and rain. On the eve of the storm, Max was still living above the boat house, their plan having been to move him in the following day. Even though Dilly had wanted him to move in at the start of the relationship, she also wanted the time to date and enjoy the first flush of love. There had been something magical about the nights they'd spent apart and she'd cherished waking up alone in the lighthouse and glancing out of the window to see Max across at the boat house. He would greet her with a playful message using the semaphore flags, their private romantic code that made her heart skip a beat every time. It had become a charming ritual that she loved, and they had fallen into a way of life together that felt effortless and right.

Still, she had been looking forward to his moving in, and being able to wake up and see his smile in her bed, rather than across the bay.

The wind was howling that day and Dilly had had a niggle in her belly all morning. The Braxton Hicks were playing havoc across her stomach, leaving her uncomfortable. With a throw wrapped around her shoulders, she'd sat on the bedroom floor using the binoculars to watch Max. He'd somehow known she was watching as the signal soon came: the three flashes of light telling her he was about to send his last message via the semaphore flags from the boat house.

I L-O-V-E Y-O-U

She'd smiled. Even though Max had shared those words with her out loud, he'd never spelled it out via the flags. She'd known he was waiting for her return message so she'd bent down to pick up the flags … and taken a sharp breath.

'Woah!' she'd said as the tightening across her chest took her breath away and she felt a warm, unexpected rush of wetness spreading down her legs. Her eyes widened as she realised that her waters had just broken.

As soon as the contraction eased, she'd thrown open the window to give Max a clearer view of the message. The wind howled and the rain was lashing down as she spelled it out.

H-U-R-R-Y B-A-C-K I-M I-N L-A-B-O-U-R

Max had been looking at Dilly through binoculars and as soon as he'd deciphered the message he'd dropped them and sprinted across the harbour towards the jetty.

'The babies are coming!' Dilly had gasped as he rushed through the door. She clutched her stomach as another contraction rippled through her, making her knees buckle.

Max had grabbed her hand. 'Dil, the causeway is closed. The tide is in. The storm is raging, and we can't get you to the hospital.' His voice was panicked.

'Call Betty. She's done this before!'

Soon the lighthouse was alive with activity as a long line of people hurried up the jetty, battling against the howling wind and sheets of rain. Ralph, Betty, Annie and Clemmie had burst through the lighthouse door, their clothes soaked, faces flushed with urgency and determination.

As Ralph set about making tea to steady everyone's nerves, Betty and Max had disappeared up the spiral staircase to the bedroom. For over an hour, the group downstairs had waited until finally, through the howling wind, they'd heard the cry of newborns echoing down the staircase.

'We have two healthy baby girls!' Max had shouted down to the others. 'Mother and babies are both doing well.'

Now, hearing a rap on the door, Dilly was pulled from her memories.

'Aunt Annie!' she exclaimed as she opened the door. She kissed her aunt on both cheeks.

'I'm reporting for duty!' Annie announced cheerfully as she slipped off her coat and hung it on the stand at the back of the gallery. Since discovering her new family, Annie had taken a bold leap, moving all the way from Devon. She was now renting Seaside Cottage, the very place where Selby had lived her whole life after moving from Lightkeeper's Cottage.

'Thank you again for helping to cover for me while I'm on maternity leave.'

'I'm loving every second of it,' Annie replied, her gaze drifting to the painting of Eva. As with anything noteworthy on Puffin Island, the news about Selby having had twins had spread quickly, and although it had initially shocked the community, they had welcomed Annie with open arms. In just five months, Annie had become an integral part of Dilly's life, and her support had been invaluable.

'And where are the beautiful babies? Can I grab a cuddle before I open up the gallery?'

'I think they're still sleeping but we'll all know the second they wake up.'

'And do we have any names yet?'

'Not yet, Aunt Annie, but soon! I'll go and get myself ready. Here's the keys to open up – and thank you again, you've been amazing. Oh, and take a look at the newspaper!'

Dilly climbed the spiral staircase to the nursery and as she gently pushed open the door, a wave of pure joy washed over her. Max was fast asleep in the armchair in the corner, both babies nestled snugly against his chest.

Max had embraced fatherhood with such ease, effortlessly changing nappies, feeding the babies and grabbing cuddles wherever possible. He stirred and opened his eyes, a warm, sleepy smile spreading across his face. 'I can't move,' he whispered, careful not to disturb the twins.

'That is such a picture of happiness,' Dilly replied, laughing softly. 'How long have you been there?'

'For a few hours, but I don't mind, you needed your rest. I think Twin One needs her nappy changing.' He wrinkled his nose.

'Aunt Annie's just arrived and she's asked me about names again.'

Max's eyes twinkled as he continued in a hushed tone, 'You do know everyone's expecting us to announce their names at this afternoon's family dinner? We can't keep calling them Twin One and Twin Two.'

Dilly nodded. 'I know and I've been thinking ... I like

Selby Eva and Violet Annie. Four strong, remarkable women. What do you think?'

Max looked down at the twins then back towards her. 'I think that's perfect.'

She leaned down to kiss him on the top of his head and then each baby's forehead. 'Selby and Violet, which one of you will be the most trouble?' she mused aloud.

Max's smile widened. 'I don't think these two will ever be trouble.'

Gently, Dilly picked up Selby and placed her in the Moses basket whilst Max changed Violet's nappy. After Violet was placed in the basket next to her sister, Max wrapped his arm around Dilly's waist, drawing her close. Together, they watched their daughter's sleep.

'Even their breaths sync,' noticed Dilly, watching the gentle rise and fall of their chests. 'Could you have ever imagined, five months ago, that we'd be here … together … living in a lighthouse and watching the most beautiful set of twins sleep?'

Max squeezed her. 'Not in my wildest dreams. But here we are, living the most perfect life.'

Just at that moment, Selby stirred and let out a cry that quickly awakened Violet. The twins' cries soon grew louder and more insistent, as if they were in a playful competition.

Dilly's laughter bubbled up. 'It's Selby who's going to be the troublemaker. I can feel it!'

Max, with a grin, declared, 'I'll get the bottles. It's all hands on deck!' His voice rang with enthusiasm as he dashed towards the kitchen.

In that moment of joyous chaos, surrounded by the comforting glow of their lighthouse and the unwavering love they shared, Dilly knew that their life together would be an adventure filled with love, laughter and the occasional challenge, and she was going to embrace every moment of it. She brimmed with love for her family and the life she had created.

'I love you, Max Harrington,' she shouted.

'I love you, Dilly Waters,' Max shouted back.

Acknowledgments

Writing a book is never a solo journey, and I have so many people to thank for helping me bring this novel to life.

First and foremost, a massive thank you to my incredible editor, Laura McCallen! Your insights, support, and uncanny ability to wrangle my wandering plotlines into shape have turned this story into something I'm truly proud of. I'm so grateful to have you as my wing woman – every writer needs a Laura in their life! Thanks for always believing in me (even when I wasn't sure what my characters were doing). Here's to more adventures and fewer red pens!

To Charlotte Ledger, the best boss anyone could ask for – thank you for always being there with your endless encouragement and wisdom (and for not minding when I occasionally send too many emails filled with excessive exclamation marks and babble). Working with you and the amazing team at One More Chapter is such a joy – it's like a never-ending book club, but with deadlines! Here's to many more chapters together (pun absolutely intended)!

A huge shoutout to my trusty copy editor, Tony Russell, who has bravely stuck by my side through the whirlwind of Love Heart Lane and now finds himself washed ashore on the wilds of Puffin Island. I'm not sure if he's here for the adventure or if he's just developed a strange affinity for small fictional islands, but either way, he's still here – and that deserves a medal! Tony, thank you for surviving my endless plot twists, comma catastrophes, and occasional bouts of writerly chaos. Here's to more puffins, plot holes, and proofreading!

To my amazing children, Emily, Jack, Ruby, and Tilly – thank you for your endless love. Tilly, a special shoutout to you for coming up with the name of the main character in this book, Delilah Waters. Not only are you an academic weapon, you are a true creative genius too!

A big hug to Nellie, my writing partner in crime, I adore you with all my heart.

A special mention to Woody, who sadly passed away at the very end of this book. You loved me every moment of your life and I'll miss you every second of mine. I feel incredibly lucky to have been a part of your life. My heart is broken.

A huge thank you to Anita Redfern – my best friend for life! Your unwavering support, endless encouragement, and the fact that you've survived my occasional meltdowns make you an absolute legend. I couldn't imagine this wild ride called life without you by my side. You're basically stuck with me now, forever!

To Julie Wetherill, an amazing friend – thank you. Whether you like it or not, I make you read all my books – but I know deep down, you love it!

Catherine Snook, thank you for giving me the Canadian adventure of a lifetime! Not only did we see the wonders of the Great White North, but you also taught me some life-changing lessons along the way. I now (finally) know my left from my right – no GPS required! I've learned that everyone truly does need a Mustang Sally in their life, preferably one that can hit the open road with country music blasting. And, of course, I'll never look at a seagull the same way again – because every single one of those squawking feathered friends is, without a doubt, named Steven. Thank you for the laughs and the memories on our amazing trip.

To Bella Osborne, thank you for all the puffin memes and videos that have kept me entertained (and occasionally stopped me from getting any work done). I'll definitely miss our annual outing to the HarperCollins bash of the year – no one else makes mingling that much fun! But I'm *really* looking forward to our upcoming adventure on a real Puffin Island later this year. Let's hope the puffins are ready for us!

A big thank you to Glynis Peters and Deborah Carr for the daily support in our writing group. Writing may be a lonely job, but with you two around, it's never short of laughter, random tangents, and questionable snack choices, Yum Nuts! I'm so lucky to have you both in my creative circle – whether we're brainstorming or just procrastinating together, it makes all the difference!

Thank you to all the book bloggers, booksellers, and library staff for reviewing and recommending my novels! You're the real MVP – without you, my books would just be lonely, gathering dust on the shelf. And of course, a huge shoutout to my lovely readers! I wouldn't have the best job in the world if it weren't for you choosing my books to read. You make me feel like a literary rock star – minus the groupies and the tour bus, of course!

I have without a doubt enjoyed writing every second of

this book and I really hope you enjoy hanging out with Dilly and Max on Puffin Island. Please do let me know!

Happy reading!

Warm wishes,

Christie x

ONE MORE CHAPTER

YOUR NUMBER ONE STOP

FOR PAGETURNING BOOKS

The author and One More Chapter would like to thank everyone
who contributed to the publication of this story...

Analytics
James Brackin
Abigail Fryer

Audio
Fionnuala Barrett
Ciara Briggs

Contracts
Laura Amos
Laura Evans

Design
Lucy Bennett
Fiona Greenway
Liane Payne
Dean Russell

Digital Sales
Lydia Grainge
Hannah Lismore
Emily Scorer

Editorial
Kara Daniel
Simon Fox
Charlotte Ledger
Ajebowale Roberts
Jennie Rothwell
Tony Russell

Harper360
Emily Gerbner
Jean Marie Kelly
emma sullivan
Sophia Wilhelm

International Sales
Peter Borcsok
Ruth Burrow
Colleen Simpson

Inventory
Sarah Callaghan
Kirsty Norman

Marketing & Publicity
Chloe Cummings
Grace Edwards
Emma Petfield

Operations
Melissa Okusanya
Hannah Stamp

Production
Denis Manson
Simon Moore
Francesca Tuzzeo

Rights
Helena Font Brillas
Ashton Mucha
Zoe Shine
Aisling Smythe

Trade Marketing
Ben Hurd
Eleanor Slater

**The HarperCollins
Distribution Team**

**The HarperCollins
Finance & Royalties
Team**

**The HarperCollins
Legal Team**

**The HarperCollins
Technology Team**

UK Sales
Isabel Coburn
Jay Cochrane
Sabina Lewis
Holly Martin
Harriet Williams
Leah Woods

eCommerce
Laura Carpenter
Madeline ODonovan
Charlotte Stevens
Christina Storey
Jo Surman
Rachel Ward

**And every other
essential link in the
chain from delivery
drivers to booksellers
to librarians and
beyond!**

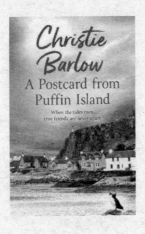

Verity Callaway is running away.

The plan is simple: hop in her reliable camper van and cross the Channel, headed for a rendezvous with her best friend in Amsterdam to kick off six months of travel. But when Verity stumbles across a decades-old postcard while preparing her cottage for its temporary tenants, her life takes an unexpected turn, and she finds herself on a ferry to Puffin Island instead.

Verity's childhood was filled with tales of adventures set on the picturesque island, but she'd always thought her beloved granny had made it all up. Now, knowing the stories and the setting were real, Verity is determined to find the postcard's sender and uncover the secrets of her grandmother's past … even if it means setting off a sequence of events that will change not just her own life, but also that of the sleepy island's close-knit community…

Available now in paperback, eBook and audio!